CASH COOPER

ALSO BY LYNN ELDRIDGE

Desire In Deadwood

Hearts and Mountains

Kindred Spirits

Remember the Passion

Skyrocket to Surrender

Tame the Wild

Triple C Ranch

Chase Cooper

Chloe Cooper

CASH COOPER

TRIPLE C RANCH
BOOK THREE

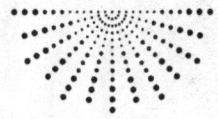

LYNN ELDRIDGE

WOLFPACK
PUBLISHING
— EST 2013 —

Wolfpack Publishing
701 S. Howard Ave. 106-324
Tampa, Florida 33609

wolfpackpublishing.com

Paperback ISBN 978-1-63977-498-2
eBook ISBN 978-1-63977-454-8
LCCN 2024930913

CASH COOPER

CHAPTER ONE

COLORADO SPRINGS

Triple C Ranch-East whipped tenderfoots into cowboys.

"Who agreed to this all-female dude ranch week, Sam?" Cash Cooper's grumble was half teasing and half serious as they left the stables on horseback. "Especially with the Fourth of July barbecue coming up on Friday?"

"You did, boss." Sam Reynolds, his longtime ranch foreman, smothered a grin.

"Yeah, that's what I thought," Cash said as they rode their horses past the rambling farm-style house built by Clarence Cooper, Cash's uncle.

Sam, black-haired and bearded, chuckled. "You told the owner of *Ranchers and Ranges* we'd turn 'em into cowgirls. Our wranglers are looking forward to working with a bunch of inexperienced women as opposed to the know-it-all greenhorn men we sometimes get."

Cash and Sam both gave a wave to Chase and Derek in the helicopter overhead flying due north. Then Cash pulled down the brim of his dark-brown, natural straw cowboy hat as the sun rose higher in the cloudless blue sky on this final morning in June. *Ranchers and Ranges* was Cash's favorite monthly magazine, thus he had a subscription. The magazine not only focused on a variety of ranches; dude ranches, cattle ranches, and horse ranches, but reported on the 3,000 miles of ranges making up the Rocky Mountains. Equally beautiful, the hundred mountain ranges were divided into four main groups: the Canadian and Northern Rockies, the Middle Rockies, the Southern Rockies, and the Colorado Plateau.

"If anybody can turn a bunch of city gals into ranch gals, it'd be our guys," Cash said.

"You know it, boss," Jeff Reynolds agreed as he reined in his horse and trotted alongside them. Jeff was Sam's son and lead wrangle on Triple C-East. Without the beard, he was a tough, younger version of his father both in good looks and good manners. "We can outride, rope, and herd horses better than any wranglers on any ranch anywhere."

"That, we can," Sam said.

Cash asked, "But what possessed me to claim we could whip a group of haphazard, first-come-first-served contest winners into cowgirls in one week?"

The magazine owner, Kirk Devereux, had come up with the idea and contacted Cash with an offer of a three-way split for expenses. The magazine was covering a third of the cost, the guests were paying a third of what they'd normally owe, and Cash was receiving the publicity for his third of the expense.

"What do you think, Sam?"

"I think Devereux isn't taking it nearly as seriously as we are, Cash."

"He said his wife liked the idea of placing a group of city ladies into the hands of a bunch of country cowboys," Cash told them. "She says it will add romantic suspense to the magazine."

Jeff nodded. "I'm with Mr. and Mrs. Devereux and the guys in the bunkhouse. I like it."

"I forgot you're single again," Cash said and laughed.

"Oh yeah," Jeff said and grinned. "Like you, boss."

"Single works well for me."

Cash hoped none of the women were redheads. He had a weakness, a fondness, no, an all-out preference for women with red hair. People often had types and his had red hair. Medium auburn. No, a rich burnt orange-red to be exact. No, that was *not* the right color, either, but close. He had a gut feeling this week was going to be challenging enough without the added distraction of a random redhead in the mix.

"Technically, we only have to turn ten of the twelve women, who will be arriving any minute via a van, into cowgirls," Sam pointed out, watching the highway for the van.

"Why only ten?" Jeff asked.

Cash explained, "Discounting the male magazine photographer, who's agreed to sleep in the bunkhouse, one of the women is an assistant to the writer and the photographer. The other woman is the journalist who's writing the human-interest story on this ranch and its legacy."

Triple C Ranch-East had been in the Cooper family since the 1800s. Cash's ranch, at 40,000 acres, represented one-third of the 120,000 total acres owned by himself and his two siblings. In square miles of Colorado land, the Coopers were responsible for 187.5.

To the west of his dude ranch, Chase Cooper, his older brother by five years, owned Triple C Ranch-Central, a 40,000-acre Black Angus cattle ranch with hundreds of cows, heifers, bulls, and calves. Chase had inherited the childhood homestead from their parents who'd been lost to COVID. Chase lived with his wife, Jade, and their two young children, Colton and Courtney, in a mountain-style house, built of stone and wood. At 10,000 square feet, it was the largest of the three main houses. Among other attributes, his brother and sister-in-law's homestead boasted a *Gone with the Wind* staircase, an elevator, and on the basement level, an Olympic-size indoor pool. Jade was a mental health therapist whose practice consisted of elementary school-aged clients. In addition to talk and play therapy sessions, she offered equestrian therapy to the children, provided by the American quarter horses on Triple C-Central. Crawford Cooper, the patriarchal grandfather of the Cooper clan who went by Coop, had built and lived in a log home also on Triple C-Central.

A few miles past Chase's ranch, toward Pikes Peak, lay Triple C Ranch-West. Cash's older sister by two years, Chloe Cooper Brevard, operated a newly constructed bed-and-breakfast near the original country-style house built by their Uncle Chester Cooper. Prior to marrying her husband, Derek Brevard, Chloe had run her bed-and-breakfast business in the country-style house. But these days, Chloe and Derek were glad to have the home to themselves, their son, Cooper, and the twins; a boy, Austin, and a girl, Abilene. Chester, having had a competition of sorts with his brother, Clarence, while building their respective houses, had agreed only to keep the square footage similar. Each was determined to build the more unique home. On Triple C-West, Chester had an indoor fishpond, two dumbwaiters, and an outdoor swimming pool. Derek, a former Marine sniper and deputy sheriff, was responsible for adding the new bed-and-break-fast beside it. After leaving law enforcement, Derek had returned to his family's roots of horse ranching. On Triple C-West's 40,000 acres, he'd also built state-of-the-art stables for Percheron stallions and mares which he bred and trained for mounted police throughout the United States.

At thirty years old, Cash had his parents, Carson and Elle Cooper, grandparents, Crawford and Zoe Cooper, Uncle Clarence Cooper, and ancestors to thank for his property and house. Grateful to have this ranch, he was a serious steward of the animals, wildlife, land, and natural resources for which he was responsible.

"What do you think your uncle would say about this all-female dude ranch week?" Sam asked as they neared the wide front gate separating the driveway from the main road.

Sam had worked for Clarence Cooper up until the day Cash's uncle had keeled over in a corral from a heart attack seven years prior.

"Seeing as how he was a confirmed bachelor, I think he would have enjoyed the ladies," Cash replied.

Uncle Clarence had always described himself as a sometimes rowdy yet mostly refined cowboy. He had never married and had no children. At least none he'd known about or who had come forward. Yet. There was a codicil to Clarence's will to be acted upon should an heir come knocking. The family knew two things; his heir would most likely be the child of one Charlotte Fleming and the codicil expired soon. Anyway, Uncle Clarence had been roping and riding when the heart attack struck. He was gone by the time he hit the ground. Cash was there, learning the ropes, and had consoled himself thinking it was the way his uncle would have wanted to go.

"I think you're right about your Uncle Clarence," Sam said with a chuckle.

"I know he would have been glad you stayed on, Sam, and didn't let me run Triple C-East into the dirt."

"You were young, catching on fast, and just needed a hand," Sam said, like the humble man and close friend he was to Cash and all the Coopers. "This is home."

"Yeah, it's home," Jeff agreed with a nod. At twenty-two, he lived in the ranch bunkhouse with the other wranglers. His parents, Sam and Kellie, lived on one side of a large duplex. Someday, Cash figured, Jeff might want to get married and live on the other side. Kellie was not only an RN which came in handy on a ranch, but she was in charge of all things to do with the daily meals for their guests. "Who's gonna be on this bus?"

"We're about to find out," Cash said as he spied an oversized van headed their way.

The van slowed and Cash reined in his horse, Captain Jack Sparrow, Captain for short, to the right of the gateway to the ranch so that he would be on the driver's side. Sam and Jeff halted their horses to the left and the bus turned onto the paved drive under the Triple C Ranch-East wooden arch.

"Hello," the driver of the van said. "I'm Jacob Berger, a photographer for *Ranchers and Ranges*. Here in the passenger's seat next to me," the man with short, light-brown hair gestured to a blond woman— "is Donna Smith, assistant to myself and the journalist." Cash, out of habit, assessed both to be in their mid-forties and in good enough shape to perform their magazine jobs while riding a horse. "I think you're expecting us."

"Yes, sir, we are," Cash replied. "I'm Cash Cooper." There was some whooping from the ladies inside the van, and Cash tilted his head forward in acknowledgment. "On the other side of your van are two of your companions for the week, father and son, Sam and Jeff Reynolds." More hooting and hollering inside the van. Might be a fun week after all or a really long one. "If you follow us, we'll lead you down the side road and around the back of the main house to our guest cabins. You can unload the van there and then bring it back around the front to park."

"You got it, Mr. Cooper. Lead the way," Jacob said.

"Cash," he said with a tip of his hat.

"Please call me Jacob."

Cash nudged Captain and they were off with Sam and Jeff flanking him. Where the driveway split, with the blacktop road on the west side leading to the house, Cash rode east leading them around his 6500 square foot, two-story home which Uncle Clarence liked to describe as an upscale farmhouse to fit the upscale dude ranch. Actually not as all-inclusive and exclusive as the ranch could be, an idea had been rolling in Cash's head as to a major upgrade.

Cash skirted the front yard of bluegrass and followed the blacktop to a back road, which ran all the way from his ranch, past Triple C Ranch-Central to Triple C Ranch-West. This route took them past Cash's four-car garage to the guest cabins. A circular drive made drop-offs and pick-ups of luggage and guests easy and separated the main house from the five, two-bedroom, comfortable log cabins. Each of the guest cabins had a porch with two rocking chairs and its own hitching post.

Cash indicated a spot in front of the middle cabin and Jacob parked the van. Dismounting Captain, Cash left him at the hitching post closest to the huge building which housed his combination Triple C Ranch-East Western Store & Stables. Cash thought his uncle would have approved of the building he'd added and the business he'd grown since Clarence had passed.

"This is impressive," Jacob said, hopped out of the van and slid open doors.

"Thank you. Welcome to Triple C Ranch-East," Cash said to the guests, as Sam and Jeff also dismounted their horses and joined him.

"These will be your homes away from home this week," Sam said, indicating the cabins.

As the women alighted from the van, Cash noted they were all shapes, sizes, and ages. Athletic ability or lack thereof, he'd been informed by Kirk Devereux that none of the ladies had much if any experience with horses. No matter. They would be appropriately, which meant safely, matched to their mounts. The women, chatting as they looked this way and that at their surroundings, quieted and gathered into a group facing him, Sam, and Jeff.

"As you may have heard me say to Jacob, I'm Cash Cooper. I own Triple C Ranch-West. To my right is my right-hand man, Sam Reynolds, the ranch foreman. On my left here is Jeff Reynolds, my lead wrangler. We're happy you're here and planning to show you a great week."

"Y'all will be cowgirls when you leave," Jeff said, and with a nod at Jacob, added, "and a cowboy." Jacob and the ladies laughed and clapped.

Sam said, "I have your cabin assignments, so after we help you with your bags, we'll let you get settled in for the next half hour."

"Then we'll introduce you to the best wranglers in Colorado," Jeff said, proud of his cowboy crew. "There are six of us all together," he said, indicating himself, Cash, and Sam.

"And we'll take you on a tour of the stables where your horses await you," Cash said. "So be dressed to step into the saddle."

Sam handed out the random cabin assignments with the center cabin and the two end cabins being slightly larger than the two in between them. A couple of the gray-haired women hurried forward to speak with Cash as Sam and Jeff, helped Jacob and the ladies tote bags into their lodgings.

"Remember us? I'm Diane," the lady who reached him first said.

"And I'm her sister, Joyce," the other one said.

"I sure do remember you ladies," Cash replied as the sisters, whom he figured were in their late sixties or early seventies, took turns hugging him. "You have stayed at my sister, Chloe's, bed-and-breakfast a couple of times, right?"

"Yes," Joyce said. "And we packed the Western clothes we bought from your store when we visited your ranch."

"It's great to see you again," Cash said, fondly remembering the sweet sisters. "You'll see Chloe and Derek and their kids at the Fourth of July barbecue. It's on my ranch this year."

"We can hardly wait," Diane said and clapped her hands.

"We called Chloe to tell her we won the first two spots in your contest," Joyce told him.

Cash personally escorted Diane and Joyce to their cabin. With the van unloaded, Jacob drove it back around to the front of the ranch where there was plenty of parking allotted for guests. Cash had counted and there were only eleven women. When Jacob returned with his duffel bag, Jeff joined him, ready to walk him over to the bunkhouse.

"Wait." Cash held up a hand and asked Jacob, "Aren't we one lady short?"

"Right. That would be Tracy, the journalist who's writing the story," Jacob said.

Donna nodded, saying, "She missed the van and had to drive."

No sooner had the words been spoken than a shiny red, brand new, if Cash had to guess, Ford Mustang with tinted windows sped around the house and skid-marked to a stop three feet in front of him. Cash clenched his jaw. The driver's door opened, and a pair of black stilettos swung out of the car to the blacktop. There was movement behind the car door and then a female wearing a black Panama hat and large black sunglasses looked directly at him over the top of the door. Stepping from behind the car door her body, snug in a short black dress, was killer. He figured she was five foot five, hundred and ten pounds. Half his weight. She swept off her hat and dropped it on the driver's seat of the Mustang, then casually flipped her sunglasses to the top of her head. Full lips, a shimmering cinnamon color, tilted up in a radiant smile, as she strolled toward him, car keys in hand and hips swaying. A drop-dead gorgeous redhead. Damn. When her big turquoise eyes trimmed with thick black lashes met his gaze, Cash inwardly groaned.

"Tracy, I presume?"

CHAPTER TWO

"*H*ello," Tracy replied, hoping he couldn't detect the tremor in her voice.

Cash Cooper was even more strikingly handsome than his photograph on the Triple C Ranch-East Internet website.

"Hello," he replied.

"Sorry I'm late," Tracy said to the cowboy who had not flinched a single inch when she'd nearly plowed into him.

"Uh-huh."

Mirroring her voice, her body trembled over that skiddingly close call. At least six foot four, the powerfully built man stood unmoving in the middle of his blacktopped drive. The dark-brown cowboy hat didn't quite conceal the frown creasing his forehead. Broad shoulders and bulging biceps filled out the snug, button-down, light-blue shirt he wore with sleeves rolled up his tanned forearms. Large hands with long fingers splayed at his tapered waist where a brown belt and large silver buckle rode low on a pair of jeans. Those jeans hugged his muscular thighs and pooled around dark-brown cowboy boots. Suddenly realizing this man was waiting for her to confirm her identity she snapped her head up and looked into eyes. Cobalt blue.

"Tracy Dalton, the journalist."

"Cash Cooper, the owner."

"Also, I apologize for almost running into you, Mr. Cooper."

"It's not like you meant to, Tracy." Donna stepped up beside her and smiled at Cash Cooper. Divorced, Donna was a platinum-blonde, with brown roots and brown eyes. She was the first to claim her ample bosom was her best feature which she admittedly drew attention to via her jiggles, low décolletages, and accidentally-on purpose-brushes. Looking at Cash Cooper, Donna shook her head and breasts, assuring him, "Tracy's just a terrible driver."

"That's not true," Tracy said. Donna initially seemed like a friend but more often of late she was a mixed bag of tricks. "Well...maybe in this particular instance it's true."

"Well..." Cash Cooper echoed. "Here on Triple C Ranch-East, we don't race our vehicles around folks and horses, Miss Dalton.," he said, hands remaining on his hips.

"Duly noted," Tracy replied. He wasn't a pushover.

With the guests settling in their rooms, Jacob pulled out his camera. Jacob, single and reliable, possessed an easy-going and friendly personality. He had done his college internship at *Ranchers and Ranges* and had been hired by the magazine's owner even before he graduated. As intelligent as he was helpful, Jacob knew all the ins and outs of his job. Tracy was grateful to have him as her photographer on her first big assignment. Jacob was already busy snapping photos of the surroundings. Perhaps taking that as a hint to perform her job as their assistant, Donna removed Tracy's bag and purse from the Mustang. Apparently, Tracy was in the middle cabin as Donna placed her bag on that porch. She wondered if there was any remote possibility that Donna was not her roommate for the next week. Tracy rebuked herself for the unkind thought and remembered she had her own job to do. Jacob smiled and snapped a picture of Cash and Tracy's conversation.

"Please call me Tracy, Mr. Cooper."

"You can call me Cash, but first things first, one of us is

going to *slowly* drive your car around to the front of the property where guests park away from our horses."

Tracy reached out and at chest level, dangled the car keys. To her utter dismay, her hand shook so when Cash held out his steady hand, she quickly dropped the keys into his big, square palm. Though it was not her intention, she got the feeling he had taken her actions as a direct challenge as his thick fingers snapped shut around the keys.

"It's a Ford Mustang Dark Horse 500-horsepower with a 5.0-liter V8 engine," Tracy said in explanation of her inept control of the vehicle. "It's a six-speed manual. And for the record, its official color is *Race* Red. If you're going to attempt to drive it, this, I have to see."

"Okay," Cash replied nonplussed. To Jacob and Donna, who were nearby, he said, "Excuse us." He walked to the car and opened the passenger's door. The passenger's door? Tracy was confused and didn't move until he said, "You have to see this. Right?"

"Right." Tracy walked to the car and slipped into the passenger's seat. Her heart began to *race* as Cash closed her door and then swaggered around the front of the car. She snatched her hat off the driver's seat before he slid behind the wheel and handed her his cowboy hat. When he adjusted the rearview mirror, she asked, "Ever driven a standard transmission, Cash?"

"Yeah." Cash's left cowboy boot came down on the clutch. With his right foot on the brake, he started the engine and shifted into reverse. Carefully avoiding the guests who were meandering in and out of their cabins, he backed up. Shifting into first gear, he smoothly headed the car south, toward the front of the ranch. Driving around the house, he expertly shifted into second gear and then downshifted again before pulling into a parking spot next to the van.

"Obviously, you can drive a stick shift," Tracy said as they stopped.

"Since I was twelve."

"Okay then," Tracy said and saluted him a bit mockingly. "Well done."

Without a word, Cash exited the car and came around to her side as he'd done when he let her into the vehicle. He opened her door and extended his hand. Making her first bodily contact with Cash, Tracy placed her hand in his. Her hand tingled. Tingles? Ridiculous! Those tingles traveled all the way up her arm. Cash tugged her out of the passenger's seat and let go of her hand. He closed her door, and she handed him the cowboy hat.

"That's how we drive on Triple C-East," he said, putting on his hat.

"Are you always such a gentleman?"

"No ma'am," Cash said with the slightest cock of a rakish, nearly black brow. And with that, he placed a thumb and finger between his lips and let out a shrill whistle. A moment later a beautiful horse galloped around the house. It slowed to a trot and stopped beside Cash. "Ever ridden a horse, Tracy?" he asked similarly to how she'd asked if he'd ever driven a stick shift.

"Not since I was *twelve*…once at a carnival…on a small horse tied at the end of a pole and walking around a circular pen." Tracy's shoulders sagged at the memory. "It was sad."

"Should be outlawed," Cash said as he patted the auburn-colored mane of the reddish-brown horse. "This is Captain."

"This is the biggest horse I've ever seen in person."

"He's a red dun stallion, standing seventeen hands tall which is how horses are measured. He's an American quarter horse, bred and raised here on my ranch."

"Nice to meet you, Captain," Tracy said, keeping a safe distance from him as Cash mounted the huge horse.

"Come on," Cash said and took his left foot out of the stirrup.

"What?" Tracy glanced down at her dress. "How?"

"Sidesaddle."

She shaded her eyes against the morning sun and looked up at him to say, "I'll walk."

"Sissy," Cash taunted. "Put your left foot into the stirrup and grab my arm."

"No, really I'll walk," Tracy said, having traded the tingling for trembling. She changed the subject with, "So do you live in this great big house all by your lonesome?"

Cash's cell phone rang and he answered it instead of her. Tracy decided it was her chance to escape riding that huge stallion. With a toss of her hair over her shoulder, she left Cash in her wake and took off on the trek around the imposing house. Daring as fast a clip as she could in her stilettos, Tracy heard him speaking to someone about escorting the guests to the stables to choose horses.

It was an absolutely beautiful summer day. In town or in the country, the blue skies of Colorado were endless. On this sprawling ranch the combination of flat land and rolling hills beckoned. She and Jacob had been working tirelessly for weeks, inside the downtown office building, on several small articles for the magazine. They'd turned them in, and Tracy knew Jacob was looking forward to this outdoor working vacation of sorts as much as she was. With a quick glance to the rear, she saw Cash slide his phone into his back pocket.

Tracy turned her attention to studying the house and was a ways down the road when the trotting of hooves sounded from behind her. Suddenly, an arm slid around her waist and she was effortlessly hoisted into the air and seated in front of Cash. With both her legs dangling over the left side of the horse, Tracy locked her arms around Cash's waist. His chest was hard and the arm holding her across his spread legs felt as solid as a metal pipe. They trotted around the wide curve of his house and the cabins came into view in the distance. Holding on for dear life, she noted Donna standing in the doorway of the center cabin. Was the woman scowling at them or was the sun making her frown?

"Yes, I live in that great big house all by myself. But I'm not always alone."

Cash's deep voice was so close, Tracy felt his breath move her hair. "I inquired on behalf of the article I'm writing, Cash. That's all."

"Are you afraid of horses, Tracy?"

"Of course not."

He chuckled. "You're afraid of horses."

"Give me the wildest one most likely to buck me off."

"You're ridin' him," Cash said.

Like an electric shock, excitement zinged through the center of Tracy's body. Did Cash mean him or his horse? Not afraid of horses? Having fallen off that one carnival horse she'd ridden and almost trampled by the one following him, she was terrified. When Cash headed his horse, named Captain, she remembered, into view of the stables several of the women clapped. She saw another frown, maybe concern or possibly disapproval, briefly cross Donna's face and then it was gone. Jacob, always with a smile, took pictures of her riding sidesaddle with Cash.

Outside a huge building with a sign reading Triple C Ranch-East Western Store & Stables, Cash reined the stallion in at a hitching post. Loosening his grip around her waist, he let her gently slide down the side of the horse to the ground.

Wow. Just wow. Cash Cooper made that wild pick up and tame drop off seem so easy.

"Thanks for the lift," Tracy said a bit flippantly, her knees wobbly.

"All part of the show," Cash replied before dismounting.

Cash turned away from her and spoke to a couple of men she assumed worked on his ranch. Tracy's skirt had ridden up a bit, so she melted into the crowd of ladies and tugged it into place. She smiled at Donna who gave her a 'what in the world' look before handing her a notepad for jotting down facts, statements, and ideas while writing her magazine articles.

Tracy had applied at the magazine during the last online

semester of her bachelor's degree in communication. By that time, she'd been hired by the small Kit Carson newspaper. But when *Ranchers and Ranges* offered her a job, with much trepidation and Grandma's urging, she resigned her job at the local newspaper. The newspaper's headlines had read; *Our Dalton Darling Goes to Colorado Springs*. It had been almost a year since she'd left her little hometown and moved to the big city. Soon after, Donna Smith had been hired at the magazine. Full disclosure on Donna per Jacob; Donna had been labeled as a flirtatious busybody who acted more like the magazine owner instead of a relatively new employee. Tracy had noticed that as well but hadn't commented.

Upon being hired, Tracy had been assigned to Gerald Moles, the human-interest stories editor and a fairly new hire as well. Also per Jacob, everyone loved Tracy. Not so much Gerald who, for reasons unconfirmed, was on probationary status at work. Word to the wise, Gerald was a womanizer with a dubious past and rumor had it he and Donna were sleeping together. Gerald also might have a sexual harassment accusation against him and there was talk of possibly getting high on the job, both probable causes for his probationary status. Gerald had voiced to Jacob that he'd taken a liking to Tracy and claimed he was the reason she had gotten this big break; a week on a dude ranch—Triple C Ranch-East no less, and the Mustang. As a man with black hair and a short beard walked toward her, Tracy forced aside her work concerns.

"You missed out on the introductions earlier, ma'am. I'm Sam Reynolds, the ranch foreman," the man said with a tip of his cowboy hat. As a second man joined them, he said, "And this is my son, Jeff."

"Nice to meet you," Jeff greeted her, also politely tipping his hat.

"It's a pleasure to meet you both as well."

"All right, ladies and Jacob, come on," Cash said in a jovial manner and strode down the middle of the enormous stables full of horses. With Sam and Jeff on opposite sides of

Tracy, the group followed the ranch owner. "Let's take a tour, learn a few facts, and pick out your horses." Amid the excited chatter and nervous titters among the ladies, Cash turned toward Tracy and those cobalt eyes captured her. "Ready or not, I'm gonna teach you to ride, tenderfoot."

CASE COOPER.

CHAPTER THREE

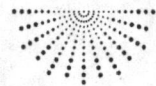

*C*ash purposely steered away from Tracy Dalton inside the stables.

"Our wranglers keep their horses in a separate barn next to the bunkhouse. You'll meet the rest of our crew shortly," Cash said to the guests, beginning the tour of horses. "In addition to renovating our guest cabins here on Triple C-East, we've enlarged the stables. We now have thirty horse stalls. Twenty of them are occupied with American quarter horses. My brother, Chase Cooper, who runs a cattle ranch on Triple C-Central, also has quarter horses. They start fast, turn fast, and stop fast which makes them excellent at cutting cattle from herds."

"Are they the horses often seen in rodeos?" Tracy asked politely, all business.

"Yes, quarter horses are highly competitive in rodeos because they excel in cow-horse competitions, calf roping, reining, cutting, and intricate maneuvers like barrel racing," Cash replied with the same professionalism. As Tracy bent her head to make a note in her notepad, he said, "On a dude ranch the quarter horse's strong desire to please, make them a popular choice for beginners as well as experienced riders." He answered questions from other guests and then said, "We also have five Percherons, which are draft horses. They were bred and born on Triple C-West. My brother-in-law, Derek Brevard, runs a large and successful Percheron horse ranch alongside my sister's bed-and-breakfast a few miles down the main road."

"We've stayed at Chloe Brevard's original bed-and-breakfast and her new one," Diane piped up with a glance around at the other ladies. "It's fabulous."

"We highly recommend it," her sister Joyce said, as the other ladies eagerly listened.

"I'll tell Chloe you ladies said so," Cash replied.

"I'm familiar with American quarter horses," Jacob began, "but not Percherons."

"Percherons are often used by law enforcement because of the horses' intelligence, willingness to work, and their docile nature in crowds. Here on Triple C-East, Percherons have proven to be an excellent addition to our stables. Despite their large size, they are gentle and even-tempered, also making them well-suited for the novice or advanced rider. Like our quarter horses we love and respect our Percherons." With a wave toward the nearest horse stall, Cash said. "This first horse is a quarter horse, a mare named Dandelion." Walking to the stall, he patted the nose of the palomino. "Mares are female horses typically over the age of four. Dandelion is gentle and friendly."

It was a good thing this tour was something Cash did all the time, because Tracy had zapped him like a red-hot thunderbolt. He wasn't sure he could have gotten all the words out as easily as he was doing if it weren't part of his regular routine. When he had swept Tracy off the ground and across his lap she'd settled against his chest and between his spread legs like she belonged there. He'd had to concentrate to keep his lower body from responding. He caught her looking his way and smiled. She made eye contact but didn't smile in return.

"Horse number two is a quarter horse named Lobo," Cash said. "A longtime friend of mine, nicknamed Lobo, suggested the name saying this horse was as fast as his Harley."

Cash had always been attracted to women with all shades of red hair; from strawberry blondes to auburn brunettes and had dated redheaded classmates at Falcon High School. While attending the University of Colorado, he dated mostly redheads and had celebrated graduating, with dual bachelor's degrees in business and animal science, with dual redheads. But this woman, this—Tracy Dalton—was the epitome of the perfect redhead. Her hair, not too light, not too dark, was just the most beautiful shade of red he'd ever seen. Long and thick, it framed her gorgeous face and swung in sexy waves around her slender shoulders.

"This fifth horse is Frederick." Sam had apparently taken over for Cash and was saying, "A gelding which, if you'll recall, I explained, is a castrated male horse."

Somewhere, along the way, Cash had become so lost in thinking about redheaded women and wondering why Tracy hadn't smiled back, he'd completely lost track of the introduction of horses numbers three and four; a mare named Lizzie and a gelding named Rocky. He chuckled to himself. Evidently, he wasn't getting all his regular words out after all.

The women petted the horses' noses and manes as Jacob snapped pictures. Cash glanced at Tracy again, who was taking notes as Sam spoke. All of the guests including Jacob, who'd no doubt been escorted to the bunkhouse by Sam or Jeff, had changed into riding attire; shirts, jeans, and boots. Only two women weren't wearing boots. Tracy, in her dress and stilettos, stuck out like a sore thumb. He figured she stuck out in any crowd.

"This next horse is good ol' Ben," Sam said. "He's wise and kind and ready to retire," Sam finished with a fond pat to the horse's neck.

"I want good ol' Ben," Diane said, raising her hand and catching Cash's eye.

"Done," Cash said with a smile at Diane as Jeff made a note. "Ben's best friend is Bess, a sweet lady by all accounts."

"May I have Bess?" Diane's sister, Joyce, piped up.

"Absolutely," Cash said and nodded, as Sam wrote it down. "Good choices."

As Jeff introduced the next three horses, Cash covertly watched Tracy who had not made any eye contact with him since he'd smiled at her.

The group walked forward to the next stall and Jeff said, "This is a sorrel mare. Sorrel means the horse has a copper coat lacking any black. Matching her color, we named her Penny."

Cash added, "The most noticeable difference between my red dun horse, Captain, and Penny is Captain's mane being a darker red than his coat."

Cash saw Tracy glance from Penny back to Captain, tethered beside the Western store near the entrance to the stables. Though the two horses' colors were similar, Penny's coat and mane were both the same shade and she was darker than Captain. Cash had noticed earlier that Captain's mane was the exact same shade as Tracy's hair, while his coat was a lighter red. Cash watched Tracy put the tip of her pen between her cinnamon lips and then open her mouth.

"I'd love to ride Penny," Donna said quickly, standing next to Tracy. Cash could have sworn Donna looked sideways at Tracy before speaking up. "Please, Cash?"

"Sure," Cash replied since Donna had addressed him personally. No matter, because he had another mare in mind for Tracy. "We'll make a note, Donna."

He saw Tracy smile and graciously nod at her assistant. Damn, Tracy was sexy. Per his record with women, so far his attention and interest had always been reciprocated by every woman to whom he'd shown interest. Having dated blondes and brunettes, too, he had enjoyed more than a decade of carefree fun and sex with women. It was his lifestyle. Why then, among countless women, had this woman hit him like the proverbial ton of bricks?

He wasn't sure. Nor was he ready for it, for—*her*.

"Boss?" Jeff said. "Jacob likes Chief, what do you think?"

"Good choice, Jacob," Cash said. "Chief is a Percheron and a gentleman."

"Okay, great," Jacob said, petting Chief's nose.

Needing to concentrate on the contest winners, and not the one redhead in the group, Cash gave himself a mental shake. Jeff and Sam led the way down one side of the stables, made a turn and toured everyone back down the other side. Eventually, they'd introduced twenty-four of the twenty-five horses. All of the ladies had mentioned a favorite horse or two except for Tracy.

"This last horse is a red dun American quarter horse, like Captain," Cash said. "However, instead of a stallion, she's a filly which is how we refer to a female horse younger than four years old."

Notepad in hand, Tracy asked him, "What is the definition of a stallion?"

"An uncastrated male horse used as a stud for breeding," Cash answered, with a slight challenge in his voice. "Captain approves of this filly's spirit."

"I might switch horses," Donna said, which Cash ignored.

"What's the filly's name?" Tracy asked, head down and writing.

"Spitfire," Cash replied.

"Spitfire?" Jeff echoed but said no more.

"Since you haven't picked out a horse yet, why don't you give Spitfire a try, Tracy?" Cash asked.

"I was joking about giving me the horse most likely to buck me off," Tracy said, evidently concerned about the horse's name. "I'm not planning to ride anyway, just write."

"There won't be anything to write if you're not in the saddle with the rest of us," Cash informed her. "We'll be out riding the ranch and trails every day, with a night of camping."

The other wranglers, Beau, Ed, and Larry, all good guys,

arrived on the scene. The five guest cabins could comfortably accommodate up to four guests per cabin. Since this was considered a luxury dude ranch, it meant extra attention from wrangler to rider, so there was one wrangler assigned to each cabin. When a cabin held only two guests, groups could be combined and a wrangler would use that week to do other needed work on the ranch or take a week off. If someone was sick, Sam adjusted the schedule accordingly. In an emergency they could always call on one of Chase's cowboys to fill in for a day or two. The sixth man ran the Western store.

Cash had selected this week for the contest winners because there were only thirteen guests as opposed to twenty. With July Fourth on Friday, the barbecue being held on Triple C-East meant extra work for the staff, so fewer guests eased the workload. Between Monday and Friday, the wranglers would teach, ride with, and help the guests care for their horses.

Sam had made the assignments and announced he would take Diane and Joyce, Ed, an affable good ol' boy from Georgia was assigned to Beth and Lisa, who were closest in age to Diane and Joyce. Larry, a former high school buddy of Jeff's, had ladies by the names of Natasha, Michaela, and LeAnn. Jeff would ride with the three youngest and potentially most energetic of the contest winners: Patience, Brittany, and Daphne.

"Okay," Cash said and, knowing his crew as he did, noted the wranglers silently appreciating Tracy's standout beauty. Positioned near Jacob and Donna, he said, "That leaves me with Jacob, Donna, and Tracy."

"Yay!" Donna unabashedly whooped.

Cash acknowledged that with a nod and turned to Tracy to say, "For safety reasons you need to change into jeans and boots."

"I don't have boots," Tracy said, tapping her pen against her notepad. "Because—"

"Because you weren't planning to ride," Cash finished

for her and crooked his finger. "But since you are, let's find you a pair of boots. Anybody else who needs to buy or rent some boots, follow me. I'll introduce you to Beau who pulled shopkeeper duty this week."

"I need some," said Beth, a short woman with short hair, maybe fifty-five. "Be back in a jiffy," she said to her cabin and riding partner, Lisa, and their wrangler, Ed.

While Sam, Jeff, Larry, and Ed began their usual instructions, demonstrations, and safety rules with those who had come fully prepared, Cash led Tracy and Beth into the Triple C Ranch-East Western Store & Stables. A good-sized store, Cash and Sam kept one-half fully stocked with cowboy hats, shirts, jeans, and boots. On the other side there were saddles, saddle pads, bridles, reins, stirrups, leathers, horse blankets, and grooming tools for those who fell in love with horses and riding.

"Beau will take care of you," Cash said to Tracy and Beth, as well as Jacob, who was tagging along to take photos. "The store stays busy and everybody takes a turn running it, including Sam and me."

"Welcome, ladies," Beau said. Tall and nice looking, he was the best salesman out of all the wranglers. The store would be even busier than usual due to the upcoming holiday weekend and Cash was glad to have Beau with his skills in the shop. "I see we need boots," Beau added with an appreciative smile at Tracy and then a smile for Beth. To Tracy he asked, "And jeans?"

"Got jeans. Just boots," Tracy said.

"Right over here, ladies," Beau said, leading them to the boots.

Leaving the women in capable hands, Cash headed to the door, and found Donna waiting for him. Cash had occasionally run into guests like Donna, and frankly, they could be a pain. Whenever that had happened in the past, he'd often elected to work in the store that week. But with his ranch being the subject of the magazine's story, he didn't figure that was the right thing to do this week. He walked Donna past the filly he'd referred to as Spitfire, to the mare named Penny, which she'd originally said she wanted to ride. Cash began the instructions as he would with any guest but kept an eye out for Tracy.

When Tracy emerged from the shop, Cash grinned. Not just because she looked fantastic, but because despite the fact she said she only needed jeans, Beau had her fully outfitted in Western wear in the color known as cinnamon. From the buckskin Elsa-style cowboy hat on her head to the snug white shirt with cinnamon-colored stripes and cinnamon pearl snaps to match, to the form-fitting blue jeans, down to the cinnamon leather boots with black soles and heels. She looked more delicious than anything made with cinnamon that Cash had ever tasted. And now he had a name for the color of her hair.

Since there were only a couple of other customers who were regulars in the shop, at the moment, Beau escorted Tracy to Cash and Beth to Ed. As Tracy and Jacob spoke, Beau paused beside Cash and nodded to the mare next to Captain.

"She thinks her mare's name is Spitfire," Beau said quietly. "I think between the two of us and *Spitfire*, we're gonna turn your journalist into a cowgirl sooner than later."

Cash chuckled. "Yeah, don't tell her the real name of her horse."

Donna had overheard. She brazenly tugged on Cash's sleeve, leaned in close enough to brush her bosom against his arm, and asked conspiratorially, "What's her horse's real name?"

"For now, it's Spitfire," Cash replied. Thanking Beau who returned to the shop, he casually stepped away from Donna to Tracy and Jacob. "Jacob, I hope you got before and after photos of your journalist. She's made quite a trans-formation."

"Yes, I sure did," Jacob said. "May I get a picture of you and Tracy outside of your Western store?" Cash moved in front of the glass door to the store and when Tracy came to stand beside him, Cash shoved his hands into his front jean's pockets. "Tracy, loop one arm through Cash's and put your other hand on your hip."

"Like this," Donna said as she hurried to do so, on the other side of Cash.

Tracy posed as Jacob asked and he took photos that included Donna. That done, Cash worked with the three of them pointing out features of *Spitfire*, Chief, and Penny. He also showed them the saddles and put names to the other gear they would be using to ride the horses. Tracy was taking notes when she got a call on her cell. She walked away to take the call, but Cash saw the expression of concern on her face. As he continued with instructions that Tracy needed for her safety and for her story, Cash was making note of what she'd missed.

Forget about the human-interest story on his ranch. What was Tracy's story? Why had she been late today? Boyfriend? Boss? What? Who?

"Is everything okay?" Cash asked as Tracy returned.

"Yes," Tracy said distractedly. "No." With a halfhearted laugh she said, "I don't know."

"Can I help?"

"Oh, no. No." She shook her head and then yanked on both sides of the brim of her new Elsa hat as if to make sure it didn't fall off. She was spectacularly adorable in the hat. A city girl or maybe a small-town girl, instead of a country girl, but sensational. "Thank you, though, Cash."

"Let's not wreck your new hat on the first day," Cash said and demonstrated with his hat how to adjust it by touching the top instead of dragging down the brim. "Try that next time."

Tracy had watched and nodded seriously. "I will," she said as she received another call.

The jangling of the ringer on the triangular sides of the chuck wagon bell signaled lunch in the outdoor kitchen and dining area where the sign above the wooden roof read; *Cooper Café*. With sides that pulled down, heating for the winter months and fans for summer, it was simply and fondly referred to as the café. Sam's wife, Kellie, would have all the fixings for a great welcoming first meal for the guests and wranglers.

"Let's go to the café and eat!" Cash called. "We'll saddle up after lunch." Everyone started filing toward him, and with a glance at Tracy, he asked, "Coming?"

CHAPTER FOUR

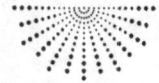

"$\mathcal{B}$e right there." Tracy forced a smile.

Worries weighed so heavily on her that even when Cash, surely the best-looking cowboy on earth, had smiled at her earlier she'd not even had the presence of mind to respond in kind. She walked out of the stables and placed her cell to her ear.

"If you're late to lunch you have to feed the chickens later," Cash warned her as he led the chitchatting guests past her. As the group walked toward tables and chairs housed under the roof of the café, Tracy sincerely wished the chickens were the worst that could happen. Cash added, "There're a hundred of 'em."

A hundred? Tracy flinched but gave the handsome cowboy a thumbs-up. Listening to the voice on the other end of the line, she wondered how bad it would be if she were to bow out of this dude ranch week. Bad. Most likely the magazine would fire her—kind of bad. Her gut said chance it. Her heart wanted to believe everything would be all right. Her brain warned her this was the beginning of the end.

Her cell still pressed to her ear, she sat down on a wooden bench just outside the entrance to the stables and listened. What would she do if she got fired? Who cared? Maybe she needed to get to Wild Horse at all costs. But what would she do without income? She had less than a thousand dollars in savings. Other jobs? Here? In journalism? Not if the biggest magazine south of Denver let her go. She had recently finished writing her first two children's picture books but was still working on the illustrations for the second one. Unpublished books weren't going to pay her bills. Was the life she was trying to build for the two of them in Colorado Springs not meant to be? There was definitely no future in Wild Horse. But he was there. What about him?

"Okay, I'll stay here," Tracy heard herself say to the caller. "For now." She rubbed her forehead, felt the brim of her Elsa hat touch her fingertips, and glanced around Triple C Ranch-East. She had looked forward to this assignment and to writing her first big ranch story for weeks. "But I want to see you. I *need* to see you." She listened, looked east toward Wild Horse, and nodded. Head down, shoulders sagging, she said, "Remember how much I love you." The sentiment was returned, and Tracy whispered, "Bye-bye." She clicked off her cell but stared at it.

Tracy glanced at the café. She was missing the first meal of her dude ranch adventure. Jacob wouldn't say an unkind word. But Donna would have an opinion. So far she'd arrived late, nearly run over the ranch owner, and been unprepared to ride. What was Cash Cooper thinking of her? That she was a loser with a capital L?

Not one to feel sorry for herself, Tracy raised her chin, squared her shoulders, and took off with purpose in her step toward the people, food, and tables. Pasting a smile on her face, she walked under the arched roof to the serving line. There were oblong metal pans positioned over candles no longer lit. The first pan held a single barbecued rib, the center pan had half a scoop of fried potatoes in the corner, and in a third pan baked beans were all but gone. Tracy picked up a tin plate as a lady, maybe in her late forties, walked behind the serving tables with two nearly empty pitchers. One pitcher appeared to have been filled with iced tea and the other with lemonade.

"I'm Kellie, Sam's wife and Jeff's mom," the tall, slim woman with short, black hair said, setting the pitchers aside. "You're Tracy, the journalist?"

"That's the rumor," Tracy said self-consciously with a laugh and a smile. "It's nice to meet you, Kellie. I'm sorry I'm arriving late to my first meal on the ranch."

"No problem," Kellie said, putting on oven mitts. "Hungry?"

"More than I realized," Tracy admitted.

"Good. I've got you covered." Kellie opened the oven and removed a tin plate filled with barbecued ribs, fried potatoes, and baked beans. She gestured for Tracy to discard her plate and carrying the warm one, she said, "Follow me." Kellie set the tin on a picnic table where there was an empty spot next to Jacob and across from Jeff. "Sweet tea or lemonade? Cash's Aunt Rachel makes the best sweet tea in Colorado. She and I brew it the same way."

"Sweet tea, please," Tracy said.

All smiles, Jacob said, "Pick up that rib, Tracy, and let's get a shot."

Tracy already felt better, sitting with Jacob and Jeff. Kellie was back with sweet tea, napkins, and utensils. Tracy took a bite of the most delicious barbecued rib she'd ever tasted. Her eyes opened wide in delight and she nodded her appreciation at Kellie.

"Yeah, Mom's a great chef," Jeff said and grinned.

Tracy covertly glanced around the other tables. She didn't see Cash. She caught Donna staring at her, but in the blink of an eye, Donna smiled. Jeff and Jacob talked about the ranch. As Tracy quickly ate, to catch up with the others and more ravenously than she would have thought possible, she spied Cash. Standing near a corral, where several horses were saddled, he was speaking to a strawberry blonde. The woman reached out and took his hand. Tracy remembered how her own hand had tingled when Cash held it. She silently acknowledged an odd stab in her stomach as the woman stepped closer and placed her other hand on Cash's chest which Tracy knew was rock hard with muscle. When Cash shook his head, the redhead seemed to be trying to cajole him into something. Tracy said nothing and looked away as Sam Reynolds joined them.

"I see Rusty is back. Again," Jeff said to the man with the black hair and beard.

"Yeah," Sam replied but didn't elaborate, instead greeting Tracy and Jacob.

Tracy concentrated on finishing her food and when she dared look up again, it was due to the sound of Cash's voice. He was at the picnic table where Ed and two older ladies in the group sat. The redhead named Rusty had vanished. Where? The house? The stable? Down the road?

"Guess who's feeding the chickens this evening?" Cash asked on his way to the table where Tracy sat. He stopped at the opposite end of the table and looking at her, said, "That girl."

"Chickens don't take well to strangers," Jeff said seriously and shook his head.

"Any experience feeding chickens?" Sam asked her.

"No, I've been told they're dangerous," she said.

"Not if they don't peck you," Jeff replied.

"Oh, they'll peck her," Cash said.

Tracy's only encounters with fowls had been at a distance. "They're peckers?"

"They can be," Kellie said with an arched brow aimed at her husband, son, and boss. "Ignore these men, Tracy, but wear your boots around the chickens. They nip bare toes."

Everyone laughed, including Tracy. Wranglers began filing out of the dining area, stacking their plates on an empty table. The guests assigned to them followed their lead.

"See you later," Sam said to his wife, then stood and gave her a kiss on the cheek.

Tracy, Jacob, and Cash stood as well. Then it was back to the stables and time to saddle the horses. She realized the wranglers' horses were the ones already saddled and in the corral. As the men instructed, demonstrated, and did most of the heavy lifting, Jacob engaged Donna in helping him get some shots of the action.

"First bit of information," Cash said as Tracy pulled her notepad and pen out of her jeans pocket. "You've got barbecue sauce on your lip."

"Oh no." Tracy didn't have a tissue. Not only that, she realized she'd left her lipstick and cinnamon mints in her purse. So, no lipstick and maybe barbecue breath for the rest of the afternoon. Swell. To rid herself of the barbecue sauce, she slowly ran her tongue around her upper and lower lips. Then she puckered them for Cash to see. "How's that?"

"Hot."

"What?"

With a grin tugging on one side of his mouth, Cash replied, "Let's saddle you up." Like his wranglers were doing, he began showing her how it was done. "This is a trail saddle and weighs about twenty-five pounds." He swung it onto the pad resting on the horse's back and secured it in place. Pulling the reins to the horses over their heads, he handed Tracy the reins to the filly she hadn't planned to ride. Holding on to Captain's reins, Cash swung his hand toward the oversized door to the stables leading outside. "After you." When Tracy stood unmoving, he said, "You realize you missed a good amount of the tutorials."

"I know. I apologize for being so rude."

"You have to stay focused around here to remain safe," Cash said seriously. Tracy knew it was an opening for her to confide in him. It was the second time he'd offered, the first being when he asked her if everything was okay and if he could help. "Think you can do that?"

"Yes, sir." That came out more flippantly than she'd intended. With a smile, she saluted. That only seemed to make things worse as Cash grimaced. To move past the awkwardness she asked, "Shall I get on the horse now?"

"We don't *saddle up* inside the stables. Should the horse

buck or bolt, it's safer to mount out in the open. Tug on the reins and the horse will follow you."

"Oh."

Tracy couldn't remember having made such a horrible first impression anywhere as she had on Triple C Ranch-East. Hoping not to do anything else stupid, wrong, or rude, she took a step and tugged on the reins. The beautiful horse followed her just like Cash said she would. They walked their horses out of the stables. Tracy listened intently to Jeff and Sam who took turns demonstrating and explaining how to mount the horses. Wranglers stood by, offering hands-on help as needed. When the ladies began saddling up, Tracy took a deep breath, hoping she would saddle up correctly.

"Okay, Spitfire," Tracy said and glanced at Cash. "Let's do this."

"Talk to me as you mount," Cash suggested.

"Hold both reins in my left hand just above the withers," she repeated what Sam had said and touched the highest part of the filly's back, at the base of her neck. "Along with the reins, grab a handful of mane. This prevents excess pressure on Spitfire's mouth and saddle."

"Good," Cash said, standing a few feet from her.

"Turn the stirrup iron toward me and slide my left foot in?"

"Correct."

Tracy grabbed the filly's mane and recalling what Jeff had said, she recited, "Point my left foot down, so as not to kick her in the side and give myself a bounce on my right foot. Stand up in the left stirrup and swing my right leg over her —what was it?"

"Croup. The croup is the highest point of a horse's hindquarters," Cash reminded her. "Do that and you'll be in the saddle."

"Let's hope." Tracy nodded. She slid her foot into the stirrup, hopped, and swung her right leg as told. With a grin, she was sitting on top of the horse. "Woo hoo!"

"Right foot in the stirrup?"

"Oh right." She looked down her right side and found the stirrup. "Now it is."

"Yeehaw," Cash said and mounted Captain.

"Yeehaw!" Tracy hoped she sounded confident.

She was scared but determined to improve her image in Cash's eyes. Not just for her sake, but for that of the magazine. She glanced at Jacob who was smiling as he trotted up to her on the gelding called Chief. She noticed Donna, staring at Cash. Tracy's gaze also drifted back to Cash. His vibrant blue eyes met hers and when winked at her, Tracy's heart skipped a beat. Sam offered to let anyone who wanted to practice, by riding around in the corral, the opportunity to do so. Otherwise, they were headed down a back road of the ranch. Everyone voted to head onto the back road, rather than be cooped up in the corral. Jeff took the lead and the horses began to move. At this point, Tracy and Cash were in the rear of the group of guests and wranglers.

"You do well on this ride and I'll help you feed the chickens," Cash said. "What do you think, spitfire?"

"Spitfire thinks you've got yourself a deal."

Cash gave Tracy a cocky, sideways grin. "Does she?"

"Yes, she does," Tracy said, carefully leaning forward to pat the horse's mane.

As Captain walked forward, Tracy's horse followed him on her own. Tracy recalled Cash saying Captain liked Spitfire's spirit. Obviously, Spitfire liked Captain's spirit too.

Cash casually said, "By the way, your filly's real name is Cinnamon."

CHAPTER FIVE

*D*aybreak this time of year was around five thirty a.m.

Cash didn't need an alarm to wake up, but he usually set it anyway. As he lay in bed, his first thought this morning was the memory of feeding the chickens with Tracy Dalton. His eyes still closed, he chuckled. There was no rule on the ranch about having to feed the chickens if you were late to lunch. He suspected Tracy knew that, but she'd been a good sport and played along.

When he'd started shooing dozens of white, black, and red hens across the fenced pen containing grassy areas and natural shade, toward the large A-framed chicken coop with glass windows, a regular door, and a pop door, Tracy had shooed them too. He'd chuckled as the chickens clucked at Tracy who occasionally shrieked and jumped out of their way.

"We call all the white hens Lily, the red hens Goldie, and the black hens Iris," Cash had said as he plucked up a big black chicken before she could dip underneath the ramp leading to the door for the coop. Placing her into the coop he said, "Once we get them all past this pop door we close it to keep 'em safe from predators for the night."

"Why's it called a pop door?" Tracy had asked.

"Because the chickens pop in and out of the coop," he'd said.

Tracy's turquoise eyes had sliced a sideways glance at him evidently not knowing if he was serious about the pop door or pulling her leg. He'd assured her that he was completely serious. All but a couple of the chickens were safely in their coop when Tracy had spied a stray. She'd looked cute and sexy in her Elsa hat and snug jeans, as she bent over at the waist and tried to coax a little red chicken out from under a bush.

"This chicken doesn't want to be caught," Tracy had said, hands on her slim hips.

"Can't give up on her."

"Goldie!" Tracy huffed. "Come here, chick, chick, chick."

"Thatta girl."

Cash had taken up a position on the other side of the bush, and blocking the chicken's escape route, chased her toward Tracy. With all of Goldie's dramatic clucking and wing-flapping and Tracy's squealing and prancing, it was highly entertaining. He'd laughed and then cheered when Tracy had finally succeeded in catching the chicken.

Eyes still shut and reliving it all again, Cash grinned now as he had then. No sooner had Tracy caught Goldie than the little hen had escaped her arms and flown across the ground toward Cash. He'd caught Goldie and demonstrated holding the chicken like a puppy. Surprising him, Tracy had held out her arms. He had handed her the hen and on her second try, Tracy had made it to the coop with her. Closing the pop door, he had taken Tracy inside the coop. There, he had opened a plastic tub of cracked corn, distributed it, and scooped mealworms out of a canister. He gave Tracy a handful and her expression of disbelief was priceless when he'd told her she was holding mealworms. To her credit, she didn't drop them and run.

"Why aren't the chickens cock-a-doodle-do-ing?" Tracy had asked as she sprinkled the mealworms for them.

"Because they're hens, not roosters. Only roosters crow."

"I know for absolute certainty hens cock-a-doodle-do. I've heard them."

"I know for absolute certainty what you heard were roosters."

With an outright laugh now, Cash rolled out of bed, wondering if Tracy was awake. On Tuesdays, the wranglers usually took the guests out for a ride, let them have lunch along a trail, and then rode back to the ranch. In the afternoon, guests could rest, walk the trails, or ride again if they wished to do so before supper. This was all in preparation of riding to the overnight campground a few miles away.

After showering, Cash shrugged into a dark-brown shirt with a Triple C Ranch-East logo and rolled the sleeves up his forearms. He wore jeans every day on the ranch, usually with a brown leather belt, one of his Triple C silver buckles, and brown cowboy boots.

Remembering how Tracy had held that chicken like a puppy, Cash thought once again about getting a dog. He'd been meaning to pursue finding a good-sized breed, but ranch duties kept getting in his way. His grandfather, known as Coop, had an Australian cattle dog, named Crockett, loved by all. Cash smiled, his grandfather was loved by all too.

He made his way downstairs, through the house, and off the screened porch to the backyard of the ranch. Kellie and Sam were already in the café. Jeff, Ed, Beau, and Larry were following their noses to breakfast. Cash joined them and over coffee, bacon, biscuits and gravy, they talked about the day's schedule, weather, guests, and horses.

"Thanks for breakfast, Kellie," Cash said, after setting his empty plate on the designated table near the oversized dishwasher and farm sink.

"Anytime," Kellie said jokingly as she served breakfast five, sometimes seven days a week. "Since you guys are taking guests out on the trails, I will have their sack lunches ready soon." She nodded to the table where the food would be waiting. "It's Tuesday, so I'll be making soft and hard tacos for dinner this evening to serve along with refried beans, rice, chips, and salsa. And maybe in addition to sweet tea, I'll whip up a pitcher or two of margaritas."

"Sounds good to me," Cash replied.

"Thanks," Sam said to his wife and kissed her before falling into step with Cash.

It was almost seven a.m. as Cash and Sam headed to the stables. They nodded at ladies emerging onto cabin porches. The guests would soon head to the café as they'd been advised breakfast was served from seven a.m. to eight a.m. Shortly thereafter, Kellie would ring the chuck wagon bell for folks to pick up their bag lunches.

The wranglers would be in the stables and guests were welcome to accompany the men on rounds as they checked on every horse, gave medicines to those requiring it, or distributed additional feed for horses needing extra calories. Jacob was the first guest to make it to the stables with his camera in hand. But it wasn't long before the ladies began filing away from breakfast and making their way to the stables. Cash had saddled Captain and glanced at his watch. Time to ride. And here she came. It was all Cash could do not to wolf whistle.

"About time you got here," he teased the stunning redhead as she neared him.

"I was tired," Tracy said, stopping beside him in the stables. "I had to chase chickens yesterday. A whole herd of 'em."

"A peep, flock, or brood," Cash corrected her with a grin and shake of his head. "A herd is for cows."

"I was so tuckered out after chasing a whole *peep* of Goldies, Lilies, and Irises, I overslept," Tracy said, adding a bit of a twang to her voice.

"Did the owner inform you, you had to feed that flock of chickens breakfast, too, to earn your keep?"

"No, he did not!" Tracy snapped, obviously fighting a smile as she placed dainty hands to saucy hips. Her new Elsa hat hung from a cord down her back and her hair caught the morning sunshine. Today, he noticed a few faint freckles sprinkled across her nose and wondered if yesterday's sun had brought them out on her ivory skin. She wore a snug, turquoise, three-quarter length sleeve tee shirt that matched her eyes, along with jeans and her new cowboy boots. "I'm thinking I may very well report the whole feed-the-chickens-if-you're-late-for-lunch and to-earn-your-keep scam in *Ranchers and Ranges*."

They both laughed. She placed her hat on her head, without yanking on the brim, as he'd shown her the previous day. Beau was already busy in the store as guests and wranglers led their horses past it into the open area. Ed was in charge of a pack mule, named Eloise, carting extra bottles of water. Guests picked up their sack lunches and bottles of water which went into their individual saddlebags.

The morning trail ride was on.

Cash let Jeff lead the way. Jeff, though young, had been raised on Triple C Ranch-East. He'd earned his place as lead wrangler through hard work and dedication. Along the ride over flat land past creeks and toward the hills, Sam took turns with Jeff, Ed, and Larry in telling the guests about the surrounding Colorado area. They answered random questions about everything from the American quarter horses and Percherons to daily ranch duties, rodeos, bunkhouse living, and even the brood of chickens, with pride and loyalty ringing in their voices.

Cash enjoyed the questions and comments made by the guests and replied to those in regard to his ranch such as how long it had been in his family? How had it come by its name? He said his paternal grandparents had named it after their three sons; Carson, Clarence, and Chester. How big was the ranch and did he have relatives nearby? Cash told them the acreage and described his siblings' ranches. He said his entire family planned to be present for the fireworks display. Tracy asked for some specifics as to running a year-round dude ranch.

"You have to be a businessman, hotel operator, and recreation director," Cash said. "You have to know horsemanship, livestock, ranch maintenance, and public relations. You must get along with all kinds of people."

"How did the Coopers come to own this land back in the 1800s?" Tracy asked.

Cash gave a brief accounting of how the Homesteading Act of 1862, had opened the door to his ancestors buying Colorado land. When Tracy asked about his ranch in particular, he told how he'd inherited it from his bachelor uncle.

"In the early days, Sam and Kellie kept me from running it into the ground," Cash said modestly with a tip of his hat to Sam. "Jeff and our wranglers help maintain this ranch." He always gave credit where it was due. "I could not do it without all of these friends who are more like family. They make the hard work enjoyable."

Cash especially enjoyed Tracy as she occasionally smiled at him between asking questions and taking notes. He'd also noticed her assistant, Donna, often interrupted Tracy or cut her off or worse yet, sometimes answered her questions about life on a ranch. Incorrectly. Even Jacob had frowned in surprise at Donna once or twice.

"Where are we headed now?" Jacob asked, taking photos of the woods, the hills, and the land stretching on forever.

"Fish Creek. It's up ahead in the copse of trees," Cash replied and pointed. "Those of you who want to fly fish can do so when we ride to Turkey Pond. We'll pack fishing gear for the pond and for fly fishing in the creek, in wagons which we'll hitch to Eloise and our other mule, Mavis."

"When will that be?" Diane asked.

"Tomorrow," Sam said.

"We've never fished," Joyce said.

"First time for everything," Sam replied with a smile. "We'll ride out after breakfast and camp overnight near the water."

"In cabins?" Michaela, a tall, blonde barista, asked.

"No, ma'am," Larry answered.

"In tents?" Brittany, a pretty and polite schoolteacher guessed.

"Yes, in tents," Jeff said with a nod.

"Are there indoor bathrooms where we'll be camping?" Lisa, a slightly chubby woman with a quirky laugh, wanted to know.

"No, ma'am," Ed replied with a straight face.

"No bathrooms?" LeAnn, the most petite lady of the group, gasped.

"I'm warning you now if my bare bubble butt from the Bronx touches mud, the mud will burn so hot it'll be like lava oozing from a volcano!" a brunette named Natasha warned them quite seriously. Everyone laughed. Natasha's big brown eyes rolled as she swung a hand in the air for emphasis. "I'm not kidding."

"There are his and her outhouses," Sam assured the group and chuckled.

"Yay!" Patience and Daphne whooped in apparent relief at the same time.

"We've traveled for about an hour, so we're gonna let the horses drink from the creek and rest," Jeff told them. "Then we'll travel for another hour to our lunch site."

Cash smiled at the excited remarks as they reached the creek. The ladies did well in dismounting and helping lead their horses to the creek for a drink. Back in the saddles they rode further down Fish Creek. In a grassy meadow that was a typical Tuesday stop for guests of the dude ranch, there were picnic tables under a wooden shelter. Once they arrived, everyone began dismounting and the wranglers showed guests how to tether their horses to tree branches, so they'd have a ride home.

"Who's sharing a tent with you tomorrow night, Cash?" Donna boldly asked, sidling up on his right.

"Sam," Cash replied stoically.

"Jacob can bunk with Jeff," Sam said, joining them. "Ed and Larry will tent up as usual."

Tracy had overheard and walking to them, she said, "I

assume we ladies share a tent with the person we're teamed up with in our cabins." She had directed her comment more to Donna than to Cash as if she'd detected Donna might be wearing on his nerves. "Right?"

"You're partly correct," Cash said. "There are two cots per tent. So the ladies who are three to a cabin now can split up and sleep two to a tent."

Jeff, Ed, and Larry were unloading water from Eloise, placing red and white checked cloths on the picnic tables, and encouraging guests to walk around and take in the scenery. Tracy received a text and Cash saw the same expression of concern on her face, as he had when he'd asked her if everything was okay.

He strongly suspected something or someone in Tracy's life was not okay. She struck him as a loner, with little help from anyone. Perhaps she was carrying a weight that was far too heavy and shouldn't be on her shoulders in the first place. She could be a little brash and he wondered if that was her way of compensating for some insecurity. Maybe it's how she kept herself moving forward. Since when did he try to figure out a woman? Never.

Tracy wandered away from the picnic area of chatting people and sat down on a large, flat boulder to text back. Cash gave her a few minutes and when she appeared to have finished her text, he grabbed her lunch and his. With water bottles in hand as well, he walked over to her. Cash wasn't sure exactly why he cared or why he wanted to help her. But he did.

"Hey," Tracy said, looking up from her cell at him.

"Hay is for horses," Cash said. "And you can't be too careful around horses. So before you get distracted and injured, why don't you tell me what's going on?"

"I'm fine," she said.

"Yeah?" Cash noted that same slump of her shoulders she'd had when a call had taken her out of the stables. "So you're always late to a job, miss safety instructions, and have to feed chickens?"

Her smile was halfhearted. "Not usually."

"Fair enough." Cash sat down next to her. On the flat surface of the rock, he placed their bag lunches between them. Handing her a water bottle, he asked, "How bad can it be?"

"That's just it." Tracy sighed. "I don't know."

Cash opened a lunch sack and handed her a deli-style sandwich. "Normally, cowboys eat dried meat, beans, hard biscuits, and dehydrated fruit when they're out on the trail. Kellie takes pity on the guests and treats us to much better grub."

"Let me make a note of those foods," Tracy said and quickly flicked away a single tear before reaching for her pad and pen.

"I can remind you," Cash said and placed his hand over hers as she held her pad and pen. "Is it my company that's making you sad?" he asked with a grin, hoping she'd smile.

But instead of smiling, her eyebrows drew together before she looked away. Cash pulled his hand from hers and took a bite of his sandwich. After a moment she bit into hers. He chewed and waited, wondering if she'd confide anything. If not, he didn't feel he could ask her a third time. As they ate, a summer breeze blew, catching long locks of Tracy's hair and tossing them over her shoulder. Cash imagined those cinnamon waves would be as silky soft as they looked. When a lock blew across her face as she tried to take the last bite of her sandwich, he caught the red strand and moved it over her shoulder to her back. Yeah, even softer.

"It's the company keeping someone I love," Tracy whispered.

She'd said it so quietly, Cash wasn't absolutely sure he'd heard her correctly. But he ran her words over in his head and his first thought was that she had a boyfriend who was cheating on her. If that was the case, what a fool the guy was. But how could a woman as beautiful as Tracy *not* have a boyfriend? A bunch of boyfriends. A sting of jealousy jabbed

Cash right in the gut. Then again, maybe he could be a shoulder for her to cry on.

"What does that mean, Tracy?" Cash noticed Donna staring at them as she swung her legs out from under the picnic table. He did not want the woman interrupting them and though she was technically a guest, he sent a frown her way. "Does the company involve a man?"

"Oh, yeah." Tracy nodded but didn't make eye contact.

"Look, it's none of my business. I just want to keep you safe and focused this week."

"Safe," Tracy repeated the word and looked into the distance as if she were a million miles away. "I'm not convinced he's safe company."

"Tracy," Cash said. Her glittering eyes met his. "Was that text from him?"

"Yes."

"Is he threatening you in some way?"

"No."

"What then?" Cash asked.

"Winston says she fell and sprained her ankle but is much better and not to worry," Tracy said and blinked to clear the tears gathered in her eyes.

"Is Winston your ex?" Cash asked. She didn't reply, almost as if she'd floated so far away his words hadn't reached her. "Does *she* mean your daughter?"

"No," Tracy said as if his second question had finally registered. "I'm not here to burden you with my problem, Cash. Everything will be okay." Though her turquoise eyes belied her words, her vulnerability had vanished. She stood up. "I'll try to be more punctual and focused. I promise."

"Two heads are better than one," he said. "Let me help."

CHAPTER SIX

"*I* don't need help." Tracy wasn't accustomed to lying and that was a whopper. "But thanks."

Cash Cooper was a good guy with an appealing bad-boy edge.

Tracy liked that about him. From the timbre of his deep, steady voice to the intelligence and savvy it took to run his ranch, to the confidence he exuded in everything he said and did, Tracy knew Cash could help her. At the very least, she might bounce the situation she was dealing with off him. For a male point of view.

"Okay," Cash said and stood up beside her. "Maybe you have parents or siblings or a best friend who you can talk—"

"I don't," Tracy admitted.

Cash shrugged. "If you change your mind, my offer to help stands."

"I didn't mean to sound abrupt, and I do appreciate your offer. But I'm kind of a loner from way back."

"I kind of got that," he said, mimicking her a bit. "Who taught you to drive a stick shift?"

Tracy smiled. "Believe it or not, my grandmother."

Cash chuckled. "Good for you and your grandmother."

"About my grandmother—"

"Is this a private lunch?" Donna interrupted, her bosom jiggling in a low-cut neckline as she walked to them.

"No, of course not," Tracy said, watching Donna smile up at Cash. She couldn't blame the woman. Cash was not only handsome, he exuded masculine charisma. She'd noticed Natasha and Michaela appreciating his exceptionally good looks and undeniable sex appeal too.

"Ready to roll, boss?" Sam called from a few yards away.

"Yeah," Cash grumbled, clearly irritated by Donna's intrusion. "Let's ride."

Donna, apparently oblivious to Cash's signals, walked beside him chatting him up all the way to the horses. Deep in thought, Tracy followed along and untethered the sweet filly named Cinnamon. As they rode back to the ranch, the wranglers veered off here and there taking their guests on various routes back to the ranch. Donna stuck to Cash like glue and Tracy had to smother a laugh when Jacob rolled his eyes. All too soon, they were back at Triple C-East. Dismounting near the stables, Cash and his wranglers showed the guests how to unsaddle their horses. For some the saddles were too cumbersome, but Tracy managed hers.

The ladies were given free time to rest and refresh, snack and snooze or while away the time however they chose before the chuck wagon bell summoned them to supper. With a glance over her shoulder at Cash who had headed toward the store as Beau called to him, Tracy made her way to the log cabin she shared with Donna. On the outside, the five cabins were rustic and on the inside they were modern with of course, a Western flair. Crossing the wooden porch and opening the door, she took one step into the living room. The living rooms stretched across the front of the cabins, each boasting a stone fireplace. Between the two bedrooms, both furnished with two queen beds, was a bathroom. On the western side of the cabins a bay window had a distant view of the mountains. On the eastern side of every cabin was a Dutch door.

Donna had arrived in the cabin first and taken the

bedroom with the mountain view. Tracy opened the top half of the Dutch door to the gentle air of a Chinook breeze. The Chinooks, meaning snow eaters, were famous winds in Colorado. In the winter they melted the ice on roads, leaving snow on evergreens and grass. On a summer evening, like this one, an occasional Chinook provided a pleasant respite from the sun and heat.

Tracy sat down at a desk, took out her laptop, and began transferring her daily notes onto it. She glanced at Donna who flounced into the cabin and plopped onto the couch in front of the floor-to-ceiling stone hearth. Tracy wasn't really sure how or why the magazine had sent Donna on this assignment as she'd not contributed much of anything so far.

"Are you going to make a move on Cash Cooper or what?" Donna asked from the couch. "Just about everybody else is. I think I will too."

"Isn't that what you've been doing?" Tracy asked, looking up from her laptop to Donna. "Moving on him?"

"Yeah." Donna shrugged. "But I'm not getting anywhere. I'm going to step it up."

"Don't forget we're here on an official job for the magazine, Donna," Tracy advised.

"Is that what's holding you back?" Donna pried, turning sideways on the sofa and staring at her. "Then again, I've never seen you flirt with any man. You do like men, right, Tracy?"

"Yes, I like men. But I've not come across the right one for me," she replied, wondering if the right man hijacked one's every thought like Cash had been doing to her since the moment she'd met him.

"Cash belongs on the cover of *People* as the sexist man alive," Donna said.

"Yes, he does," Tracy admitted. She had every hope and intention of Cash being on the cover of *Ranchers and Ranges*.

"I suspect I'm older than Cash by a dozen years or so. You're probably younger than Cash by half a decade...at least," Donna said with a question in her voice. "Oh well, maybe I can show him a thing or two in the bedroom."

Covering her shock, Tracy heard herself calmly say, "I doubt that. I think Cash Cooper is as much a stud as his stallion."

"You don't know, he might want to be taught, like in my case. Or he might want to teach, like in your case?" Donna asked. Tracy didn't confirm or deny her inexperience. She'd never shared such personal details with Donna, nor did she plan to start. But apparently, her naiveté with men was evident. "If Cash doesn't start flirting back, I'll set my sights on Sam or Beau."

"Sam is married to Kellie," Tracy said.

Donna got a call on her phone and looked at the number. With a glance at Tracy she hopped off the couch and went into her bedroom to take it. Tracy sat stunned at Donna's morals or lack thereof. To her relief, the woman must have fallen asleep because she didn't return. As Donna began to snore, Tracy went back to her laptop. But in her mind's eye she saw Cash on the screen instead of the words she was trying to put there. An hour later the clanging of the chuck wagon dinner bell sounded.

"Hey," Cash said through the open half of the Dutch door.

"Oh!" Tracy jumped in surprise and laughed. "Hay is for horses."

"And supper is for their riders." He grinned, gave her a *come-on* wave of his hand, and disappeared. But Tracy heard him call, "It's Taco Tuesday."

Tracy closed her laptop and met Cash at the front door. "I love tacos and I'm starving."

Cash proffered his arm and she took it. Tall and made of muscle, in walking at Cash's side Tracy felt safe and... wanted. Where had that thought come from? From the attention and strength of the man beside her. They strolled into the café, already bustling with activity. Guests and wranglers were mingled at tables talking about the day's events while chowing down on tacos, chips, and dips. In addition to water and sweet tea, glass pitchers on tables held something frosty and lime colored.

"Taco Tuesday," Kellie called to Cash and Tracy and held up a basket of chips in one hand and sauce in the other. "Follow me." She led them to a corner, not too far from and not too close to the other tables. As they sat across from each other, Kellie gave a nod to a pretty young woman and said, "Cristen's summer school class at Pikes Peak State College is over so she's back to work. Here she comes with drinks, and I'll bring your tacos."

"Margaritas?" Cristen asked. Holding a pitcher of margaritas and two glasses, she had an hourglass figure and long blond hair. Tracy figured they were about the same age.

"That's a hell yes for me," Cash said. "Thanks, Cristen."

"For me, too," Tracy agreed.

Cristen poured and left the pitcher with them. Jacob caught their attention and snapped a photo before returning his attention to Natasha and Michaela who were at his table with Larry.

"Think I can have some photo approval as to what goes in the magazine?" Cash asked.

"Absolutely," Tracy said. Cash smiled and held up his glass. Tracy held hers up, they clinked their glasses and drank. It was delicious. "Especially if they put you on the cover."

"What?" Cash asked. Obviously the thought had never crossed his mind. "The cover?"

"Yes. Donna thinks you should be on the cover of *People* as the sexiest man alive," she told him.

He shook his head and muttered, "Donna." He paused and asked, "What do you think?"

"I think I'm gonna do my very best to get you and your ranch on the cover of *Ranchers and Ranges*."

"I'm only one-third of the Triple C Ranches," he said. "As I told the group yesterday, Chase runs a cattle ranch and Jade offers equine therapy on Triple C-Central. Chloe and

Derek run the bed-and-breakfast and Percheron businesses on Triple C-West."

"Right." Tracy's eyes grew as round as their basket of chips, and she scooted forward in her chair. "I just had an idea! Do you think I could interview them? It wouldn't be nearly as extensive as your story and I'd have to run it by my editor, but I think he'd go for it." Her mind was racing. "I know I have to vacate my cabin after this week, but if I could come back next week for maybe a day, do you think your family would pose for a few photos?"

Cash chuckled at her enthusiasm. "I don't know. I guess we could ask them."

Something or someone caught Cash's attention behind her, and he raised his hand. Tracy glanced over her shoulder and saw an older man arriving for Taco Tuesday with Beau. Tracy also noticed Cristen, smiling from ear to ear, as she hurried to greet them. Beau wrapped an arm around her, and Cristen stood on tiptoes to give him a quick kiss.

"Donna will be disappointed," Tracy thought and realized by Cash's expression, she actually said that out loud.

"If you mean, Beau, he's taken," Cash said.

"Yes, I can see that. They make an attractive couple."

"What about you, Tracy? Are you taken?"

Tracy sat back in her chair and decided to answer his previous, though subtle, question and this direct one. Meeting his gaze, she said, "Yes, I think you should be on the cover of *People* too. And no, I'm not taken."

A slight grin played on Cash's lips. He'd darn well known she'd sidestepped his question earlier and said, "Thank you, Tracy." Looking past her, he called, "Coop, come over here. I want you to meet someone."

Tracy smiled at the spry gentleman with bright blue eyes sauntering toward them. Clad in a Western shirt and jeans, cowboy hat and boots, he also wore a big smile. Cash scooted back his chair and stood to greet him.

"Howdy," the man named Coop said as Cash placed a hand on his shoulder.

"Hello," Tracy replied.

"Crawford Cooper, my grandfather and winner of seven world titles for team roping, steer roping, and tie-down roping," Cash began in introduction and paused to look at Tracy to add with obvious love and pride, "Coop's in the ProRodeo Hall of Fame and the Museum of the American Cowboy in Colorado Springs." Then turning back to his grandfather, he said, "I'd like you to meet *Ranchers and Ranges* journalist, Tracy Dalton."

"A pleasure, Miss Dalton," Coop said.

"It's so nice to meet you, Mr. Cooper." Tracy extended her hand. "Please call me Tracy."

"Nobody calls me Mr. Cooper," he replied in a humble tone. "I got tired of being called Crawdad and Crawfish so everybody calls me Coop."

Cash pulled up a chair for him, and said, "Please sit."

Tracy liked Coop immediately and said, "Yes, please join us, Coop."

Taking a seat, as Cash also sat down, Coop asked, "Dalton, as in the infamous Dalton Gang of the late 1800s?"

CHAPTER SEVEN

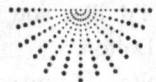

"*O*ne and the same," Tracy admitted and splayed her hands. "According to my Grandpa Lewis Dalton. And verified by an old family *Bible* and the Internet."

"No kidding?" Coop replied as Kellie brought a plate of tacos to him. Cristen accompanied her with another margarita glass and poured a round for them. He thanked them as did Tracy and Cash. "To the Daltons," Coop said as they clinked their margarita glasses.

"The Daltons." Cash looked at Tracy and asked, "As in bank and train robbers?"

"Some of the Dalton boys, not all of them," Tracy said. "The Daltons' parents were James Lewis Dalton and Adeline Younger Dalton. Full disclosure, the Dalton brothers shared the same grandfather, Charles Lee Younger, with the Younger brothers who ran with Jesse and Frank James."

"The Dalton, Younger, and James Gangs." Cash leaned back in his chair, cocked a brow, and folded his arms over his chest. "That explains so much."

"Does it, now?" Tracy arched a cinnamon brow. "I don't know if this helps to repair my terrible first impressions or solidifies them, but according to my grandpa, only Bob, Gratton, Bill, and Emmett Dalton were bank and train robbers."

"You're right," Coop said. "The majority of the Dalton children were law abiding."

Tracy's turquoise eyes sparkled as she said, "There were fifteen Dalton kids in the family and Grandpa Lew told me the same thing about most of them being law abiding, Coop."

"I can't remember all of the Dalton family members, but I know Cole Dalton was a teacher and Littleton Dalton was a sheepherder," Coop said. "They lived in California. Franklin Dalton was a much-admired Deputy US Marshal, working under Judge Isaac Parker in the Oklahoma Territory."

"Yes, that's right." Tracy smiled, nodding.

"I'm thinking you two might be kindred spirits," Cash said.

Tracy smiled at Cash and then at Coop to say, "Grandpa Lew said Franklin Dalton was tracking down whiskey runners when he was shot and killed in the line of duty."

"I read that somewhere. Sad. Franklin was a couple of years younger than you are, Cash," Coop began, with a nod at him, "when he was murdered in 1887."

"Franklin was twenty-eight," Tracy confirmed. "My dad died at twenty-eight and my mom had just turned twenty-four, like I'll be on—soon."

"I'm sorry to hear about your folks," Coop said.

"Me, too, Tracy," Cash said.

"Thank you," Tracy said. "It was a long time ago. They were in a helicopter crash during a sightseeing tour of the Grand Canyon. I was only three years old and had stayed behind with Grandpa Lew and Grandma Tammy in Wild Horse, Colorado."

"You have something in common with my granddaughter-in-law, Jade," Coop said. "She lost her mother when she was a toddler."

"So, when's your twenty-fourth birthday, Tracy?" Cash asked.

Tracy rolled her eyes and laughed. "As if the Daltons aren't firecrackers enough, I was born on the Fourth of July."

"Duly noted, *spitfire*." Cash's eyes narrowed as he also took in her red hair. In calling her spitfire, he sensed he'd thrown her off balance, just a bit. Fair enough because she rocked him to his core with every look she flashed and every word she spoke. Turning his attention back to his grandfather, he said, "Coop, I'm surprised you know so much about the Daltons."

"Full disclosure," Coop began with a twinkle in his eye, "Cade Cooper, a distant relative from way back in the day, was falsely accused of horse theft in ol' hanging Judge Isaac Parker's neck of the Oklahoma woods. Franklin Dalton, US Marshal, knew who the real thief was and spoke up on Cade Cooper's behalf. Because of a Dalton, a Cooper didn't hang back in 1885."

Never having heard that family story, Cash was taken by surprise. He looked from Coop to Tracy. Her sensual mouth had fallen open in obvious shock. Cash's eyes met hers and the corners of his lips turned up in a grin as he saw the gooseflesh covering her skin.

"Wow!" Rubbing her forearms, Tracy told them, "That gave me goose bumps."

Cash would like to be giving her goose bumps from head to toe. "Coop, I remember hearing about Cade Cooper, but never that he was accused of being a horse thief," Cash said. "As I recall he rode Mustangs in rodeos and stayed in Oklahoma instead of coming west to Colorado."

"That's right. Cade Cooper was long gone before my time," Coop said. "But because of my history with the rodeo, I've always had a soft spot for ol' Cade."

"That connection will clench your interviews with Chase and Chloe," Cash said to Tracy. Then he turned to Coop to explain, "Tracy hopes to expand her *Ranchers and Ranges* article to include Triple C-Central and West."

"You in, Coop?" Tracy asked, smiling at him.

"Yes, indeed," Coop replied. "Whatever you need."

"Thank you," Tracy said to him.

They spoke about the article she was writing, and Coop

regaled them with a few favorite stories about the Triple C Ranches. Tracy seemed mesmerized as Cash sat back and mostly listened. The time flew and an invisible rope seemed to fall around Cash, lassoing him to Tracy.

"Coop is a history buff," Cash said. "He also knows the Alamo history like he was there with Jim Bowie and Davy Crockett. A few years ago, Coop donated an authenticated Bowie knife to the Alamo," Cash said. "We all flew to San Antonio, Texas for the dedication."

"Oh, my gosh! Where in the world did you find an original Bowie knife?" Tracy asked.

"On Triple C Ranch-West," Coop told her with a glance at Cash.

"That's a story in itself," Cash said.

"I love the Alamo too." Tracy clasped her hands under her chin. "May I mention your donation of the Bowie knife to the Alamo in my article, Coop?"

"Sure," Coop said with a big grin.

"I've got so much to write, I'd better head back to my laptop and get busy," Tracy said.

As they were done with their tacos and the margarita pitcher was empty, Cash stood and said, "I'll walk you back to your cabin."

"Okay." Tracy scooted back her chair, stood and said to Coop, "I'm honored to have met you, sir."

Coop stood, too, and took Tracy's hand. "You make a great first impression." He lifted her hand to his lips and lightly kissed it. "Truly a rare pleasure, Tracy Dalton."

Tracy was apparently so moved she hugged Coop. Damn, Cash had to give his grandfather credit where it was due. Coop had received a hug from her before he had.

Standing back, Tracy said with a choke in her voice, "The pleasure is all mine, Coop."

"Coop, do you need a ride back to your place?" Cash asked.

"No, sir," Coop said. "That magazine photographer feller, Jacob, wants to take some sunset pictures of the ranch along the back road. I told him I'd show him the way."

"Jacob is a good guy," Tracy told Coop. "You'll like him."

"Yup, already do."

"Another private party?" Donna asked, sidling up between Cash and Coop.

"Not at all," Tracy said. "But I'd appreciate it if you'd help Jacob however you can when Mr. Cooper takes him along the back road for photos of this evening's sunset on the ranch."

Tracy had made the statement with such authority, that after the briefest of frowns and a slight hesitation, Donna said, "I'd be happy to."

"As we say on the ranch, sooner than later." Coop tipped his hat to Tracy and Cash.

"Sooner than later, Coop," Cash said and offered his arm to Tracy.

Tracy slipped her hand over the bicep muscle of Cash's left arm, and he walked her away from the café with a wave of his right hand to Sam, Kellie, and others still there. Jeff was leaving for the bunkhouse with his wranglers as they heard Sam reminding the guests to have whatever they planned to take on the camping trip ready to pack into saddlebags the next morning. It was a warm evening with just the right amount of breeze and the trip to Tracy's cabin went all too fast.

"Would you care to come in?" she suggested. "If you have time, I'd like to ask you a few questions for my story."

"Grab your laptop and we'll do it at my house, where we won't be interrupted." Cash turned as two women called his name simultaneously.

"Famous last words," Tracy teased him.

Cash muttered, "Delilah and Desiree, the barrel racing twins. Hell." With an apologetic glance at Tracy, he said, "Excuse me."

"No problem. I can catch up with you tomorrow, Cash."

"I'll be back for you shortly."

~

TRACY DIDN'T BELIEVE THAT AND DIDN'T REPLY.

She entered her cabin and shut the door. Her heart pounded but not in a good way. Moving to a window and standing back just enough to see but not be seen, she watched the women, both with long brownish-red hair, coming after Cash. They stopped mere steps from the cabin's front porch. Obviously, they were familiar with the ranch and with Cash. His left arm, which Tracy had recently held, was seized by one of the women as the other one grabbed his right arm. With so many redheads vying for his attention, evidently Cash had a type. Tracy wondered who would be the one to catch him. Certainly not her.

"We want to see it, Cash." The voice and a giggle from one of the women drifted to her.

"Please? We brought our suits," the other one assured him.

Tracy had heard and seen enough. With a knot in her stomach, she walked away from the window. She sat down at the desk and turned on her laptop. She made some notes from her Taco Tuesday dinner with Coop and Cash. But she couldn't concentrate enough to write them into the story, so she shut her laptop down. While no man had ever shaken her mentally and emotionally like Cash Cooper, she instinctively knew Cash was in his element with the women who'd come for him.

Be back for her? Fat chance.

Catch Cash Cooper? Since when did she wonder about catching a man? Since meeting Cash. The three women she'd seen vying for his attention so far apparently knew what they were doing. Tracy hoped she came off as worldly, but in truth she was anything but. She'd grown up in Wild Horse, for heaven's sake. It wasn't even considered a town, it was a village.

Tracy couldn't resist peeking out of the window again. Delilah and Desiree had convinced Cash to go with them and they were off in the distance now. She wondered what they wanted to see and what kind of suits they'd brought. The barrel racers had the look of experienced women and were probably the most popular girls in their high school. Although he had shrugged out of their grasps, Cash was indeed leaving with them.

Tracy had attended Kit Carson School which, in a town with a population of three hundred, was kindergarten through twelfth grade. She'd planned to leave Wild Horse as soon as she graduated. But the summer after her sophomore year, Grandpa Lew's health began to fail. Thus, her grandma had been the one to teach her to drive. Shortly after she'd graduated from Kit Carson School, her grandpa had fallen outside their home and died. Grandma had urged her to move to Denver or to Colorado Springs or anyplace Tracy could establish the writing career she wanted. But no, her grandmother would not move with her. For reasons known only to Grandma, Tammy Dalton adamantly refused to leave her house.

Look to these walls, Tracy, she recalled Grandma saying in the living room of their two-bedroom house next to a tool shed on an acre of land. *It's our nest egg. I will stay behind and guard it for you.*

Tracy had stayed too. She'd begun studying online to earn her bachelor's degree, not sure when or if she'd ever get to use it. She'd streamed endless podcasts, videos, and documentaries soaking up big city facts and fashions so she could blend in—if she ever got the chance to live in the city. Then one day, into the village lumbered Winston.

Winston Smith had been a school bus driver spanning the fourteen-mile distance between Wild Horse and Kit Carson, so the Daltons had known of him for years. Tracy figured he was probably a decade or more younger than her grandmother. That sort of concerned her. Then again there weren't many singles in Kit Carson, much less Wild Horse. When Tracy was in her last year of her online college program, Winston had stopped by the house to say hello. Saying he had retired and was bored, he seemed harmless and began showing up on a daily basis.

Tracy had worked on finishing up her degree, while also writing for the local newspaper. Winston had helped Grandma Tammy revive her garden which had been taken over by weeds after Grandpa Lew had passed. After a few trips in and out of the old shed, where the garden tools were stored, Winston had shown up with paint. Though the paint was foul smelling he didn't seem to mind and used it to paint the shed. Where the window had given way to dry rot in the shed, Winston had gone to the trouble to board it up and painted it as well. Tracy had to agree with her grandmother; it was an improvement.

Then Winston had brought those two chickens. She and her grandmother knew nothing about chickens. But the ones Winston had come up with had been so crazed, crowing, and nipping at his legs, Tracy wondered if he'd found them in the wild somewhere. He'd warned Tracy and Tammy the *hens* were dangerous when protecting their eggs and to stay away from them. He'd do the egg gathering. Thus, Tracy had been truthful with Cash as to her unfamiliarity with chickens, except for being told they could be dangerous. She and her grandma didn't go near the tiny coop Winston had built. He gathered the eggs, the *hens* crowed, and Tracy had let it drop when she should have Googled chickens.

But thanks to Cash, Tracy now knew those so-called chickens were roosters and could not have laid those eggs. Winston had bought the eggs to endear himself to Tammy. In Tracy's opinion, Winston Smith was working too hard at something. Or was he just a nice guy who was too embarrassed about the roosters not being hens that he'd tried to cover up his mistake?

Whatever the case, Grandma Tammy seemed to enjoy his company. As his presence in the small house increased, Tracy had decided her grandmother would be looked after and she could leave upon completing her online journalism classes. Finally, with her degree in hand, she'd started looking for something beyond her newspaper job in Kit Carson. After a few months, she'd landed the position at *Rancher and Ranges* in Colorado Springs. Grandma had offered her the truck but Tracy had refused to take her only transportation. Grandma had given her two thousand dollars and assured her everything would be fine. With her hectic schedule, Tracy hadn't been back to Wild Horse since she'd left. But was everything fine?

"Should I call her again?" Tracy whispered. No, it was no use. She sighed and decided to pack for the overnight camping trip.

CHAPTER EIGHT

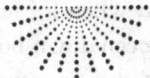

"*L*ike I've said before, please call first before you drive all the way out to the ranch," Cash reminded them more politely than he felt. They had wanted to go inside, up to his bedroom, and onto his balcony. He'd turned them down flat. "I'm a rancher running a business here, ladies."

"Fine, we'll leave for tonight," Delilah whined as they stopped beside her truck.

"But we'll be back," Desiree promised, clinging to his arm again.

"Call first," he repeated firmly.

He'd recently told Rusty the same thing and was dead serious about it. He suffered kisses to both jaws, which as usual, sported a day's growth of beard. Since when did these twins kissing him count as suffering? Since it was Tracy he'd rather have kissing him. He stepped away from the women and turned his back on them. As he walked toward his house, truck doors opened and closed. The engine started but shouts of seeing him again reached his ears. He didn't look but waved a hand in goodbye over his shoulder.

Out the back door of his house, Cash made his way across the acreage. He checked in with Beau who was closing the store for the day. Jeff and Sam caught up with him and by the time they were done discussing the upcoming overnight camping trip, the sun had set.

A soft yellow light glowed in the bedroom of Tracy's cabin. So she had come from Wild Horse. Never in a million years would he have guessed that. The way she'd arrived in that Mustang and with no Western wear, he'd taken her for a city girl. She was well-spoken and well-educated. With Coop she'd been gracious and when it came to owning up about the Dalton Gang, she'd been down-home humble.

Tracy Dalton was a city *and* a country girl with class.

Cash liked that about her. What Tracy wasn't—was pushy, clingy, or needy. She was her own woman. Maybe growing up in such an isolated area of Colorado, she had to be. Reaching her cabin, he noted the Dutch door in the dark living room was still open but decided to knock on the front door. As he raised his fist, he heard a bang and a scream from inside the cabin.

"Tracy?" he called.

"Help!"

Cash jiggled the knob, but it was locked. He leaped off the front porch and sprinted around the side of the cabin. Looking through the Dutch door he saw her as moonlight glowed past him into the room. Tracy wore a sleeveless, white nightgown that was somehow stretched tautly across her full breasts and shapely hips. With terror on her face, she stood as still as a statue. He had no idea what was going on.

"What's wrong?" Cash asked.

"Something has a hold of me," Tracy whispered, her eyes like saucers as she gingerly pointed an index finger over her shoulder.

Cash pulled out his cell, leaned into the top half of the door, and turned on the flashlight. Her laptop had fallen off the desk, landed on the wooden chair, and with a bang had pinned her nightgown to it. He couldn't recall ever having seen a woman so sexy, so vulnerable, and so funny all at the same time in his entire life. Until Tracy Dalton—at this moment.

"Do you think it's one of the chickens?" he whispered. "I've heard they're dangerous."

"I guess they could have flown in through the Dutch door when I was in the bedroom." Tracy's voice trembled. "Dear God! I'm barefoot."

"You're gonna leave Triple C-East missing some toes."

"Cash, help me!"

Cash hopped over the half door and into the room. He walked to Tracy, reached around behind her, and picked up her laptop. The gown floated back into place, the moonlight twinkled, and the woman fainted.

"Tracy!" Cash caught her with one arm and set her laptop on the desk. Scooping her up, he carried her through the cabin to her bedroom where the lamp on a nightstand covered them in its yellow glow. "Tracy?" he repeated. Her nightgown was sheerer than he'd realized, and he wanted to look down her body. With a will of iron, he didn't. He patted her ivory cheek. "Tracy, hey, wake up."

"Hay is for horses!" She sat up in bed and smacked his arm.

Cash tried his best to smother a chuckle but couldn't and howled with laughter. "If only you could have seen yourself with that big, bad laptop holding you hostage."

"Oh!" Tracy huffed, but he could tell she was fighting a giggle. Trying her best to frown at him, she gave him a shove and he stood up beside the bed. She scooted off the bed, poked him in the chest, and said, "You're the only thing big and bad around here, Cash Cooper!"

"Yeah," he said, growing serious as they stood inches apart, him fully dressed and Tracy in the flimsy gown. "And you're the only spitfire around here, Tracy Dalton."

When Tracy stared up at him, Cash cupped his hands to her face. As he lowered his head, he saw her eyes close. When his mouth made contact, he realized something was amiss. It took him a second before he realized she'd sucked her lips between her teeth. He chuckled, raised his head, and let her go.

"Don't you have a menagerie of redheads waiting for you?" she asked.

"No. Don't you know how to kiss?"

"I know how to kiss."

"Like you know how hens cock-a-doodle-do?"

"Like I know how roosters are peckers!"

"Kiss me like you know how." Cash didn't think she'd take the challenge.

But in the next breath Tracy grasped the open collar of his shirt, pulled herself to him, and stood on bare tiptoes between his cowboy boots. Sliding her hands to his shoulders, she closed her eyes, and tugged him closer. He lowered his head and this time his mouth met silky soft lips with a cinnamon flavor. Supple and full, her lips and mouth were the sweetest he'd ever tasted. He placed his hands on her waist and though he wanted to move them to her breasts, he restrained himself. When her fingers delicately threaded through his hair at the back of his head, goose bumps covered his skin. He pictured tossing her onto the bed just before she broke their kiss. Lowering herself from her tiptoes, she took a step back and smiled confidently.

"Do I know how to kiss?" Tracy asked, flipping a long lock of hair over her shoulder.

Cinnamon hair, lips, and breath, Tracy was princess of the cinnamon kiss. "Not bad."

"Not bad?"

"Not as good as a kiss from me, but not bad."

"What?" Tracy's mouth fell open. She pointed past the bedroom door. "Get out, mister big'n bad!" When Cash chuckled, she grabbed his hand and led him through the cabin. "Out!"

"I'm going," he said. She let go of his hand and slashed her index finger at the front door. He raised both hands in surrender. "We have to be up with the sun, so get a good night's sleep."

"Go!" she snapped and opened the door.

Shimmering moonlight haloed the gorgeous woman.

Through the gauzy nightgown, there was a hint of her nipples and the vee between her legs.

"When we get back on Thursday, I'll give you a tour of the inside of my house if you'd like to see it. For the purposes of your story."

"I would appreciate a tour," she admitted. "Thank you."

"I'll show you something new I recently added on the balcony facing Pikes Peak. You'll be the first one to see it."

"What is it?" Tracy asked, but he shrugged. "Tell me, Cash."

"Maybe I'll kiss you under the stars on the balcony." With that, he sauntered out of the cabin. "And maybe I won't." Crossing the porch he stopped at the edge and turned to her. Looking her up and down he cocked a brow and said, "Racy Tracy, don't bring that nightgown out on the trail. I can see right through it."

"Good night!" Tracy snapped and smacked the cabin door shut.

~

"RACY TRACY?" SHE REPEATED.

Tracy looked down at her gown, realized Cash was right, and hugged herself. She picked up her laptop and returned to the bedroom. She flipped back the bedspread and sheet and settled herself in the bed. Nothing she could do now about what he may or may not have seen. But she'd follow his advice and not take this gown on the overnight camping trip. She leaned against the headboard and sighed.

What was Cash planning to show her on that balcony? Would he really try to kiss her under the stars? Just in case he did, Tracy warned herself not to respond any more to him than he had to her when she'd kissed him. During that kiss Cash had kept his hands safely on her waist. But if he hadn't, how far would she have gone with him? Farther than she'd ever gone before? She wanted Cash to—

"I'm back," Donna called from the living room and

slammed the front door shut. Tracy hoped if she didn't answer, Donna wouldn't leave her be. "Knock, knock," the woman said at the same time she rapped on Tracy's bedroom door.

Her thoughts of Cash interrupted, Tracy reluctantly replied, "Come in."

Donna opened the door and leaned against the doorjamb. "I just ran into Cash and he brushed me off. As usual," she complained. "I don't know how that red-blooded, all-American, gorgeous rancher can resist all of this—" she waved a hand over her bosom— "voluptuousness."

Tracy shrugged and mumbled, "I don't know."

"And Beau! Handsome wrangler that he is, taken by simpering—" Donna huffed the name, "Cristen."

"Cristen is really pretty and so sweet," Tracy said. "She and Beau are cute together."

"Whatever. Even when Sam's wife isn't around, he's standoffish toward me. Jeff is too young and still wet behind the ears. I guess that leaves Ed and Larry."

"Leaves Ed and Larry for what?"

"A roll in the hay." Donna had apparently amused herself and laughed.

"Just for sex?" Tracy asked, probably showing her backward village persona.

"Umm...yes." Donna wiggled her head all around and repeated, "Just for sex."

"Do you even like Ed and Larry?"

"I like what's in their jeans."

"Those guys could be married like Sam, or maybe have a girlfriend like Beau."

"*Maybe* I'll find out on the trail tomorrow. At the campsite." Donna turned away. "Two at a time." She wandered away into the living room. "In their tent."

"Donna," Tracy began but heard her bedroom door slam, "please don't get us fired."

CHAPTER NINE

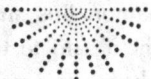

"Wednesday morning," Cash muttered, realizing Tracy's assignment was close to halfway done.

The chow bell clanged, officially announcing breakfast. He strode from the stables with Sam. They and the wranglers had already saddled the horses. For this overnight adventure, they would hitch both mules; Eloise the brown one and Mavis the black one to midsize, covered wagons. The guests always got a kick out of the mules and wagons on the overnight trips. The wranglers had gone ahead of Cash and Sam to eat so they could be ready to assist guests with saddlebags and saddling up. For some reason, Kellie had decided to accompany them on the excursion which meant packing an extra tent for Sam and Kellie to share.

That also meant Cash would be alone in his own tent. Never once had Cash shared a tent with a guest. But he sure as hell wanted to share one with Tracy. He'd gone to bed the previous night, tossed and turned until he fell asleep, and then dreamed of her. It had been so real when he had awakened he rolled over in bed and reached for her. But dammit, she hadn't been there.

He and Sam reached the café and took places across from

each other at a table. Halfway through his stack of pancakes, Cash saw her. An Elsa hat atop cinnamon waves, surrounding a beautiful face with those alluring turquoise eyes, she swayed toward them. Perky breasts filled out a shirt Cash recognized from his shop. At her waist, where his hands had rested the night before, the shirt was tied in a knot across her belly button. Blue jeans hugged her hips and thighs. Glistening cinnamon lips smiled as cowboy boots walked her closer. As he'd said to the barrel racing twins, Cash reminded himself he was a rancher running a business. Where Tracy was concerned, he'd rein himself in today.

"Is this seat taken, Cash?" Jacob asked, with a plate of food.

"No, sit down, Jacob," Cash said, pulling his eyes off Tracy.

"Your grandfather, Coop, is one of the nicest gentlemen I've ever had the pleasure of meeting," Jacob said, setting his plate on the table. "I got some great sunset photos."

"Good deal," Cash said and heard Donna's sharp, odd laugh. She had met up with Ed and Larry near the corral. "Yes, thanks, we all think Coop's the best too."

Turning in his chair, Jacob called, "Tracy," and waved her their way.

Cash hoped Tracy joined them before Donna could as she linked arms with the wranglers and tugged them toward the café. Those guys knew how to handle themselves. He wasn't concerned.

"Morning, gentlemen," Tracy said a moment later as Jacob pulled out the chair beside him. Setting her breakfast tray down on the table, she took the seat directly across from Cash. She smiled at him and said, "I'm excited about our camping trip."

Cash nodded. "It's never dull."

"I was telling Cash that thanks to Coop, we've got some fantastic shots of the sunset here on Triple C-East," Jacob said as Tracy sliced into her pancake.

"That's great, Jacob." With a glance to include Cash,

Tracy said, "At sunrise or sunset, the beauty of your ranch is nothing short of magnificent." Cash smiled and Tracy took a bite of pancake. Then back to Jacob she said, "I emailed Gerald last night and told him that along with Cash and Coop, I'd like to include some photos and quotes from the families on Triple C-Central and West."

"Emailed...like on a laptop...in the dark?" Cash asked innocently.

"Yes," Tracy said. Her eyes widened playfully warning him against telling Jacob about the laptop episode. "I had time to send an email last night since I wasn't chasing chickens."

"Good to know they weren't holding you hostage." Cash's lips twitched as he tried not to grin. When Jacob glanced away at Donna, who was heading their way without Ed and Larry in tow, Cash gave Tracy a wink of conspiracy as to her laptop. "Who's Gerald?"

"My editor at the magazine," Tracy told him.

"He's smitten with Tracy," Jacob said, back in the conversation as he nudged her in the arm with his elbow. He looked across the table at Cash to say, "Gerald will give Tracy whatever she wants whether she asks for it or not. Like a badass Mustang to drive on assignment."

"I'm sure that's not true." Tracy laughed, but Cash could see on her face she suspected Jacob's assessment was accurate. "As for our assignment, the owner, not Gerald, has final say about this article."

"Feel free to invite Gerald to the Fourth of July barbecue," Cash offered, figuring he might as well get a look at the competition. Competition? Was he vying for Tracy's attention? What had happened to not being ready to give up his living alone, casual sex, bachelor life? "So that Mustang's a rental?"

"Yes," Tracy said, finishing the last of her pancake. "If I'd been accustomed to driving it, I wouldn't have been going so fast or almost run you down."

"I see," Cash said, noting the cute blush staining her cheeks.

"The only other standard I've ever driven is a truck," Tracy said.

"The old clunker truck?" Donna snickered and plopped down next to Cash.

"I said my grandmother called it a classic not a clunker," Tracy countered as Donna shrugged.

"How is your grandma, Tracy?" Jacob asked with genuine concern.

Cash saw Tracy flinch before she replied, "I thought she sounded better this morning when I spoke to her. Thanks for asking, Jacob."

"Boss?" Sam asked, walking to the table. "Ready to go?"

"Yeah," Cash said to Sam and stood. "Let's ride."

"I just started eating," Donna said, diving into a double stack of pancakes. She began shoveling food into her mouth and snatched up her plate as Cristen neared. "I'm not done!" When Beau neared and greeted Cristen, Donna said around a mouthful of food, "Hi Beau!"

"I'm ready to go," Jacob said evenly, stood, and pulled out Tracy's chair for her.

"Got your personal belongings ready for the saddlebags?" Cash asked.

"Yes," Tracy and Jacob both said at once.

Out in the open area, Cash paused to take count of guests, wranglers, and horses. Kellie and Sam loaded some last-minute food items into the covered wagon hitched to Mavis. The wranglers had the horses on standby waiting for their riders. Cash headed toward Captain tethered next to Cinnamon. Jacob walked with Cash and Tracy, stopping when he reached Chief. Donna came running and chewing and was the last to mount up. At the front of the pack, with Patience, Brittany, and Daphne, Jeff nodded to his parents who were chatting with Diane and Joyce. Ed, Beth, and Lisa were to the left of them as Larry, Natasha, Michaela, and LeAnn sat ready to ride on the right. When Jeff glanced at him, Cash tipped two fingers off the brim of his cowboy hat. Jeff tipped two fingers off the brim of his hat in return.

Sweeping his arm forward Jeff hollered, "Wagons ho!"

~

"Do you always carry a gun, Cash?" Tracy asked, come late morning. "I noticed you had one yesterday when we rode to Fish Creek."

"Yes," Cash replied. "This is my ranch revolver, a Ruger Blackhawk 357 Magnum. You never know when you'll meet up with a snake."

"We never had a gun so I don't know anything about them," Tracy said and let the subject go at that. Glancing up at the clear blue sky as a refreshing Chinook breeze blew past them, she said, "Another beautiful Colorado day."

Cash's cobalt eyes swept over her, making her tingle as he said, "Yup."

Tracy listened as Cash, Sam, Jeff, and the wranglers talked with guests about the dude ranch, local wildlife, and previous excursions. Riding here and there, but mostly near Cash, she took mental notes. Jacob snapped photographs. Donna flirted outrageously with Ed and Larry. Although the men behaved themselves, some of the younger female guests in particular noticed Donna's flirting, too, and giggled or rolled their eyes. Cash ignored it.

"Fish Creek dead ahead and Turkey Pond on down the trail," Jeff called.

"Is the fishing pond fed by the creek? Is that why it's called Fish Creek?" Tracy asked.

"No, but I can see why you'd think that," Cash said. "Turkey Pond is spring-fed from the water that comes out of the hill behind it." He indicated what was basically a mountain decorated with ponderosa pines about halfway up it. "The pond is nearly twenty feet deep and gets cold about four feet down because of being spring-fed."

"So no skinny dipping?" Tracy asked. Where on earth had that come from?

"I didn't say that," Cash replied. "But not in the pond."

Shocked at herself, Tracy didn't ask where they might skinny dip. Instead she asked, "Are there turkeys around Turkey Pond?"

"Yes, and that's why my great-grandfather named it Turkey Pond. The turkeys live in the higher elevations of Colorado like these foothills." He pointed in a wide circle at the trees. "Sometimes we see them and we almost always hear their loud, throaty gobbles."

"You might be right about hens not cock-a-doodle-doing," she admitted.

"You don't say."

"Winston brought chickens to the house to impress my grandmother with eggs. Except the chickens never laid a single egg. But they crowed every morning. I'm convinced Winston bought the eggs and said the hens laid them."

"Who the hell is this Winston?"

"A retired school bus driver, who we've known of for years. He became a friend of my grandmother's after Grandpa Lew passed."

"The first red flag about Winston is." Cash caught her eye and said, "He's a liar."

"Yes, I know that now thanks to you."

"How old is he?"

"I heard he retired early, so maybe sixty, sixty-two. Probably more than a decade younger than my grandma. Maybe as much as fifteen years."

"At the risk of sounding politically incorrect, that could be a second red flag."

"Yes. I totally agree," she said. "Wild Horse is a hundred miles due east of Triple C-East," Cash said. "I'll go with you to check things out, Tracy. Anytime."

"Thank you, Cash," Tracy said sincerely. "My grandmother assures me Winston is just a friend who is helping her with the yard and chores." Swallowing her concern, she told him, "This story, featuring your Triple C Ranch, is by far my biggest article ever for *Ranchers and Ranges*. She wants me to send her a copy when it comes out."

Cash nodded but with a slight frown. They rode in silence for a few miles to Turkey Pond. It was large, more like a lake than a pond. The area was as serene as it was green. Tracy heard appreciative oohs and ahhs from the guests. After everyone had dismounted, the horses were watered along Fish Creek. The wranglers set up the tents with help from the guests. Nine tents were arranged around the pond not too far apart, yet with enough distance to allow for some privacy. Along one side of the tent Tracy was to share with Donna were the two girls Tracy had come to think of as Pretty Patience and Delightful Daphne. On the other side were Beth and Lisa, both sweet as could be. Ed and Larry's tent was on the far side of Natasha and Michaela, who could make you laugh with just a roll of their eyes. As others chose tent-mates, Tracy wasn't sure who was rooming with whom. She helped Cash set up her tent while Donna chatted to Ed and Larry without lifting a finger.

Kellie had a cooking area set up and running in no time flat. The delicious smell of burgers filled the air. Served on paper plates atop tin plates, the burgers came with chips and an apple. Sam helped Kellie serve lunch and Tracy found that she was starved.

When Cash sauntered up beside her, Tracy said, "Putting up a tent along with riding a horse all this way can work up an appetite."

"Yeah." Cash's grin was as cocky as his deep chuckle. "Let's eat and go fishin'."

"I need to make notes on my story."

"Your phone will work, but your laptop won't have a signal out here."

"Not to worry, I've got a pen and paper. And more questions for you."

"Let's do it by lantern light," Cash said.

"You mean work on my story?" Tracy asked.

"Sure." His smile was cocky and her heart raced. "That's what I mean."

Kellie placed a burger, chips, and an apple on their plates. They each grabbed a bottle of water and walked to a picnic table. Tracy sat in the middle and Cash slid in beside her. Even as he ate his lunch, this man thrilled her with his virile masculinity. He hadn't touched her since kissing her the previous evening, but shivers spread through her from head to toe. That was due to just sitting next to him on the bench. As she took a bite of burger, Tracy wondered if he were to kiss her, much less touch her while doing so, how she would react. Could she resist this man? Did she want to? Why would she? Well, for one thing, because she was a professional, serious journalist. She hadn't taken this assignment looking for anything but a great story. For another thing? She couldn't come up with another single thing.

"Boss, you gonna fish?" Jeff asked, standing over by the wagons.

"Probably, but don't worry about me," Cash said. "I'll get my gear when I need it."

"We got it," Sam called, standing next to his son. "And we set up your tent while you were helping Tracy. Your gear's outside your tent."

"Thanks, guys," Cash called, seeing his tent was ready to go. They finished their lunch as had Larry and Ed who had somehow escaped Donna and were unloading the wagons. Cash said, "I have a fondness for Eloise and Mavis. Let's give them an apple before we go fishing."

"The mules?"

"Yup." He chuckled. "Come on."

Cash tugged her off the bench and they put their paper plates in trash bags and stacked their clean tins on a table. Tracy assessed this part, like every part of her dude ranch experience, as a well-oiled machine. They each grabbed an apple and made their way to the mules. As soon as Cash got close enough, the mules rubbed their noses against him and flicked their tails.

"Grandpa Lew always said animals know a good person from a bad one," Tracy said.

Cash smiled his thanks. Feeding his apple to the brown mule, he said, "This is Eloise."

"Hi Mavis," Tracy said to the black mule and held her apple to the animal's mouth as Cash had. "I miss my dog."

"You have a dog?" Cash asked, and she nodded. "Where is your dog this week?"

"Doggy day care in the Springs," Tracy said.

"What breed?"

"German shepherd. A year and a half old," she said. "He was an owner-surrender at the pound. I made sure that the complex I chose to live in allowed for animals. I adopted him the same week I moved into my apartment. He's been a great companion this past year."

"I wish I'd known. We make exceptions for breeds that are typically good around horses. I would have let you bring him with you."

"I had no idea."

"Yeah." Cash chuckled and shook his head as if in disbelief. "Coop has an Australian cattle dog named Davy Crockett. Crockett for short. But I've recently been thinking of getting a dog and a German shepherd had crossed my mind."

"German shepherds are really smart and protective."

"My brother-in-law, Derek, who's a former cop, was saying that just the other day," Cash said. "The house I grew up in has a *Gone with the Wind* staircase and my sister has a big, black cat named Scarlett O'Hara." He chuckled. "I'll give you one guess what they named their German shepherd puppy."

"Rhett Butler?" Tracy said with a romantic sigh.

"Hell no." Cash laughed, enjoying teasing her. "Spike." Tracy laughed and with a pat to the mules' noses, Cash said. "Come on, let's go catch our supper." As they made their way to Cash's tent, the most secluded of all the tents, he asked, "So what's your dog's name?"

"He was used to his name by the time I adopted him when he was six months old, so I kept it," Tracy said. Cash cocked a brow while waiting for her to answer. "When I tell you his name, you'll laugh."

"Try me."

CHAPTER TEN

"Dude." Tracy smiled.

"Seriously?" Cash asked and when Tracy nodded, he chuckled. That was an ideal name for a dog on a dude ranch. Would he have come up with it for his dog? No idea. "Dude is a perfect name," he said. Could this girl be any more perfect? Perfect hair. Perfect face. Perfect body. Perfect personality. Perfect dog. "I'd like to meet Dude."

"I'm sure Dude would like to meet you too," Tracy said a bit shyly.

Cash wondered if Tracy had just opened the door to him visiting her in the Springs. They had reached his tent and, like Sam had said, his fishing gear was waiting for him. Outside each tent were two camping chairs. Inside were lanterns, pillows, and bedrolls on cots.

"I never get tired of this," Cash said to Tracy, looking around the campsite, pond, creek, trees, hills, and endless land.

"I'm going to quote you on that simple but telling statement in the story," Tracy said, just as Jacob walked toward them. "Jacob, can you take a picture of Cash in front of his tent?"

"Absolutely. I'm getting a bunch of great photos today,"

Jacob said and snapped a couple. "I'll take some of the folks fishing down by Turkey Pond too."

Cash picked up his gear and handed an extra pole to Tracy. They made their way down to the pond where ladies and wranglers were sitting here and there. Ed and Larry tossed in their lines and helped some guests do the same while Jeff and Sam walked to the creek to assist those who wanted to fly fish. Still, others preferred to relax while they watched and enjoyed nature. There was a wooden dock that extended out over the water. Cash walked almost to the end of it and set his tackle box, net, and pole along one side of the dock.

"We've got canoes and paddleboats in that barn across the way," Cash told her as they sat down on the dock side-by-side.

"I'm going to stick my toes in the water," Tracy said and took off her boots.

"Okay, do that."

"You do it with me, Cash."

Tracy inched forward and dipped her toes into the pond. When she nudged him and grinned, Cash realized he hadn't done so since he was a kid. Without thinking twice, he pulled off his boots and socks and rolled up his pants legs. Sinking his feet in to the ankles, Tracy gently seesawed her feet back and forth in the water. Cash watched her feet with reddish-orange toenails wiggle in the pond.

He teased, "This is a well-stocked pond with plenty of largemouth bass and channel catfish. The reason we don't skinny dip in this pond is because bass are predators and catfish are scavengers. Either way, they'll think your toes are pyracantha berries and have a nibble."

"Yikes!" Tracy giggled and pulled her feet back onto the dock. Sitting crossed-legged and barefoot, she said, "Between your chickens and your fish, I'll be lucky to go back to Colorado Springs with all ten toes."

Having so much fun with her, Cash laughed. "Oh come

on, we can spare a toe or two. Stick your feet back in the water. But don't splash or you'll scare the fish away."

With a laugh, Tracy eased her feet into the pond. Cash helped her bait a hook and showed her how to toss the line into the water. They laughed and fished and talked. As often as Cash had camped here, he couldn't remember having a better time at this pond. All because of Tracy. The wind caught her hair and tossed it around her face. It occurred to him that might be how her hair would look after a tumble in his bed. Cash caught a six-pound bass and said he'd caught his dinner and hoped she didn't starve. When he caught about an eight-pound bass, he said maybe he could share a bite or two with her. Tracy frowned in determination and caught a fish about half the size of his first fish. Cash was more excited for her than he'd ever been for himself. Tracy jumped up with the fish dangling on her line. As she raised her fishing pole out of the water like Cash had done, her belly button peeked out from under the knot of her shirt.

"This is the ugliest fish I've ever seen!" Tracy squealed as it flipped back and forth.

"Catfish are ugly," Cash agreed with a laugh as he stood. She did a curtsy at the end of the dock to acknowledge the hoots, hollers, and applause from folks around the pond. Damn, this woman was one sexy spitfire. "But they taste good."

"Thank you, Cash," Tracy said as he took the fish off the hook for her. "I've never fished. This was a fun experience."

"You're welcome." In Cash's opinion the whole day had been...fun. Yeah, fun and perfect. They soon gathered up their fish and gear. Slipping on their boots, they walked along the dock, both smiling. "Let's take the fish over to Kellie's kitchen."

Where Kellie had set up her outdoor kitchen, Cash demonstrated to Tracy, Natasha, Michaela, LeAnn, and Jacob how to clean and gut a fish in preparation for cooking it. Jacob had caught a fish and gave it a try. The ladies watched and then Tracy volunteered to try her hand at it. When she closed one eye and squinted with the other, Cash said she had to watch what she was doing with both eyes wide open or risk losing a finger which might hurt more than a toe. She opened her eyes, he helped her, and four fish were ready to cook. Other people began showing up with fish and Cash knew no one would go to bed hungry.

After supper, he left Tracy talking to Jacob. In front of the large horseshoe circle of tents, individual campfires crackled, burning brightly. Cash made his rounds as host, visiting with the guests and his wranglers. All were chatting, chuckling, and having a grand time. He noted Tracy's so-called assistant was far more interested in Ed and Larry than touching base with Tracy and Jacob. But as long as Ed and Larry did their jobs, which they were currently doing by seeing to the horses, it wasn't his call if Donna wasn't doing hers.

Cash walked to his tent and took a seat in one of the camping chairs. He gazed down the gently sloping hill to the pond and watched Tracy. As people gathered in groups of two or three, she made a point to speak with everyone. Her tinkling laugh floated to him on a breeze. Even as she and Jacob helped Joyce and then Diane up from where they sat on the dock, Tracy moved with grace. As the sun lowered behind the ponderosa pines, people began drifting to their own tents. Cash wished Tracy was sharing his tent tonight. Hell, more than tonight. She glanced his way, and he lifted his right hand from the armrest of the chair.

Hips swaying as she walked up the slight grade she asked, "Are you tired?"

"No ma'am," he replied as she reached him. He cocked a brow, looked her in the eye, and with meaning said, "Just enjoying the scenery." A turkey gobbled in the nearby trees and Tracy jumped. "Turkey." Cash chuckled and swung a hand to the empty chair. "Sit a spell."

Tracy sat and they talked, easily drifting from one topic to another, finding an occasional similarity among the differences in their lives and backgrounds. Everything about Tracy mesmerized Cash. He definitely wanted to take her to bed. But he was enjoying getting to know her outside of the bedroom too.

"It's late, I should head to my own tent," Tracy said.

"You won't be able to sleep," Cash said and nodded.

Most of the guests had turned in for the night. Outside of the tent Tracy was to share with Donna, the moonlight showed the woman standing and holding onto the forearms of Larry and Ed as if trying to prevent them from going to their own tent. Voices drifted to them and then when the men sat back down, Donna did as well.

"I'm sorry about Donna," Tracy said softly, looking in the direction where Donna was tipping a bottle to her mouth. "Jacob is fed up with her. I can honestly say I wouldn't want her on another assignment with us."

"I saw her slide a bottle of vodka in her saddlebag," Cash told her. "I think she's had too much to drink."

Tracy sat forward in her chair, preparing to stand. "I'll go over and try to intervene on behalf of Ed and Larry."

"No, stay where you are," Cash said, and waved her back into her chair. "Ed and Larry can handle her. Not their first rodeo in a case like this." He kept an eye on the situation as Tracy also watched with obvious concern. "Before she passes out, one of them will help her to her cot," he added from experience. "Ed and Larry will go to their tent and no one will be the wiser if you spend the night in mine."

Tracy's head swiveled in his direction and her lips parted in surprise. "Your tent?"

"Two cots to a tent," he said with a shrug.

"Actually...that would be great, Cash," Tracy said quietly but with relief in her voice. "Donna snores like a grizzly bear." Finally, something about Donna was unexpected music to Cash's ears. "I don't mean to sound unkind, but sharing a cabin with her has been torture. I've tossed and turned and slept in spurts with a pillow over my head since we got to the ranch."

Sam gave them a wave and disappeared into his tent

with Kellie. Jacob looked at Tracy and raised both hands, palms up, regarding Donna. Tracy splayed her hands as well and then Jacob waved before heading into the tent he was to share with Jeff.

"I don't know how comfortable you'll be on our camp cots. They're the bare minimum and lightweight so that Eloise and Mavis can manage them. But at least they're up off the ground." With a grin, he said, "You can tell me in the morning if I snore." Tracy nodded. "Why don't you get settled in first while I make a final round of the campsite?" Cash suggested and stood. He offered a hand to Tracy and when she took it, he tugged her out of the chair. Entering the tent, he lit the lantern, exited, and said, "If you need to use one of the outhouses during the night, watch out for grizzly bears lurking in the trees."

Tracy's turquoise eyes grew wide. "Are there grizzly bears in these woods?"

"No," he said. She was so cute to tease. "But there are turkeys and snakes."

"I'll be on my cot," Tracy said and darted into the tent.

Cash grinned. He'd sleep on his cot too. But he hoped it would be the first and last time he slept alone in Tracy's presence.

CHAPTER ELEVEN

"*W*hat am I doing?" Tracy whispered to herself. Here in this tent, she would spend the night in the closest of confines with the most handsome and irresistible man she'd ever laid eyes on. The lantern, hanging from a hook, cast a pale glow across the tent. She glanced from side to side. The camp cot to her left boasted a pillow and a blanket covering it. On top of the cot to the right lay a rolled-up blanket with a pillow atop it. She grasped the pillow of the cot on the right and tossed it toward the far end.

Quickly, she unzipped her jeans, pushed them down and sat. Whoa! Okay, so sitting on a cot was not like sitting on a bed. She'd almost tipped it over. Carefully repositioning herself she shed her boots and jeans. She tossed her jeans to the end of the cot, untied her shirt, and smoothed the tails over her tummy and hips. Carefully lying back on the cot, she shook the blanket out over her legs and torso. Whew. Done. Before Cash got back. For the next few minutes, she concentrated on breathing evenly trying to calm herself.

"Are you decent?" came his baritone voice at the entrance to the tent.

"Yes." Tracy heard the tremor in her reply and swallowed. "I'm good."

Cash pushed open the flaps of the tent and entered. "I'll bet you are."

His compliment and rakish grin made her tingle. The tent had seemed roomy until Cash filled it. He couldn't stand up straight. Sitting down on his cot, he grinned across the short span between them. Rolling to her side to face him and careful to keep her blanket in place up to her waist, she almost tipped the cot over again. Cash shook his head and chuckled.

"Any sign of Donna?" Tracy asked.

"Didn't see her, but I heard snoring when I stopped to thank Ed and Larry for getting her inside her tent to her cot."

"I told you about the snoring, didn't I?" Tracy asked as Cash nodded. "I will repay Ed and Larry with a photo and nice quote about them in the magazine article."

"Got everything you need for now?"

"Heck no," Tracy said incredulously with a soft laugh. "I need to brush my teeth, wash my face, take a shower, shampoo my hair, blow it dry, and put on my nightgown." When Cash nodded and took off a boot, she said, "But we're roughing it tonight, right?"

"Kinda." He set his boot aside and took off the other one. "Roughing is when you're moving cattle for days on end. My brother, Chase, and I grew up doing that on Triple C-Central. He doesn't go on those drives much these days because he and Jade have two young kids; my nephew, Colton, and my niece, Courtney. But driving cattle is roughing it."

"I need to make a note of that for my article."

Tracy carefully sat up so as not to wobble the cot, and keeping the blanket in place across her lap, she grabbed her jeans. Reaching into the back pocket, she pulled out her phone and made a note. As Cash unbuttoned his shirt, she wondered if he'd take it off. She wanted him to. She was curious. Though she didn't know exactly what to expect, as he certainly did, she'd bet he was *good* too. She stole a quick glance and saw that he had removed his shirt and placed it on top of his boots. Wearing his jeans, instead of covering himself with the blanket, he'd stretched out on top of it. Hands stacked under his dark head, chest bare, and ankles crossed, he had easily settled onto the cot.

Prolonging her view of Cash, she let her gaze roam from the jeans at his feet, up his calves, to the snug fit around his thighs and hips. Below his indented belly button, dark hair swirled and disappeared beneath a brown belt with a silver buckle. Above the belt and buckle, she admired a flat stomach and muscular chest belonging to the *sexiest man alive*. Then back to the crotch of Cash's jeans she visually caressed the masculine bulge.

"Done?" he asked.

Tracy snapped her gaze back up his body, and his blue eyes seized her. "Done." She clicked off her phone and placed it beside her. "Thanks."

"Anytime."

Cash turned the lantern off and moonlight streamed in through the netted windows. Tracy carefully lay back in the cot. Her heart was pounding. Wildly! She hoped he couldn't hear it and to make sure she folded her hands over her heart. If this man could elicit such a reaction from four feet away and not touch her, however would she survive a kiss? That is if he decided to kiss her…under the stars…on the balcony of his house.

"Good night, Cash."

She detected a slight groan in Cash's, "Night, Tracy."

Tracy closed her eyes and after a long, busy day and two nights of little sleep, she hit dreamland. Visions of Cash played with her in slumber; he was in the saddle, the owner, the man in charge, the leader. He set her straight about the Mustang and swept her onto his stallion. Cash sent her heart racing, her knees wobbling, and her skin heating. She kissed him. He was completely unmoved. Unaffected. Not touching her. Uninterested.

Then as dreams often do the scene changed and Tracy

found herself wrapped in Cash's muscular arms. He'd taken command in what had to be his bed. His lips touched hers, his hands slid around her body, and he tugged her on top of him. Tracy rolled with it and—splat!

"Oof!" she said, waking up on the floor of the tent.

The lantern spread its soft glow. She lay on her stomach with the cot on top of her. The cot was hauled off her and put right side up, where it started.

"Are you okay?" Cash asked.

"Yes," she mumbled, mortified. She pulled the pillow, which was on top of her head, close around her face. The blanket lay underneath her and she realized too late that her shirt had ridden up her back with the movement of her arms. Her bikini panties and bare legs had to be in full view. She prayed for the ground beneath her to open up and swallow her whole. It didn't. "I meant to do that."

Cash's deep chuckle put a grin on Tracy's lips, but it stayed hidden underneath the pillow. It was the middle of the night, and she could tell he was doing his best to rein in his amusement so as not to wake the camp. Had this been during the day, she absolutely knew he would have hooted and hollered in a belly laugh. She would have too.

"This little episode is going in *Ranchers and Ranges* if I have to write it myself," Cash informed her.

"No!" Tracy said as she pulled the pillow off her head. She looked up at Cash as he snapped a flash photo of her with his phone. Leaning forward as he sat on his cot, his forearms rested on his spread knees. He turned his phone to show her the shot of her looking up at him; eyes big, hair in wild disarray, and her bikini-clad fanny clearly exposed. He grinned down at her and she pleaded, "You can't tell anyone! It's our secret! Pinkie swear!"

"Hell no," he said around another chuckle. "This is too damn funny to keep secret."

"We'll never speak of this again!" she insisted and held up her pinkie finger. "Swear!"

"No." Cash snagged her pinkie with his and turned off the lamp. "C'mere, spitfire."

Keeping Cash's pinkie finger wrapped with hers, he tugged and she found herself on her knees between his spread thighs. Through the split in the tent opening, moonlight showed her the handsome face of the powerful man who had her in his clutches.

"Pinkie swear, you'll delete that photo, big'n bad?" Tracy whispered, using the nickname that described him.

"I'm keeping that photo in case I need to blackmail you."

Cash's voice was husky and he let go of her pinkie. He placed her arms around his neck and settled his hands at her waist. His head lowered and his eyes closed. She shut her eyes and his mouth came down on hers. Leaning into him, she tightened her arms as his hands slipped under her shirt. She threaded her fingers through the thick dark-brown hair at the back of his head. So much for not responding to him, she thought. Cash groaned, and it sounded a lot like the groan that had escaped him when he'd said good night. As they kissed, his hands flattened to her back and moved lower. When he cupped both hands to the cheeks of her fanny and squeezed, every nerve in Tracy's body jolted like she'd been touched with a live wire.

"Cash!" She gulped, breaking their kiss and opening her eyes.

"Yeah." He slid his hands up to her waist and winked. "Sorry."

"Are you?" she whispered.

"Do you want me to be?"

"No."

Cash molded her to him for another kiss and this time his hands moved up her ribcage. Never in her life had Tracy experienced a predicament like this. Because she'd never allowed herself to be in a situation like this. Wanton craving flooded her entire being for this man and only this man. She yearned for him to do this and…and… What? More. He cupped her breasts.

She gasped. But, oh yes. Her nipples beaded against the thin fabric of her bra separating her skin from the palms of his large hands. She arched her body, pressing her breasts into his hands.

"I'm not made of steel, Tracy."

"You feel like steel." Tracy trailed her fingers across his broad shoulders and down his muscular arms. "More, Cash."

"Any more and you're liable to get it all," he warned. His hands slid to her waist, and he scooted her from between his legs. "Racy Tracy, crawl back onto your cot."

With her hands on his knees, she said, "Only if you pinkie swear you'll delete that pic."

"If I don't promise you that, it's a win-win for me. Win because I keep the pic and win because we're gonna make love right now," he clarified and cocked a brow.

Tracy thought it would be a win-win for her, too, but didn't say so. Grabbing her blanket and pillow, she carefully snuggled back onto her cot. She heard Cash mutter a couple of mild oaths, something to do with holy water and hellfire. He rolled to his side, facing away from her. Maybe he wasn't as unmoved, unaffected, and uninterested as she'd assumed.

"Night," she whispered.

"I hope so."

Tracy closed her eyes and it felt like only minutes later when she heard birds chirping. Morning? Already? She opened her eyes and saw Cash's empty cot. He was up and gone. She was instantly wide awake. The whole camp would know she'd spent the night in Cash's tent. She yanked on her jeans, stepped into her boots, and tied her shirt. Looking for her phone and running her fingers through her hair, she cringed at how she'd thrown herself at Cash Cooper. He was no doubt used to it. But for her it was a first. She stepped to the tent flaps and peeked out at the camp. Quiet. The pond glistened in the early light from the sun peeking out behind the hills.

Widening the tent flaps, she saw Cash sipping from a cup and sitting in one of the camp chairs. She had no choice but to face him and yet another bad impression. Why had she ruined their night together? His cowboy hat sat low on his head, shading those cobalt-blue eyes from the sun. The stubble of a black beard added to his rugged, masculine appeal. He wore a different shirt today. The tails were tucked into his blue jeans which bunched around his boots.

"Is the coast clear?" she asked.

"Yup, come on out," he said. When she had sat down in the other camp chair, he handed her a cup of coffee. "Damn, you're pretty in the morning."

Tracy felt herself blush and began, "Thank you, and about last night—"

"What about it?" A slow, sexy smirk played across Cash's lips.

Holding her tin cup with both hands, she said, "I just wanted to tell you that I don't come onto guys. I mean I've never done that."

"Done what?" he asked. "Fallen out of their bed?"

"No, I've never fallen out of their bed. Or my own bed. Anybody's bed." Tracy felt flustered and shook her head. "But that's not what I mean." She would not allow her wrong impression to stand uncorrected. In the few days she'd known Cash, he'd impressed her. It was important to her that he knew she wasn't what? Loose? "I'm not usually *racy*." She glanced away from him to say, "I've never spent the night with—" When he didn't reply, she looked at him. "Do you know what I mean?"

Cash cocked his head. "You're a virgin."

"Yes." Tracy had noted it wasn't a question. And instantly she knew that's why he'd stopped and sent her back to her own cot. Her blood warmed and her heart melted. She did her best to ignore both. Raising one shoulder in a shrug, she said, "Full disclosure."

"Full disclosure, I'm flattered." Cash winked and drained his coffee cup. The chow bell clanged and he held out his hand to her. When she took it, he tugged her out of the chair and then let go. "I'm hungry."

CHAPTER TWELVE

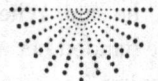

*Y*eah, hungry for Tracy. Only for Tracy.

What kind of holy water or hellfire could cure him? None, he knew of.

As she walked by his side along Turkey Pond, Cash didn't want the previous night to be his first and last with her. He'd made this camping outing on the ranch countless times and never gave a thought to who was with him. Until he'd ridden his horse alongside Tracy. Fished on that dock with Tracy. Shared a tent on his favorite hillside with Tracy. Cash reasoned if he took her to bed she would be out of his system. That was always the case. Tried and true. But she was a virgin. *More*, she'd whispered to him. He'd been with virgins. Granted it had been a while. Probably not since college. To be honest, being with a virgin wasn't nearly as enjoyable as being with a woman who knew what she was doing in bed. So far.

"Hi Jacob," Tracy called and waved as they saw him and Jeff standing outside their tent, drinking from tin cups. "I don't see Donna anywhere," she said as they neared the breakfast line.

"Me neither," Cash replied, looking past the table Kellie had laden with breakfast burritos, which were easy to eat when out on the trail. "Mornin'," he said to Kellie as they stopped. Tracy picked up a burrito and he took two. He spoke to wranglers and guests who were lining up for breakfast. Then to Tracy he said, "I usually eat down by the pond."

"Sounds good." They moseyed to the pond and sat near the water's edge. Cash had finished his first burrito and Tracy was halfway done with hers when she asked, "Do you bring people here just during official dude ranch excursions or do you come here for private getaways as well?"

"Are you asking me if I bring women here?"

"That was a magazine question, not a personal one."

"My magazine answer is I come here mostly on ranch excursions." Cash wondered if she'd ask him where he went for private getaways. But in the next second Donna burst through the flap of her tent, stumbled down the slight incline to the pond, and knee deep in the water upchucked whatever it was she'd last eaten. Or drank. Cash frowned. "That did not just happen."

"I'm afraid it did," Tracy said as Donna heaved again before sloshing out of the water and traipsing back up the hill. "I'm so sorry, Cash." Before entering the tent, Donna turned and scanned the campground until she spotted Tracy. Tracy waved directly at her but without acknowledging her, Donna disappeared inside the tent. "Honestly, I wouldn't blame you one bit if you threw the two of us off your ranch and let Jacob stay."

"And miss out on things like almost being run over, sideswiping you into my saddle, watching you chase chickens, or rescuing you from a laptop? And then there's the whole cot kerfuffle."

"Kerfuffle?" she repeated.

"Commotion." He chuckled. "So, no chance, I'll throw you off the ranch. Who knows what other entertainment you might provide?"

Tracy's turquoise eyes had grown wider...until they narrowed dangerously. Raising her index finger and wagging it at him, she teased him back, "You swore a pinkie promise."

"No, ma'am." He grabbed her finger. "I sure as hell did not." Letting go of her finger, he laughed. "From now on, I'll be telling the story about how my tent mate moaned herself right off her cot."

"Did I moan?" Tracy gasped.

Cash only grinned. "You're fun to tease. You aren't offended over every other word or deed and you laugh at yourself. You give as good as you get." He took a deep breath on purpose and admitted, "You're a breath of fresh air, Tracy Dalton." Her expression conveyed that was not what she'd expected to hear from him. It wasn't what Cash had expected to say. But the words were true. "Couple of clichés there," he acknowledged with a shrug. "I'm not a writer."

"You're a rancher," Tracy said as if it were high praise indeed. "Thank you, Cash."

"I call it like I see it."

"Boss?" Jeff said as he walked toward them. "Are we gonna fish or head home?"

"Ask the ladies," Cash said with a roundabout gesture toward the tents. He got to his feet and extended his hand to Tracy, helping her to hers. "If they're ready to go now, you could take them on the longer, more scenic route back to the ranch."

"That's what I was thinking too. We have provisions for lunch."

"Since it's Thursday and the barbecue is tomorrow, I've already saddled Captain and after I break down my tent, I'm taking the shortcut home."

"Got it. We'll load your tent." Jeff left with two fingers off the brim of his hat.

Cash turned his attention back to Tracy. "What would you like to do?"

"If you mean fish or head out with you, I'd like to go with you," she said, and when he grinned, she blushed. "If you meant take the longer more scenic route back to the ranch—"

"You're going with me. I'll saddle Cinnamon while you get your stuff. Meet me at the horses and Tracy," he glanced over her shoulder, "please don't let Donna come with you."

~

"You look drunk, Donna!" Winston Smith blared as he stared at the cell phone screen of his FaceTime call.

"I'm not!" Donna spat right back at him. "I'm hungover."

"You're still on that magazine job with her, aren't you?" Winston spewed a chaw of tobacco out of Tammy Dalton's truck window. Sitting behind the wheel and parked on the far side of the shed, he eyed Tammy's little house. Having returned from the grocery store, he was holding four eggs to warm them, as if they came from the chickens. Luckily Tammy was ignorant about them being roosters. "Has the *Dalton Darling* figured out you're in cahoots with the magazine guy?"

"No, she's too busy with the ranch owner." It really bugged Donna that the Kit Carson newspaper had bestowed the darling pet name on Tracy with a front-page sendoff when she had landed the big-time magazine journalism job. "And just so you know, I *had* to drink to make it through the night in a freaking tent in a godforsaken woods. The only reason I'm still here is because you're paying me to spy on her."

"With a big payoff coming."

"So you've been saying for months, Daddy dear," Donna said sarcastically. "How much longer do I have to follow the little bitch around?" When her father didn't answer, she glared into the phone at him and snapped, "How much longer?"

"I told you, until I get the old lady's money in my hands and preferably her property in my name too."

"What good does that do me exactly?" Donna

demanded. "I sure as crap don't plan to live in Wild Horse. There are no men within a thousand-mile radius."

"Stop exaggerating. Besides, her property's all mine," he reminded her. He spewed tobacco again and wiped his mouth with the hand holding his newly purchased gun. "But with your share of her buried cash you can live anywhere and get any man you want."

"Not any man," Donna said and glanced away from the phone.

"Are you looking for Tracy?"

"Shit no," Donna said. "I'm trying to spot that good-lookin' rancher she's writing about. I don't see either one of them."

"You gotta be Tracy's best friend and stay close so you can keep me informed of her comings and goings, Donna," he insisted for the hundredth time, admiring the gun from the pawnshop. Staring back at his phone, he said, "We agreed; keep your friends close and enemies closer. I'm doing my part. Do yours."

"I've tried, she's not buying it. And I think Cooper's interested in her."

Winston almost choked as he fingered the gun. "That's all we need is for some man to intervene on her behalf before I get the money, if not the property. Sidetrack Cooper."

"Cooper's hotter than hell and I'd like nothing better than to sidetrack him away from Tracy," Donna griped with a frown wrinkling her brow. "But he's not buying it, either."

"I've seen to it that Tammy fell and sprained her ankle. She can barely hobble around. I'll try to speed things up. Work on being Tracy's confidant, keep tabs on her, and make sure she stays away from Wild Horse. Like I said, do your part."

"The only thing keeping her from visiting Wild Horse is Tammy telling Tracy everything is okay. Keep doing your part!"

"I've got an idea of how to buy some time and keep Tracy away." He opened the console and put the gun in it.

"Gotta go. If Tracy Dalton shows up here, you get zilch, Donna."

"Screw you, old man."

"CATTLE SHOW UP ON MY RANCH NOW AND THEN," CASH SAID.

Tracy was thoroughly enjoying this exclusive tour with Cash. Wearing her Elsa hat to shade her eyes, she followed his gaze. They'd watered the horses along Fish Creek and then veered off on what Cash told her was one of his favorite shortcuts. Shortly thereafter, he'd spotted a cow and her calf grazing down in the meadow. The valley rolled with sloping hills on either side and was populated by evergreens, wildflowers, and glimpses of the creek. As they sat atop Captain and Cinnamon, still a couple of miles north of Cash's house, he explained the cows belonged to his brother, Chase, and had wandered off Triple C Ranch-Central.

"What a beautiful scene, Cash. It looks like something out of a movie," Tracy said with a sigh, watching the animals graze. "I can certainly understand why your heart and soul belong to Triple C Ranch-East."

"Yeah, it's always been home. Do you miss your home?"

"I miss my grandmother." Struck by the sound of his voice, interested and caring, Tracy turned to look at him. "I've been so busy with my job, I've not visited her. I talk to her often but I feel guilty for not making the trip to see her in person."

"My guess is that she fully understands and wants the best for you."

"Yes, she and my grandpa always encouraged me to leave Wild Horse. I stayed until I graduated with my online bachelor's degree. That's about the time Winston came knocking."

"I've never been to Wild Horse. But I've heard it referred to as a ghost town."

"Yes." Tracy nodded with a sigh. "That's a fair description. Wild Horse was founded in 1869, as a cavalry outpost. The Kansas-Pacific Railroad brought people through on their way to Denver. But there was a fire in 1917, which burned down most of the businesses. The Depression and the Dust Bowl of the 1930s helped wipe out what was left. There's a former one-room schoolhouse, a post office, and a few scattered older homes."

"How many people would you guess live around there?"

"Thirty, thirty-five?" Tracy shrugged. "Just like Grandpa Lew, my grandmother's friends are dead or long gone. She's completely isolated."

Cash tilted his head and asked, "Would she move to Colorado Springs?"

"I've asked. She won't. She's never lived anywhere but Wild Horse. I think she fears not being able to adapt to a big city like Colorado Springs, but if I can, she can." Tracy shook her head. "However, Winston's in the picture now."

"Do you think Winston's a good guy, even though he's younger? Maybe he's lonely and doesn't want to move away from Wild Horse, either?"

"I want to think he's a good guy." She smiled and said, "Like you, Cash."

"Yeah, well, I've had my share of detractors now and then."

"Female detractors?" she teased. Suddenly picturing Rusty, Delilah, and Desiree, jealousy stabbed Tracy. When she realized she'd placed her hand to her heart, she batted her eyelashes at him and asked like a southern belle, "Detractors who are smitten but rebuffed?"

"Like the editor who is smitten with you at the magazine?" Cash teased her right back. "What's his name?"

"Gerald Moles. Carefully rebuffed, since he's my supervisor."

"Did you invite Moles to the barbecue?"

"I did. If he shows up, I'll introduce you."

"Can't wait," Cash said. "Wanna help me wrangle a

couple of cows back to my ranch and into the corral? One of Chase's guys can come fetch 'em later."

"Yes! Wrangling cows will be a fantastic addition to my article."

"Yeehaw!" Cash whooped and nudged Captain down the incline.

"Yeehaw!" Tracy echoed and followed him.

CHAPTER THIRTEEN

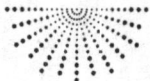

$\mathcal{T}$racy was a slow burn under Cash's skin.

He led the way down the hill. The cow and her calf began moving along as if knowing they were lost and not in the right pasture. Cash rode alongside them with Tracy following close behind. She had taken to riding a horse like she was born to it. He couldn't help, didn't want to help, visualizing how she might ride him in bed.

Flanking the mama cow and her baby, they began leading them safely back toward Triple C-East. He told Tracy about the upcoming barbecue as they moseyed along flat ground with tall grasses. Though they'd taken a shortcut, Cash hadn't hurried, not to mention the cow and her calf slowing down their return to the ranch. The morning sun was high in the sky as they approached a stack of boulders on the left.

"Just about everybody from all three ranches shows up on the Fourth for the barbecue," Cash said.

Tracy's horse became curious about something in the grass to their right. She pranced sideways and snorted. Cinnamon hadn't been on the ranch long but thus far had proven steady and reliable. Cash sensed rather than saw the problem.

"Cash, what am I doing wrong with Cinnamon?"

Snakes spooked horses. A bite might not be as fatal to a horse as it would be to a small dog, but Cash wanted to avoid an injury of any kind if possible. Nudging Captain forward, sure enough, Cash spotted a diamondback slithering toward them and the rocks where it no doubt had a dark cool den between the crevices.

"Rattlesnake. Don't panic," Cash said calmly, pointing with his left hand as he pulled his gun with his right. "I'm gonna shoot it. Press your knees against Cinnamon to hold on in case she spooks. Don't let her buck you off on top of the snake."

"Oh my gosh," Tracy replied but nodded. "Okay."

Cash hoped the horses stayed calm. However, the snake, feeling the vibration of horse and cattle hooves, reacted. Rattling its tail the snake raised its head to strike at the closer horse which was Cinnamon.

BOOM! The shot from Cash's Ruger Warrior blew the venomous snake's head off.

"Whoa!" Tracy called out as Cinnamon's front hooves left the ground.

"Cinnamon!" Cash barked with authority.

Cinnamon whinnied and pranced to her right. Twisting sideways, trying to see the rattler, Tracy's right foot slid out of the stirrup. Her hat fell off and hung down her back on the cord as she slipped precariously to the left in the saddle. Reining Captain up beside her, Cash pulled Tracy across his lap. Wrapping her arms around his neck, she clung to him, shaking.

"Is Cinnamon safe?" Was Tracy's only concern. "Or did she get bitten?"

"I think I killed it before it could strike her," Cash said. Both their hearts were pounding. "You were brave," he praised, holding her close.

"You're an excellent shot," Tracy said, staring down at the headless rattlesnake.

"Yeah." Cash closed his eyes and kissed her. She hugged him even tighter, kissing him back. He loosened his grip and said, "Let's make sure I was fast enough." Cash let Tracy slide to the ground and then he dismounted. He checked Cinnamon, confirming she had not suffered a snake bite. He picked up the rattler by the tail, held it out, and looked at it. "Diamondbacks start mating in late July, so even though this is early July there could be others nearby."

"Eww." Tracy grimaced, staring at the snake. Then reaching for her phone, she said, "Jacob would want me to take a picture for the magazine."

"Make a note that we don't kill nonvenomous snakes here on the ranch because they take care of barn mice and other rodents," Cash said. "But it's not illegal to kill a rattlesnake in Colorado. Especially one about to strike. I'll skin this guy and make a hatband for your hat."

"No way."

"Yes way." Cash chuckled. He coiled the reptile into a circle, pulled a red bandana out of his saddlebag, and tied the snake in it. Hanging the bandana over the saddle horn, he asked, "Ready to ride?"

"Yes."

They mounted and rode to his ranch. Beau was busy in the shop with customers and none of the wranglers and guests were back, yet. It was quiet as they unsaddled the horses and brushed them. Making sure the stallion and filly had fresh water and plenty of hay, Cash glanced at Tracy. She may have been afraid of horses on Monday, but today she had both arms around Cinnamon's neck. Tracy's long copper waves blended with the filly's deep copper mane. The beautiful writer gave the pretty horse a kiss on the side of her face and suddenly, Cash could not imagine anyone but Tracy riding Cinnamon. They were both new to the ranch, had victoriously survived a near catastrophe, and seemed to go together. Tracy stepped out of Cinnamon's stall, which was right next to Captain's and turned to Cash. When her full lips curved up, her smile reached her turquoise eyes.

This woman flipped every switch in Cash's system to red-hot and rock-hard.

"Didn't I say I'd turn you into a cowgirl?"

With a pat to Cinnamon's mane, Tracy gave him a saucy grin. "I think you said, ready or not you were gonna teach me to *ride*."

Sexual electricity zinged in the two-foot expanse between them.

"We're halfway there." Cash's voice was husky. "C'mere."

"You come here, big'n bad."

"You ornery little spitfire."

Cash snared her wrist and yanked her to him. She giggled all the way. Her arms twined around his neck and he felt her breasts slide up his chest as she stood on tiptoes between his booted feet. When his lips touched Tracy's, her tinkling laugh turned into a soft moan. His hands flattened to her back and all he could picture was teaching her how to ride in his bed. Her lips left his and she stepped from between his feet.

"I should go work on my article."

"I need to skin that snake and work on preparations for the barbecue," Cash said. "But Cristen's in the café, so let's rustle up something for lunch first. Sounds good?"

"Sounds great."

Cristen waved as they approached, already busy working on the supper meal. She offered to make them lunch and Beau, catching a break between customers, joined them. BLTs with chips and iced tea hit the spot. Cristen told them there would be a variety of pizzas, pasta with meatballs, breadsticks, and fresh salad with blackberry pie for dessert. As they ate, they told Beau and Cristen about fishing, camping, and the rattlesnake. After lunch, Cash walked Tracy to her cabin and then reluctantly headed to his home office.

The picnics were a tradition these days. They used to be held on Triple C Ranch-Central, but as marriages and kids came along, that had changed. Memorial Day picnic was on Triple C-Central, Fourth of July on Triple C-East, and Labor Day on Triple C-West. In any event, the celebrations were a fairly well-oiled machine at this point and everyone pitched in to help. The beef came from Chase's ranch, of course. Family, friends, and neighboring ranchers all brought side dishes. There would be live music, as always, and Cash was picturing a dance or two with Tracy.

Cash glanced at the clock in his office and headed to his master bedroom for a shower. Stepping out of the shower and wrapping a towel around his waist, he left the bathroom and crossed the bedroom toward his walk-in closet.

"Cash?" came the voice of a redhead outside his bedroom. "Hello? Cristen let me in."

Not the redhead he wanted. Hell. Cash's smile turned into a frown.

CHAPTER FOURTEEN

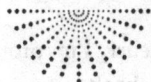

*T*racy couldn't stop smiling.

"Grandma, thank you for the early birthday wish," Tracy said into her cell phone.

"I was afraid I might have spotty cell service on the highway tomorrow," Tammy Dalton replied.

"I'm so glad you're getting out of the house. A visit with Winston's daughter in Punkin Center will be a nice road trip. I vaguely recall Winston having a daughter. I think she's about twenty years older than I am so we never crossed paths in school. What's her name?"

"Brenda," Grandma said. "This will be my first time meeting her."

"Punkin Center is almost halfway to Colorado Springs," Tracy said. "It would be wonderful if you could talk Winston into extending your road trip another sixty miles."

"He's nodding," Grandma told her.

"Great!" Tracy said and listened. "How long will you be staying with Brenda?" When her grandmother didn't answer right away, she figured she was discussing it with Winston.

"Winston says a week, maybe two. Then we can head toward the Springs."

"Grandma, the very best birthday gift you could give me is seeing you," Tracy said, her heart feeling light and happy.

"For me, too," Grandma said. There was another pause and then she asked, "Are you still on your ranch assignment?"

"Yes, and it's been a thrilling experience." Tracy knew it was Cash who made it thrilling. "I'm hoping Kirk Devereux, my boss, will extend my time to work on the story a few extra days so that I can interview additional members of the Cooper family."

"Wonderful, sweetheart. I'm proud of you. I love you. Tracy." Grandma's voice broke.

"Hi, Tracy," came Winston's voice. "Your grandmother is overcome with happiness."

"Me too," Tracy said. "Thank you for talking her into a trip, and thanks in advance for bringing her to Colorado Springs."

"My pleasure," Winston said. "She and I are taking good care of each other."

"I'm glad to hear that. I really appreciate it, Winston. I only have a one-bedroom apartment, but I want you both to stay with me when you get here. I can sleep on the sofa."

"No, no. Don't worry about me. I can sleep on the sofa, or the floor for that matter."

"We'll figure something out," Tracy assured him, so grateful. Feeling guilty for misjudging him, she said, "Thank you so much, Winston. May I say goodbye to my grandma?"

He chuckled. "She's waving, sniffling, and saying goodbye. We'll see you in a couple of weeks, our Dalton Darling."

"Okay! Great! See you when you get here. Grandma has my address, Winston." Then more loudly she called into the phone, "Bye-bye, Grandma."

The line went dead and Tracy held the phone to her heart. She'd see her grandmother soon. Everything was going to be okay. With a happy sigh, she looked at her few outfits, wondering what to wear for the evening. Deciding, she hurried into the shower. While shampooing her hair she wondered if Cash would stop by and walk her to supper. It occurred to her that he didn't have her cell phone number. She needed to rectify that. For the sake of the magazine story. She smiled. Sure, for the magazine story. After shaving her skin smooth and rinsing away soap, she stepped out of the shower. Blowing her hair dry, she gathered it high on her head in a ponytail. With some mascara, blush, and lipstick she was ready to get dressed. Since riding was over for the day she had decided on a dress for a change. Casual, it was a snug, white sleeveless shirtdress that hit her above the knee. She snapped the turquoise buttons up the front and slid into a pair of white sandals.

She worked on the magazine article, leaving out the cot kerfuffle and adding the close call with the rattlesnake. Wondering how much longer it would be before Jacob, Donna, and the others returned from Turkey Pond, she took a break and wandered across the living room. At the window, overlooking the distance between the cabins and the back of Cash's sprawling farmhouse, she imagined the area filled with friends, family, neighbors, guests, and wranglers. She was excited to meet Chase and Jade as well as Chloe and Derek and Cash's little nieces and nephews.

Tracy hugged herself. As an only child raised in a ghost town by her grandparents, she longed for a big, extended family. She looked forward to having children. Two at least. She wondered if Cash wanted children. Oh for heaven's sake, she'd known the man for four days. Even so, she smiled. As if thinking about Cash made him materialize, she saw him exiting the Western store. He held the door open for someone and then the woman named Rusty followed him outside. Wearing a cowboy hat and folding a bag under her arm, she grabbed his hand. Tracy's smile faded, and she stood back from the window. Cash and the strawberry blonde walked away from the stables toward the front of Cash's house.

Tracy's entire body could not have been more jolted if she'd been snake-bit.

She stared but lost sight of Cash and the redhead as wranglers, guests, and horses returned from the overnight camping excursion. Ladies and gentlemen began dismounting. Eloise and Mavis, pulling the covered wagons, joined the horses at the water trough. The wranglers began gathering up reins, unhooking the mules, and leading the animals into the stables, no doubt to be fed and brushed.

No more sign of Cash. But when Tracy spotted Donna walking toward the cabin, she decided to avoid being trapped inside with her. She stepped onto the boardwalk in front of the cabins and waved to Jacob, Natasha, Michaela, and LeAnn. She'd go find Cristen in the café. Maybe she could use some help since Kellie had been out on the trail. Perhaps that would take her mind off Cash and Rusty. Unlikely.

"I thought we'd never get back," Donna snapped, stomping toward Tracy.

"Are you not having fun?" Tracy asked, pausing for a minute.

"Not much," she said, brushing dust from the trail off her jeans.

"Why did you push so hard to come along, Donna?" Tracy had wanted to ask her that question since before they left Colorado Springs. "Surely you knew what to expect."

"Men?" Donna asked mockingly as if she should know that. "Ranchers and wranglers?"

"Right," Tracy commented. "I thought maybe you and Gerald—"

"You thought wrong."

"Okay," Tracy said, wondering if Cash would be back for pizza, pasta, and pie.

Donna held up a finger and complained, "First and foremost, Cash has made it clear he's not interested. Second, Sam let it be known he's happily married." Adding a third finger to finger number two, she said, "Beau only has eyes for Cristen." Holding up finger number four, she said, "Larry has a puppy-dog crush on some woman named Fern at a neighboring ranch." She rolled her eyes and holding up all five fingers, she mumbled, "And Ed claims he has a girl-friend. But I think Ed and Larry are lying. Which is a slap in my face."

"There are lots of single men back in Colorado Springs, Donna."

"Lots of men are coming to the barbecue too," Donna said. "I overheard Diane and Joyce saying that Chase Cooper is drop-dead gorgeous like Cash and that Derek Brevard's wife refers to him as a handsome-hot, bad boy."

"Diane and Joyce are loyal friends of the Coopers."

Donna snickered. "And old enough to be the mothers of those two men."

"Joyce and Diane are just complimenting Chase and Derek," Tracy said. "I've heard those ladies also say more than once how beautiful and kind Chloe and Jade are."

"Those two old broads better stay out of my way."

"Donna, I'm going to speak my mind," Tracy said as they somewhat squared off on the porch between the rocking chairs. Fists going to her hips, Donna tilted her head. "You have become increasingly aggravated as this week has progressed. Why is that?"

"Maybe my life isn't as easy and carefree as yours, Tracy."

"Really?" Tracy asked. Easy? She was scratching out a living, working all the time. Carefree? She had lost her grandfather and was constantly worried about her grand-mother. And now there was Cash. Where had he and the strawberry blonde gone? "I'm happy to listen and I'll try to help."

Donna laughed. "I don't think so!"

"All right. Fine." Tracy raised her hands in the air. "But as I've said before, we're on assignment and here as guests," she reminded her. "Please don't cause any more trouble."

"More trouble?" Donna spat. "Are you referring to the lousy food making me puke into that scum pond?"

Tracy didn't comment. "If you'll excuse me, I'm going to see if Cristen needs help preparing supper."

Donna waved her off and headed into the cabin. Tracy continued to the café. She'd been so happy when talking to her grandmother. Then seeing Cash with Rusty and dealing with Donna had weighed her down. Donna was one thing. But knowing Cash was interested in the redhead after the night they'd spent together in his tent, hurt. Darn it.

In the kitchen, she found Cristen more than busy. Evidently, Kellie had been there unloading supplies from the camping trip, but Cristen had shooed her off to rest for a bit. The Western shop had since closed, and Beau apparently had the same idea as to helping out.

"Hi Cristen. Hi Beau," Tracy said, stopping in the dining area. "What can I do to help?"

"Hi Tracy. Nothing really," Cristen said pleasantly, if somewhat distractedly, and turned back to Beau. "Are you sure he's not mad at me? Because I definitely did not let her into the house. Rusty barged past me as I was carrying out some extra plates and silverware."

"I'll place the silverware and these napkins on the tables," Tracy said quietly, picking up a pile of silverware from the end of the serving table that she figured had come from Cash's house, along with a stack of napkins.

"Thank you, Tracy," Cristen replied with a sweet but worried smile.

"If he's mad at you, he might as well be mad at me too," Beau said. "Rusty ordered a cowboy hat and instead of coming to the shop to pick it up, she went to the house. She found Cash and told him the store was locked up. That was not true."

"We're back," Kellie called, seemingly unaware as she and Sam joined them.

"You and Sam are guests this evening," Cristen said. "Beau and I have this. And Tracy's helping too."

"Something's up. What?" Sam asked pointedly, apparently knowing them well. When they shrugged, Sam looked at Beau. "Beau, what's wrong?" Placing silverware and napkins on tables, Tracy couldn't help but overhear as they told him about Rusty. "Hell, you both know Cash better than that," Sam said. "Guarantee you he's got it all figured out. His only regret will be that Rusty caused you both grief."

And just like that, Tracy's spirits rose again. Cash Cooper was a good guy through and through and she liked him more every day. But she had a magazine article to write, her grandmother's pending visit, and a more immediate concern was hoping to prevent Donna from causing anyone on the ranch more *grief*. Having completed her silverware and napkins job, she turned and saw Cash swaggering, as only he could, toward the dining area. In his hand was the cowboy hat that Tracy knew had been on Rusty's head only minutes earlier.

"Got something for you, Cristen," Cash said, walking into the dining area with a big smile as he held the hat out to her.

"Really?" Cristen asked. "I don't have a cowboy hat." She looked at Beau who grinned and nodded. Putting the hat on her head, she said, "I love it. Thank you, Cash."

"That's the hat Rusty just bought," Beau said with a chuckle. "What happened, boss?"

"Being called on her lies got the hat flung in my face," Cash said. "I'm starved." With a grin, he turned to Tracy and asked, "Are you in the kitchen earning your keep?"

"Yes." Tracy laughed. "I heard it was either that or feeding the chickens."

When Cash winked at her, it was like a slice of dessert before the meal. The salads, spaghetti and meatballs dinner with sides of pizza and breadsticks was the best Tracy had ever eaten. Guests and wranglers arrived and everyone else was starved too. People were treated to oodles of food on tables covered with cheerful bucking bronco tablecloths. Jacob and Jeff took seats at the table where Tracy sat next to Cash and Jacob showed them some of the photos he'd taken during the camping and fishing trip. When Cristen began serving up slices of blackberry pie for dessert, Beau helped her.

Cash leaned in close to Tracy and asked, "What would you say if I suggested we eat our pie on the balcony at my house?"

CHAPTER FIFTEEN

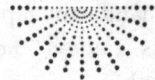

"**I**'d say yes."

"Good." Cash could get lost in those turquoise eyes and sultry voice. Get lost? Hell, days ago he'd started walking headlong into a faraway place he'd never been before because of this woman. Lost? Yeah. Turning back? No. Not yet anyway.

"If I remember correctly, you're going to show me something on the balcony that no one else has seen."

"That I am." He stood up at their table and pulled out her chair for her. When they started to leave the dining area, she asked about the pie. "There's plenty more in my kitchen."

"Where are you two headed?" Donna asked.

"To do some research on Cash's farmhouse," Tracy said without skipping a beat.

"I'll tag along," Donna said. "To you know...*assist*."

"Nope," Cash replied over his shoulder. "We're good."

Tracy giggled under her breath. "You're so big'n bad, Cash Cooper."

"Gotta be, running a ranch like this." Instead of heading into the back of his house, he walked her toward the cabins and then with distance between them and the guests in the dining area, he headed down the side road. "We'll go in through the front door of the house." When she cocked her head in a questioning manner, he said. "Plausible deniability."

"That I was alone with you inside?" she asked as they reached the wraparound porch.

"Yes. For your reputation's sake."

"I'm a big girl. I can handle my reputation, Cash."

"Which up to now is spotless," he said as they climbed the three steps to the porch.

"Is something about to change?"

"Only when and if you want it to."

Tracy arched a cinnamon brow and her full lips twitched with a smile. A couple of racy images of Tracy flashed across Cash's brain. He tapped down his desire and opened the door to his house. They stepped inside where light from a six-foot-tall decorative window above the front door lit up the two-story foyer. Tracy stared straight ahead at the wood and wrought-iron staircase ascending to the second floor.

"I love that gorgeous horse carved into the banister at the bottom of the staircase," she said, then looked to her left and to her right.

"Thanks, it's original to the house."

Cash had upgraded and modernized the house over the last few years since he'd inherited it from his Uncle Clarence. Exposed wood beams that greeted them in the two-story foyer could be seen beyond in the expansive living room and wide hallway to both sides and under the staircase. An interior decorator had kept the rustic charm of the home and implemented what she'd called a neutral palette. In the large open area off to the left, an overstuffed, cream-colored sofa with big blue pillows and chairs to match beckoned folks to relax and forget it was the formal living room. A dining room that could easily seat twelve or more boasted a crystal vase on the center of the gleaming mahogany table under a sixteen light dimmable wagon wheel chandelier with crystals that reflected the sunshine from large windows.

"Wow," Tracy breathed softly.

"Come on," Cash said and headed down the hardwood floor of the hallway.

They passed open double doors to his den filled with leather furniture, a flat-screen TV, and a fully stocked wet bar. On the other side of the hall were matching double doors to a library with built-in shelves full of books. In an oblong room was a pool table with cue sticks mounted on the wall. He pointed out his office which had not changed as much as the rest of the house. He still used his Uncle Clarence's desk and leather chair. The oil painting above the fireplace seemed to have caught Tracy's eye and drew her into the room.

"Is that you, Cash?"

"Yeah. Eighteen and rebellious," he said and chuckled. Tracy walked across the office and stared up at the painting. "My folks commissioned oil paintings from their favorite photographs of my brother, sister, and me." He indicated a framed photo on the mantel that matched the painting. "That was taken the weekend before I started college."

Leaning against a corral, Cash wore a brown cowboy hat, long-sleeved shirt, jeans, and boots. His silver Triple C Ranch buckle, fastening his brown leather belt, showed above the low-riding chaps made of cowhide. The heel of his right boot was hooked on the bottom rung of the corral and the elbows of both his arms rested on a higher slat.

"I can't decide if you're smiling or frowning," Tracy said.

"A little of both, I think. My parents wanted to send me to Denver University and into the dorms. I agreed to college but said I wasn't leaving the ranch. We compromised and I attended the University of Colorado in the Springs. I lived with my Uncle Clarence, who was a bachelor, here in this house. In hindsight, it was a godsend."

"How so?"

"He keeled over from a heart attack in that same corral I'm leaning against." Cash paused and said, "I still miss him, but at least I had learned how to run the ranch before he died."

"My grandmother's favorite movie was *Giant*. Although you're physically a lot bigger, you kind of remind me of the young rebel James Dean in that movie."

"I'll take that as a compliment," Cash said. Leaving his office, they made their way back down the hall and into his kitchen. It had been completely overhauled with stainless steel appliances, an island and countertops of granite, white cabinets, and polished dark, wide plank wood flooring. Cash pulled out one of six barstools at the island. "Sit and I'll slice you up a piece of blackberry pie."

"Your home is magnificent, Cash," Tracy said and took a seat.

"Thanks," he said and sliced up a couple pieces of pie. "Come on, we'll have our pie in the den and I'll fix you a drink if you'd like."

"Okay."

In the den, Cash set the plates of pie on a coffee table in front of the big leather couch. Stepping behind the wet bar, he asked what Tracy would like. Standing on the opposite side of him, she had no idea. He poured himself a shot of bourbon and Tracy said she'd try her first shot.

"Toss it into the back of your throat and swallow," he said. She nodded and they clinked glasses. "To your magazine article."

Tracy drank and coughed. "Oh my gosh!" Her eyes watered as she looked at her empty shot glass as if it had attacked her throat. "I understand why it's called firewater."

"Good?" Cash chuckled, pouring two more shots.

"I'll need some pie before I drink that second shot."

"Deal." Cash liked the fact she was brave enough to try a second shot. With two more shots in hand, he led the way toward the sofa. He set the glasses on the table and picked up the pie. "Speaking of your grandmother, any word from her?"

"Yes," Tracy said enthusiastically as he handed her a

plate. Cash picked up his plate and they settled themselves onto the leather cushions. "She called me earlier and said Winston is taking her on a little road trip to Punkin Center."

"Sixty miles east of here," Cash commented, taking a bite of pie.

Tracy took a bite, too, and nodded at how delicious it was. "She said they are coming to Colorado Springs."

"Tracy, that's good news."

"Yes, I invited them to stay with me."

They'd eaten their pie when Cash set his plate on the coffee table and said, "If you don't mind my asking, where do you live in the Springs?"

"I live in a gated apartment complex near Coronado High School and Garden of the Gods," Tracy said, also setting her plate on the table "My front patio looks out at Pikes Peak. At the back of the apartment, I have an attached one-car garage. With a swimming pool and fitness center on the grounds, as apartments go it's truly an oasis. Most importantly to me, it's pet friendly for Dude."

"I know the complex you mean," Cash said, recalling that's where Rusty lived.

"The only problem is that it has just one bedroom," Tracy said with concern. "I hope that won't be a deterrent for my grandmother staying with me because I'd gladly give up my bed to her...or to them." She shrugged and appeared uneasy. "I don't know if they share a bed or not. But Winston offered to sleep on the sofa or the floor."

"Tracy, you're welcome to invite them to stay here," Cash said. "I'll even let you stay too," he teased.

"Cash, that's so sweet," Tracy said, turning to him as they sat on the sofa. "But we couldn't impose on you like that."

"I've got a bunch of bedrooms upstairs. Let's take our second shot and I'll give you a tour. The master suite is off the balcony I'm going to show you."

Tracy picked up her glass. "On the count of three," she said, squeezing her eyes shut.

Cash said with a grin, "One, two, three."

His bourbon went down smoothly. Tracy coughed, her eyes watered, and he patted her on the back. Grabbing her hand, he pulled her off the sofa and trailed her behind him into the hallway. At the top of the staircase was a large, decorated landing leading to the five bedrooms. There was a laundry room furnished not only with a brand-new washer and dryer but also with a walk-in linen closet, a marble sink, and racks on which to hang clothes.

"How convenient to have a laundry room up here where the clothes are," Tracy said.

"There's a laundry chute over there." He pointed. "Before the remodel up here, all the laundry went downstairs to another washer and dryer that comes in handy at times."

The four guest bedrooms were tastefully furnished with dressers, nightstands, armoires, overstuffed chairs, and a footrest or two. A couple of the bedrooms boasted queen beds, one with a canopy, and the other two bedrooms offered two full-size beds. Each bedroom came with its own private, full bath.

"My grandmother and Winston could have their pick of beautiful rooms that would certainly work for whatever their sleeping arrangement is," Tracy admitted.

"Yeah, and you can sleep with me," Cash said, back in the middle of the landing.

"Cash!" she gasped, but her lips spread into a delicious grin.

"It wouldn't be the first night we spent together," he said referring to the previous night in the tent. He winked to let her know there was absolutely no obligation on her part. "I'm teasing you. Kind of."

"Let's see this balcony of yours."

"We're almost there."

Cash snared her hand and tugged her to him. When he lowered his head, she tilted up her chin. His eyes closed and his mouth touched her silky soft lips. Making it a short kiss, he raised his head and keeping hold of her hand, trailed her behind him into the master suite.

Stepping aside he brought her into the room. His king-size bed was dead ahead flanked by marble-topped night-stands in front of wide windows with room-darkening shades. There was a sitting area off to the left with a fire-place, built-in bookshelves, and a minibar. Across from a couple of wingback chairs in front of the hearth, there was an enormous walk-in closet. Also on the right, a master bath consisted of a long granite counter with double sinks and framed mirrors. The tiled shower was a walk-in type for two. Perhaps the most unusual thing about the bathroom was the bathtub.

"Is that a horse trough?" Tracy asked. "Because I *kind of* love it."

"Yeah," Cash said with a chuckle. "It was original to the house and I liked it, too, so I left it. Stainless steel, I guess it was Uncle Clarence's version of a hot tub. Takes forever to fill it."

"I'll bet it drains your hot water tank."

"I've got a couple tanks." Cash led her to the French doors on the opposite side of the bedroom. Opening both doors led them onto a balcony made private with solid, chest-high walls. On the floor of the balcony was waterproof flooring that drained water into downspouts. Greenery in huge ceramic planters decorated all four corners. A bistro table for two and reclining lounge chairs provided places to sit and view Pikes Peak in the distance. He swept his hand toward the rock-look casing surrounding the ultimate spa tub filled with water that would foam and soak away every ache and care. With a waterfall at one end and two captain's chairs with rollover neck and shoulder jets, LED lighting, and a Bluetooth sound system, it was the definitive body lounger.

"Wow, Cash."

"This is my version of a hot tub and you're the first, besides the installers, to see it."

Cash wondered if she would have the interest to enjoy it with him. Would she be brave enough to hop in if it were just the two of them? "What do you think?"

CHAPTER SIXTEEN

"$\mathcal{I}$ think it's a party on the top floor," Tracy said.

Cash grinned. "Damn, I like you."

He backed into the privacy of his bedroom and pulled her into his arms. This man was so hot, Tracy thought she might melt into him. She not only found Cash to be the most physically handsome man she'd ever met, she connected with him mentally. She really liked who he was.

Reminding herself she was on a job, her hands flattened to his muscular chest. Way too late at this point she told herself it wasn't professional to kiss the cowboy starring in her story as she trailed her fingers up his body and twined them around his neck. When Cash's hands slid down her back to her fanny, Tracy stood on tiptoes. Every part of her body responded to Cash. Never had she been attracted to any man as she was to this one. When his hands roamed to her waist and up her ribs to her breasts, she leaned away just enough to give him access to do what he pleased. She was a red-blooded female, and she wanted this red-blooded rancher.

"If only I had my bikini with me," she flirted daringly between kisses.

"If only." Cash began popping open the snaps on the front of her dress.

Tracy shivered with desire. As Cash's lips met hers again, throwing all caution to the wind, she let Cash proceed. Nothing and no one could have convinced her otherwise. When he raised his head, his blue eyes smoldered with desire. Placing his hands on the shoulders of her dress, he paused, giving her time to change her mind. She licked her upper lip and smiled. He pulled the dress off and let it fall to the thick rug under their feet. She stood before him in a white satin bra and white satin panties. As nervous as she was excited, she suddenly wondered how she measured up to the women he'd had before her. Not in a jealous way because she knew he was a man with experience. But she prayed Cash didn't find her lacking.

Placing her hands to his waist, she pulled his shirttails out of his jeans. What was she doing? Where had that move come from? From being with Cash Cooper, she guessed. From liking him. From wanting him. Maybe even from trusting him? He unbuttoned his shirt as she tried to unfasten the silver buckle on his belt. She couldn't figure out how it worked and he winked at her just before he unfastened it. His shirt joined hers on the floor. Still in his jeans with his belt undone, he scooped her up in his arms. She twined her arms around his neck and he carried her out of the bedroom through the French doors. With the balcony on the west side of his house that put the view of Pikes Peak directly in front of them. The cabins and outdoor dining area lay to the north, but it was dark now and the guests were in their quarters. The barn-like doors of the stables were closed, and the wranglers had taken off to the bunkhouse or other places. No one was in sight.

"Hot tub in my underwear?" Tracy asked.

"That's what I'm thinking."

"Let's do it."

"Yeah, let's do it."

Cash stood her down next to the tub and with a flick of a switch the jets bubbled the water. He held her hand as she walked up the dimly lit steps. A Chinook wind tossed

Tracy's long hair as she placed one foot and then the other into the water. It was the perfect slice of warmth. She sank into the water from her ankles to her knees. She knew when she sat down her white satin underwear would become nearly as transparent as if she were naked. Boldly, she took a seat in what Cash had referred to as a captain's chair. Sultry music softly blended with the frothy water under the moonlight.

Tracy lifted her gaze from the bubbles to the man descending the steps into the hot tub. Cash, wearing snug, black boxers, lowered his muscular body into the water, settling into the captain's seat beside her. He sighed with the same pleasure Tracy was experiencing. Pulsating jets hit her neck, back, and hips in all the right places. Cash turned his head and smiled. When he reached for her, the water floated her out of her seat and into his arms. Gently he positioned her upper body at the same level as his, while her lower body glided between his spread legs. On her knees, she wrapped her arms around his neck and her eyes met his blue ones.

Serious, sensuous, sexy. Cash was the whole package of rugged masculinity.

As his lips met hers, his hands moved to her back and he unfastened her bra. She let him. His fingers slid around her ribs and his palms covered her naked breasts. Her nipples beaded. He groaned low in his throat. Tugging off her bra, he dropped it over the side of the tub. His hands moved down her ribs, caressing her bare flesh and she let him. Not only did she let him, she moaned with pleasure. Traveling lower, Cash splayed both his hands atop the satin covering her bottom. He pressed her against his body and she felt the hard length of him. He was letting her know what she was doing to him. As they kissed, he massaged her fanny, and she wondered if he was going to completely strip her. Instead, he turned off the bubbling jets and moved her to her knees. He didn't say a word, but stood up, taking her with him to the steps of the hot tub. He exited the tub first and turned to her. She was topless and being seen by a man for the first time. Tracy fought the urge to cover herself. She let him look. He took her hand and steadied her as she followed him out of the water to the floor of the balcony.

Under the stars, he tenderly cupped her face and his mouth closed over hers. For the first time his lips parted and his tongue touched her lips. As his mouth opened, hers did too. His tongue slid past her lips and explored. Her heart pounded, her nipples brushed his chest, and her legs grew weak. She vined her arms around his neck and when he began easing her panties down her thighs, she stood on tiptoes to help him.

Was this the balcony kiss Cash had mentioned? Because it was mind-altering.

Tracy shivered from head to toe, and it wasn't from the night air brushing her skin. It was the fire radiating inside her. It was all that and more. *More*. She'd wanted more last night in the tent. She wanted more now. From Cash and only from him. She touched her tongue to Cash's and he groaned in approval. Realizing her panties had fallen around her feet she stepped out of them. In the next breath, his snug boxers joined her underwear on the balcony floor. He raised his head and there was an unspoken question in his eyes.

"More, Cash," Tracy whispered.

CASH LED THE ULTIMATE REDHEAD INTO HIS DIMLY LIT BEDROOM and threw back the comforter and top sheet. She pulled the band out of her ponytail and gave her head a shake. As she lay down, he admired the naked beauty in his bed. Her cinnamon curls spread across the white pillowcase reminding him of fire. Those mesmerizing turquoise eyes stared up at him as the cinnamon lips he'd just kissed parted. Her cinnamon breath triggered his taste buds urging him to nibble her everywhere starting with her cinnamon nipples.

"You're princess of the cinnamon kiss. You know that?"

She rested her left arm across her breasts as her right hand covered her femininity. He noted her eyes had stayed on his. She hadn't gotten up the nerve to glance down his body. He was long, hard, and aching for her.

"I know my kisses are only for you, Cash."

Good answer. And she said she wanted more, but he knew she was nervous. Cash joined her on the bed and gently swept her left arm to the mattress. Her nipples beaded. He brushed her other hand to the bed and gazed at the smooth vee between her legs. With a kiss to her lips, he trailed kisses down her neck and collarbone to the swell of her full, perky breasts. Closing his lips over her left nipple brought a gulp from Tracy and then she arched her back to his kiss. He nibbled his way to her other breast, took the tip into his mouth, and teased it with his tongue.

Never, and he meant never, could Cash remember wanting a woman like he wanted this one. He wasn't sure what kind of spell Tracy had cast over him, but he doubted making love to her just once was going to break her magic hold. Trailing his fingers down her flat tummy when he caressed the petal soft secret between her thighs, her legs spread for him. With a single finger, he explored, and she squirmed with a little wiggle. Not that he'd doubted her, but he felt proof of her virginity. Besides the barrier he'd have to break, she was going to be a tight fit. Terrifically tight. When he pulled his hand from between her legs, she moaned and held herself to him.

Lifting himself up on one elbow and looking down at her, he whispered, "If you want more, I need a condom."

"I'm on the pill to keep my periods regulated."

Again, Cash didn't doubt her. As a confirmed bachelor, he would be just as honest. "I don't have sex without using protection."

"Let's be virgins together tonight."

He'd had the no-condom offer from countless women and never taken a single one up on it. He had no intention of catching something or taking a paternity test. He'd never met a woman he wanted to have kids with and didn't plan on a shotgun wedding. But this woman was a raging fire in his blood. Making him burn red-hot with desire, Cash didn't think sex with Tracy while wearing a condom could put out these blazing flames. Letting down his guard as never before he rolled on top of her.

"Hell yeah, Tracy," Cash groaned with need. "Let's live dangerously."

Reaching between them, he opened her velvety folds and she spread her legs wider. Placing his manhood to her warm, wet entrance, he felt her hips move toward him, welcoming him. With a slight push, the tip of him met her inner barrier. He paused. She took a breath.

"More, Cash."

"Any more and you won't be a virgin when you crawl outa my bed."

"I want more."

He thrust and she gasped as they broke into never-explored territory. Sliding in to the hilt, Cash let her body adjust around his. Then, holding her to his heart, he pulled almost out. He was teaching her to ride with every long stroke and each near separation. He picked up speed. She was a fast learner, pushing against him and pulling back, matching him plunge for plunge.

"Wrap your legs around me," he said.

She did and after several strokes, he sat up, taking her with him. She smiled and tossed her hair into wild disarray. He kissed her lips and readjusted them in the bed, with her on top. He helped her rise to her knees so that they could be one again. She slowly slid all the way down him, her body gripping each inch until Cash thought he might explode.

"Are you gonna buck me off?" she asked.

"I'm gonna try," he groaned. "You're riding in the cowgirl position."

Tracy was so incredible that Cash realized what they were doing was—making love. He had never thought of having sex as making love. Until now. Until Tracy. He was making love to her. With his hands at her waist lifting her up, she slid down faster and farther. Her head bowed forward, her hair brushed his chest, and when she moaned his name it was almost his undoing.

Knowing he was close and sensing she was, too, Cash flipped her onto her back. Tracy gulped as he rolled on top of her, riding into her with a thrust of his manhood. Her nipples were beaded against his chest and with another moan, her orgasm clamped down on the length of him. Her ecstasy triggered his and as she rhythmically squeezed him, he pulsed hard and deep inside her. Over and over and over.

Their hearts pounded against each other. Furiously fast, then slower in sweet harmony.

When their breathing returned to normal, Cash rolled off her and onto the bed. Pulling her to him, he kissed her forehead and when she tilted up her chin, he kissed her lips. With her head on the pillow with his, she placed her hand over his heart. She not only fit him physically, she matched his personality. And mentally? She mirrored his deepest emotions.

Cash wanted more. More with Tracy. Only with Tracy.

He didn't allow women to spend the night. Too many eyes and nobody's business. Yet, it hadn't stopped him from taking Tracy into his tent at Turkey Pond the previous night. And nothing could have stopped him from bringing Tracy into his home and bedroom tonight. At the thought of this woman leaving him the next day after the barbecue, Cash tugged her closer. With a contented sigh, Tracy slipped a slender leg between his.

Damn, this felt right.

CHAPTER SEVENTEEN

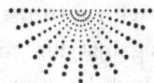

I lost my virginity to Cash Cooper, Tracy thought as she slid into her bed in the log cabin.

She had awakened at least three hours before the sun rose and smiled. She'd been snuggled to Cash in spoon fashion. Naked. As much as she didn't want to crawl out of his bed, she knew it was the right thing to do. It had occurred to her she should have offered to leave right after...well she should have already been gone. Cash had been too polite to ask her to go. Ever so slowly, to avoid waking him, she'd eased out from under his arm. In the glow of a dim night-light, she'd found her shirtdress, grabbed her sandals, and tiptoed away. With a glance over her shoulder at the door of his bedroom, she saw him roll onto his stomach. His broad back was bare as the sheet lay across his slightly rounded buttocks. He hugged his pillow and sighed.

I gave my virginity to Cash, Tracy silently corrected herself as she lay in her bed. In fact, she'd been riding on top of him at one point. Then Cash had resumed command and they had both reached what she could only describe as sizzling ecstasy. Rolling onto her side, Tracy pulled the extra pillow into her arms and hugged it as she had Cash. She had absolutely no regrets about making love to Cash and hoped he didn't either. She wondered if he'd want to do it again. She did. But only with Cash. With a smile on her lips, Tracy closed her eyes and the next thing she knew was the clanging of the chow bell announcing breakfast.

Tracy opened her eyes. Her first thought was of Cash. She was excited and, truth be told, a little nervous about seeing him. But she hopped out of bed still wearing her shirtdress and—no underwear. She hadn't been able to find her panties and hadn't even looked for her bra in the semi-darkness. In hopes of not being so late to breakfast that she missed Cash, she flew into the shower and was back out again in record time. She was headed toward the door in a tank top and blue jeans when Donna stumbled out of her bedroom. It occurred to Tracy that Donna had a drinking problem. Whatever the case, Donna was apparently none the wiser as to Tracy's foray into Cash's private world.

"Breakfast time," Tracy said to Donna just as a knock sounded on the door. Her heart instantly raced and with a smile, she flung open the door.

"Morning," Jacob said cheerfully. "Thought I could escort you to breakfast since this is our last day on the ranch. I want to be sure to get all the photos you need for the story."

Though disappointed it wasn't Cash escorting her to breakfast, Tracy smiled at her good friend and said, "Great idea, Jacob."

Cash was nowhere to be seen at the café. Everyone else was there except for Sam. Tracy asked Kellie where they were and she said most likely in Cash's office working on the day's schedule and barbecue details. Kellie went on to say they'd likely show up with work assignments for guests wanting to be a wrangler/ranch hand for the day.

Right on cue, Jeff gave the chow bell a clang to get everyone's attention. He reminded them about the annual Fourth of July barbeque later that day which was not just for the guests. They'd meet Cooper family members, friends, and neighbors. There would be fireworks set off on Triple C

Ranch-East before the guests would board the magazine's van back to the Springs. Anyone who wanted to help set tables, make side dishes, or pitch in wherever were encouraged to do so. Anyone preferring to ride, hike, or simply relax was just as welcome to do so.

"Should we find Cash and ask what we can do to help?" Jacob asked as he and Tracy sat down at a table to eat a delicious quiche of bacon, ham, and cheese. "Might be a good angle for the story?"

It was after eight, the sun was shining, and Tracy had fully expected to hear from Cash by now. Or at least see him. Was he avoiding her? Maybe regretting what had happened between them? At that distinct possibility, she inwardly cringed. Maybe she was simply a one-night stand as far as he was concerned, and she was expecting way too much.

"Jacob, you go ahead and talk to Cash if you run into him," Tracy said across the table from him as they began eating their quiches. "I'll see what I can do to help Kellie and Cristen. Then I'm going to pack up and work on completing the story I have so far. That way, if anything is missing, I can ask Cash about it later." Tracy sincerely hoped that would be the case.

They went their separate ways after breakfast. Tracy lent a hand to the ladies by helping make croissants and baking a dessert to be served at the barbecue. Donna wandered into the café and Cristen graciously served her a piece of quiche and a cup of coffee. While some of the other guests worked in the stables, Natasha, Michaela, and LeAnn worked alongside Tracy. With Kellie and Cristen telling them they didn't have to lift a finger, they enjoyed making chicken salad and fresh croissants that would be served for lunch. Donna, however, ate her breakfast and disappeared.

By the time the *fixins*, as Kellie called them, for the upcoming lunch were completed Tracy still hadn't caught sight of Cash. She guessed Jacob hadn't either as he helped Jeff and the wranglers put together a stage for the band which would play later. The guests seemed to be thoroughly enjoying watching, pitching in, or giving good-natured advice to the wranglers. Having finished with what she could do for Kellie and Cristen, Tracy headed back to her cabin to work on her story. There, she heard Donna snoring in the other bedroom and found an empty vodka bottle in the bathroom. Donna had started out somewhat positively, even making excuses for Tracy's driving. But as the week had worn on the woman had become a regular sourpuss. Was it the drinking? Or something else? What was on Donna's agenda besides men and vodka?

Around ten, Tracy meandered back outside. She knew she was shamelessly looking for Cash. She saw or spoke to all the other ladies and some of the wranglers. It was eleven when Tracy and Jacob sat in the café and enjoyed a glass of sweet tea.

Jacob asked, "Have you asked Gerald if he will allow you to expand the story to include Triple C Ranches-Central and West?"

"Not yet. But I will ask him later if he makes it to the barbecue. Otherwise, I'll wait until Monday to ask. If he does let me, I'll have to come back to interview those folks," Tracy replied.

Jacob said, "I only saw Triple C-Central and West from a distance as I took sunset photos with Coop as my guide. Triple C-Central consists of an enormous stone and wood mountain home with stables, a barn, and a multi-car garage similar to Cash's. There are corrals, horses, and cattle everywhere. Coop was a great guide and pointed out his log home and the ranch foreman's house on Chase and Jade's ranch. Down the road is the cattle ranch entrance where there's a bunkhouse and a couple of other homes."

"Wow," Tracy said. "I didn't realize it was such a large operation. But it's a working ranch with hundreds of Black Angus cows, so of course that makes sense."

"Yeah," Jacob said. "On Triple C-West, there is a huge,

country-style house with an outdoor kitchen, a lagoon-like backyard pool, and a separate bed-and-breakfast next door. Chloe and her husband, Derek, have a multi-car garage too. They have state-of-the-art stables for training the Percheron horses for law enforcement. I'd enjoy seeing more of those two ranches."

"I would too. I will plead with Gerald," Tracy said jokingly but was serious as well. With a glance around the corrals, stables, and store, she saw everyone but Cash.

"I think Gerald will let you do what you want. I hope you'll ask him to send me along."

"Of course I will, Jacob," Tracy said. "We work well together."

Jacob added, "Just don't let Gerald find out Cash has a crush on you."

"Cash doesn't have a crush on me," Tracy said maybe a little too quickly.

"Okay, sure. And you don't have one on him, either," Jacob teased her and in a quiet voice added, "If we do get to come back, I hope we don't get stuck with Donna again."

"I have to agree with you about Donna," Tracy said softly. "Since you have your camera, come with me to the cabin. I'll get my laptop and we can talk about what I've written so far. We can also pull up your photos and discuss which ones go best with the story."

"Yes, I was just thinking the same thing."

Tracy caught up with Kellie and Cristen before leaving the café and giving them her phone number and urged them to text or call if she could be of any further help to them. Then back at her cabin, she and Jacob sat in the rocking chairs on the porch while working on matching sections of her article with his photographs. Having made a great deal of progress, they had just smacked hands in a high five when the chow bell clanged to announce lunch.

"I promised to let Cash have a look at the story and photos before I submit them," Tracy said a lot more casually than she felt. "I hope he approves."

With a nod, Jacob said, "Speak of the devil."

"Where?" Tracy asked as her heart suddenly pounded.

Jacob indicated the stables and Tracy turned her head. Cash and Sam walked into the sunshine and stopped near the stage to speak with Beau. Kellie left the dining area with a thermos and paper cups in one hand and a large, insulated lunch bag in the other. Reaching the men, she handed the lunch bag to Cash and the cups and thermos to her husband. Giving Sam a kiss, she made her way back to the kitchen. Jeff exited the barn with Ed and Larry following him, and they gathered around Cash as he spoke to them.

"Time to eat again!" Donna said way too loudly, bursting out of the cabin. Her clothes and hair were somewhat disheveled, but she seemed oblivious. "Well, well, I see all the gorgeous cowboys gathered in one big group. I'll go say hello."

"Donna, it looks like they're in a meeting with Cash," Tracy said. She couldn't imagine interrupting Cash and his crew.

"I think it looks like they're ripe for picking," Donna said.

"Aren't they all spoken for?" Jacob asked.

"Cash and Jeff aren't," Donna snapped, despite having said Cash wasn't interested and Jeff was too young. With a shrug, she stumbled off the porch. Spewing a curse at tripping, she jiggled her way toward the men and stables. "Hi boys!"

"Donna is an embarrassment," Jacob muttered.

"I wish she wouldn't make a pest of herself."

Tracy wondered if she, too, had made a pest of herself with Cash. Cash had caught sight of Donna coming for them. From her rocking chair, Tracy raised a hand in the air and wiggled her fingers in a wave at Cash. But he had returned his attention to his crew and with a couple of gestures and a nod appeared to finish his instructions to them. The men split up, with Cash and Sam heading to the house and the wranglers veering off in several different directions. Donna found herself left alone in the dust.

"I don't think he noticed you wave," Jacob said, causing Tracy to slowly lower her hand to her lap. "He was too busy putting distance between himself and Donna."

Or between himself and me, Tracy thought as Cash vanished from view.

CHAPTER EIGHTEEN

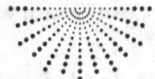

$\mathcal{N}$ever had a woman ditched Cash until Tracy Dalton.

He didn't know which was worse: a woman clinging to him as he rolled out of her bed or rolling over in his own bed and finding Tracy gone.

Finding Tracy gone.

He had only himself to blame. He'd broken his steadfast rules of not letting a woman spend the night and not using a condom. What the hell had he been thinking? Whatever thinking he'd done wasn't with his brain. Somehow bringing her into his private world had backfired.

The sex with Tracy, no—making love to Tracy, had been so incredible he'd almost convinced himself it was a dream. Maybe she'd never been in his bed at all, just in his fantasy. But as he had sat up on the side of his bed he'd noticed a spot of blood, her innocence surrendered to him, on his white sheet. It was the only tangible proof she'd actually spent the night with him. Part of the night.

"My own damn fault," Cash muttered to himself as he set the lunch bag on the kitchen table. Leaving Jeff in charge of the guests, he and Sam had a Zoom meeting in a few minutes regarding the possible purchase of some horses, thus he'd asked Kellie to pack lunches for them.

"What's your fault?" Sam asked, pouring iced tea into cups.

"Nothing," Cash said, taking chicken salad croissants out of the bag. They sat down at the table, and he took a big bite of the sandwich. It was delicious. As he chewed, he read a note from Kellie that said Tracy had made their croissants. His frown deepened.

"Is everything okay, Cash?" Sam wanted to know.

"Yeah."

By two o'clock, they'd decided on the horses they wanted to see in person to replace Ben and Bess when they retired them to pasture. He and Sam left the house and trekked to the garage. Cash noticed Jacob had parked the van in front of the middle cabin which was Tracy's. Would he always think of that cabin as Tracy's from now on? She was nowhere to be seen.

One of the instructions he'd given Jeff was to have the ladies pack and get the van loaded during the daylight. After the fireworks festivities, it would be dark and their week at the dude ranch would be at an end.

Was he at an end with Tracy? Had she already slipped away from the ranch early like she had his bedroom, during the night?

He and Sam climbed into the truck and buckled their seat belts. Driving down the side road to the front of his house Cash saw the Mustang that Tracy could barely drive. Not the car he would choose for her. Anyway, she was still here. For now. Leaving her in his wake, Cash took the highway, which was faster than the back road, to Triple C Ranch-Central.

"The boys will have hay bales and picnic tables pulled out of the barn and Jeff and I will have the barbecue grill going by the time you get back," Sam told him as Cash pulled to a stop under the two-story portico of Chase's house. "After I drop you and Chase off in Denver, I'll pick up the kegs and see you back at the ranch."

"Right," Cash agreed as Chase opened one of the double front doors. "Thanks, Sam."

"Hey, Cash. Hi, Sam," Chase called as he and his four-year-old son, Colton, approached Cash's shiny black double cab truck. Chase was tall with dark-brown hair like Cash and people sometimes mistook them for each other. Colton was a miniature of his father not only in looks, but right down to the cowboy hat, Triple C Ranch-Central shirt, jeans, and cowboy boots.

"Hi." Cash lifted a hand off the steering wheel in a wave.

"Howdy guys," Sam said across Cash.

"Howdy guys!" Colt, as he was affectionately called, echoed excitedly.

Cash had driven his truck, rather than his new Mustang Dark Horse Premium. Wouldn't Tracy be surprised to know he owned that? While her Race Red Mustang was borderline orange, his Mustang, called Rapid Red, was a deep vibrant metallic shade of crimson. He'd driven the 500 horsepower, six-speed sports car as fast as 180 miles per hour at the Pikes Peak International Raceway. Though that had been a thrill ride, it paled in comparison to his night ride with Tracy.

For this trip to Denver, his truck was the practical choice. Besides he was the only one who drove his Mustang and Sam would be driving the truck back to Triple C-East. Chase quickly installed Colt's car seat and buckled his son in. Then shutting the door, he hopped in the other side of the truck. As close as Cash was to Sam and however much he respected his ranch foreman, it was his older brother in whom Cash would confide should he decide to talk about what was on his mind.

"Jade and Courtney will meet you at my ranch later, right Chase?" Cash asked as he drove down the drive toward the main road.

"Yes," Chase said of his wife and their two-year-old daughter. "Jade is in the kitchen baking her cherry pies for the barbecue and Courtney is down for a nap."

"Has Derek completed his pilot lessons?" Sam asked as they pulled onto the highway.

"Yeah, when Derek and I flew into Denver on Monday,

he picked his private pilot's license from the FAA," Chase said. "And his new truck from the dealership. It was a productive trip."

Cash had been waiting, with Sam and Jeff, for the van bringing the contest winners to the ranch when Chase and Derek had flown over them. "Derek likes flying the chopper as much as we do."

"And he's just as good," Chase replied.

"Yes, he is," Cash agreed. "Thanks for flying the helicopter up to Denver for the annual inspection and scheduled maintenance, Chase."

"No problem," Chase replied. "I use the helicopter as much on my ranch looking for my cattle as you do flying your guests." Whenever possible, they flew the Bell 505 Jet Ranger X as a team to ensure there was always a copilot onboard. Having Derek licensed was a bonus, making flying as a team even more flexible. "We always find our cows a lot quicker in the air than on the ground, don't we, Colt?"

"I like flyin' and seein' our cows," Colton said, watching out the truck window.

Cash and Sam both chuckled. "That reminds me of a couple things," Cash said. "The journalist, Tracy Dalton, who's writing the magazine story in *Ranchers and Ranges*, was with me when we found one of your cows and her calf on my ranch," Cash said.

"Jeff brought them to me. Thanks," Chase said as Sam nodded. "What's the other thing?"

"Tracy would like to include quotes from you and Jade as well as Chloe and Derek in her magazine article. Along with a couple of photos. If you're open to it."

"Sounds like free advertising for the cattle ranch and for Jade's equine therapy with kids," Chase said. "Coop says Tracy is a descendant of the Dalton Gang."

"Yup," Cash said and headed north from the Black Forest area onto State Highway 83. "Did Coop tell you a member of the Dalton family saved a member of the Cooper family from being strung up as a horse thief by Judge Isaac Parker back in 1885?"

"Yes, how about that?" Chase said. "Coop did a little research and found out that Frank Dalton was based out of Fort Smith, Arkansas. He said that was the whereabouts of our ancestor, Cade Cooper. He said Frank Dalton had a reputation as a brave and honest lawman."

"Tracy Dalton is a looker, isn't she, Cash?" Sam prodded him.

"What's a looker?" Colton asked.

"It means she's a beautiful woman," Cash told his nephew. To the men, he said, "She's hot enough to melt dry ice."

They talked about the barbecue and the ranches then. The day was another beautiful one in sunny Colorado. The blue skies overhead had nary a cloud, and the traffic was light on this scenic back road into Denver. Their first stop was to the company that made banners and signs. After picking up the banner Cash had ordered, the next stop was only a few miles away. Minutes later, he pulled into the parking lot for the dealership of the million-dollar-plus helicopter. Once it was determined the helicopter was ready as promised, Sam took Cash's place behind the wheel of the truck and waved goodbye.

It took a little longer than Cash had expected to get the banner appropriately attached to the chopper. In addition, the wind had come up. The Chinooks weren't strong enough to keep them from flying but towing the banner would slow them down. They'd land on Triple C-East around six and the barbecue would be in full swing. No matter, he had good people in place to handle things until he got there.

The interior of the Bell 505 Jet Ranger X included the pilot's seat and the one beside it up front. Behind those seats were three seats across the back of the helicopter. Colton knew the drill and held Chase's hand as they approached the chopper. Chase helped him into the back of the cockpit and buckled him up in a window seat. Cowboy hats off all around, Chase then fitted Colton with his ear protection headset. Cash and Chase boarded and donned the headsets, which they could speak and hear through, as well. Cash started the engine, and they rose into the air.

"Yeehaw!" Colton whooped and clapped, making his uncle and dad chuckle as they started the flight back to Triple C-East.

Once they were headed south, Chase asked, "Coop likes this Tracy Dalton. The ancient history aside, I'd like to hear your take on her."

"She's intelligent, well-spoken, and accomplished," Cash said.

"And you like her," Chase replied knowingly.

"Yeah, but—" Cash shrugged.

"But what?"

"I don't know."

"Yes, you do. What's the story?"

"I don't know if she feels the same. She ghosted me in the middle of the night."

"She spent the night?" Chase asked. "At your house?"

"Yeah."

His brows raised in surprise, Chase said, "Okay. So, you *must* like her. A lot."

"Did you hear the part about her slipping away without telling me? What do you think about that, Chase?"

"I think she didn't want anyone to see her leaving in the morning," Chase replied. "For your sake and hers."

Cash looked at him. "Yeah?"

"Yeah," Chase said. "What did she say today when you asked her why she left?"

"I didn't ask her. I avoided her."

Chase frowned. "Don't let pride get in your way, Cash. Talk to her."

"If she doesn't feel the same about me, I don't want her to feel obligated."

"Only way to find out how she *feels* is to talk to her."

"I guess."

"I *guess* she'll know how *you* feel when she sees the banner."

"If she's still on the ranch."

"She'll be there."

"How do you know?" Cash asked.

"If she wants to talk to the rest of us, she realizes she needs your introductions and support."

"You think?"

"I think she likes you, too, little brother."

"What makes you say that?"

"She probably crossed a professional line by taking the risk of spending the night. She protected you as well as herself by quietly leaving. Sounds like she's a brave and self-less woman. Worth pursuing if you ask me."

"I guess I did ask. Thanks, Chase."

"No problem."

Was Chase right? Would Tracy still be there? If not for him, for his family?

As they neared Triple C Ranch-West, Cash asked his brother, "How much do you think Colt heard?"

"I heered ever'thing," Colton piped up. "Dad, look! The pool. I swimmed with Cooper, Austin, and Abilene yes'day," he told them, referring to the children of Chloe and Derek.

"That's right, pardner. You *swam* with your cousins there yesterday. We're almost home. I see your cousins up ahead of us on the back road in their new truck driving to the barbecue."

"Yay!" Colt cheered and waved.

Cash made eye contact with Chase. "Will Colt repeat anything we said?"

"It's a crap shoot."

CHAPTER NINETEEN

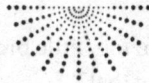

"*I* will introduce you to Cash Cooper, whenever he gets here," Tracy said to the magazine editor.

For the barbecue, she'd changed into a patriotic mini dress. With narrow straps and a deep vee neck, American flags in the shape of hearts splashed the white background of the dress. Her new Elsa hat and cowboy boots complimented the red, white, and blue perfectly.

The magazine editor, Gerald Moles, was forty and single. Wearing a white shirt, black chinos, and black patent leather loafers without socks, he appeared dressed for a cocktail at a Colorado Springs bar rather than a barbecue on a dude ranch. Gerald drove a Tesla Model 3, which he was fond of saying was the most expensive electric vehicle in the Tesla line.

Beau and Ed, according to Cash, the wranglers with the best people skills, were in charge of arriving guests and showing them where to park. When the driveway had become full, they had started directing folks to a field adjacent to the house. Gerald had called Tracy, adamantly refusing to park his Tesla in a *damn pasture*. Tracy and Jacob had hurried to greet him with Donna tagging along. By the time Tracy reached the front of the house, Beau had left Ed in the field and was talking to Gerald in the driveway. Gerald had squeezed his car in between an SUV and the front fence, near the gate. Tracy saw Beau shaking his head and indicating the Tesla was too close to the driver's door of the SUV. She gritted her teeth at the way Gerald rudely disregarded Beau who pulled out his cell phone. Since Cash was nowhere in sight, Tracy figured Jeff or Sam would be informed about Gerald and the parking situation.

Once again, Tracy had felt humiliated by someone from the magazine. Donna snickered, seeming to think the whole thing was funny. What was wrong with these two people? Tracy thought Gerald Moles should have shown better manners than to openly antagonize the people on the ranch which Kirk Devereux had gone to such trouble and expense to feature in a future issue of *Ranchers and Ranges*. She was sure Mr. Devereux would have happily parked in the field and never said a word. Tracy had experienced an inward cringe when Gerald had hugged her. She'd quickly stepped back and Jacob had extended his hand. Gerald shook hands absentmindedly with a preoccupied nod at Donna. Tracy had mouthed the words, *I'm sorry*, to Beau. Then, along with Jacob and Donna, she had escorted Gerald to the barbecue.

Where was Cash?

A country band was playing on the stage, people were dancing, Sam and Jeff were manning the fire pit grill, Kellie and Cristen were in the outdoor kitchen, and Larry was overseeing the two kegs of beer. Tracy had no idea that the Fourth of July barbecue meant a hundred people. How did Cash manage it all? There were more than three times as many people in Cash's backyard than lived in the community of Wild Horse. Tracy and Jacob stayed with Kellie's sweet tea while Larry poured cups of beer for Donna and Gerald.

"Besides the staff and cowboys from Triple C-Central and West, family, friends, former and current guests, along with neighbors and friends are always welcome at the Coopers' three summertime barbecues," Larry said affably to Gerald and smiled.

Instead of focused and polite, Gerald nodded distract-edly as if not fully present. Why?

Tracy wondered if *she* was still welcome to be here. Why had Cash ignored her before leaving the ranch? Was this how he treated a woman after she gave him her virginity? Maybe Cash feared she expected a commitment from him. Tracy admitted to herself she really liked the big'n bad rancher, but she certainly didn't expect a commitment of any kind. The best she hoped for was his friendship. Nervous, she decided all she could do was what her grandmother told her before she'd left home; *Always behave graciously like the classy young lady you are.*

Tracy admonished herself as the thought occurred to her that Cash might think she was anything but classy after the way she'd ridden him in the so-called cowgirl position in his bed. If she hadn't been holding her cup of sweet tea, Tracy would have been wringing her hands.

Or maybe Cash's neck.

Looking from where she stood in the picnic area, it occurred to her Cash was giving her plenty of time and opportunity to leave his ranch. Would he be irritated to find her still here? Tracy pictured the crowded driveway and wondered if there was any possibility she could safely maneuver that rental car she wasn't used to driving out of its parking spot.

"So where is this mystery rancher who's not here to greet his guests?" Gerald asked, tipping a third cup of beer to his mouth.

"I don't know where Cash—" Tracy began but the whirring of helicopter blades interrupted her, drawing her eyes to the sunset sky.

Behind a red, white, and blue helicopter waved a red, white, and blue banner reading, *Happy 4th of July and Happy Birthday, Tracy.* As Tracy's jaw dropped, people all around her began cheering, clapping, waving, pointing, and calling out happy birthday. Jacob snapped photos. Donna whispered something to Gerald and they both smirked.

To Tracy's complete shock, Cash sat in the pilot's seat. The words, Triple C Ranch, appeared on both sides of the helicopter. He flew in a wide circle above the ranch before landing in a grassy field beyond the five guest cabins. The banner fluttered to the ground behind the chopper and the blades overhead whirred to a stop.

"What a show-off," Gerald said to Tracy and laughed. "Next year the sign will just say Happy Fourth of July."

Ignoring Gerald and the thought of Cash cutting the banner in half, Tracy set her cup on a picnic table and walked toward the helicopter. She noticed a beautiful blonde carrying a blond little girl also heading to the helicopter.

"Hi," the blonde said. "I'm Jade Cooper."

"Hi, Jade. I'm Tracy Dalton and I've heard wonderful things about you and your family from Cash."

"Thank you, Tracy. Coop speaks highly of you."

A dark-haired man opened the closer door of the helicopter which was facing them. He lifted a dark-haired boy out of the helicopter and stood him on the ground. The boy ran to Jade.

"We're back, Mom!" the little fellow called.

"I see that, sweet boy," Jade replied. When the little girl reached for the man, who looked so much like Cash he certainly had to be Chase Cooper, Jade handed him their daughter and hugged their son.

Cash exited on the far side of the helicopter and strode around the front of it. Tracy caught a flash of uncertainty on his handsome face. So maybe he was unsure of their situation too. Some of the heaviness lifted from Tracy's shoulders and she smiled her best smile at Cash. When he grinned in return, Tracy hurried to Cash and his arms opened wide.

"Happy Fourth of July birthday, spitfire," Cash said as he hugged her.

"Thank you." Tracy didn't care who saw or what they thought as she boldly gave him a quick peck on the cheek. Breathlessly, she said, "I missed you today, big'n bad."

"Me too," Cash said and snared her hand. Walking

toward the four people near the cockpit he said, "Tracy, I'd like you to meet my brother, Chase, his wife, Jade, my nephew, Colton, and niece Courtney."

"I'm four. Courtney's two," Colton said.

"Hi Colton and Courtney." Tracy smiled at him and then at the little girl.

"It's nice to meet you, Tracy," Chase said politely.

"Tracy and I introduced ourselves just a moment ago," Jade said with a smile.

"It's my pleasure to meet you all," Tracy replied.

"She's a looker!" Colton said importantly as if echoing something he'd heard.

The adults laughed and Tracy said, "Thank you, Colton."

Colton told her, "Uncle Cash says you melt ice."

"Okay, pardner," Chase chuckled. "Look, here come your cousins."

Cash squeezed her hand and Tracy squeezed back. Cash thought she was attractive! Her heart sang. *Thank you, little Colton*, she thought. Then Tracy noticed a lovely brunette walking toward them beside an attractive man with dark blond hair. In front of them two young boys and a girl came running. Obviously, these children and their families loved each other.

"Hi guys," Cash began, "this is Tracy Dalton, who is writing the story about the ranch. Tracy, this is my sister and brother-in-law, Chloe and Derek Brevard." With a smile at the kids he said, "My nephew, Cooper, is five. The twins, Austin and Abilene, are three."

"Nice to meet you," Derek said.

"Happy birthday, Tracy," Chloe said. "We're glad you could join us."

"Thank you," Tracy replied. "It's so nice to meet all of you."

Turning to the children, Chloe asked, "Cooper, Austin, and Abilene, can you say hello?"

"Hello," the three children all said at once.

"Hello," Tracy said to them. Overwhelmed by the

warmest welcome she'd ever had, it made her eyes sting with happiness. Being raised as an only child, these siblings, siblings-in-law, nephews, and nieces of Cash's exuded an inner circle family closeness she'd never experienced in her life. "It's an honor to spend the Fourth of July with you."

Chase carried Courtney as her big brother, Colton, told the cousins how he had seen their swimming pool from up in the sky. Cooper said he'd seen Colton waving to them on the way to the barbecue. Then the boys ran ahead with twins Austin and Abilene hot on their heels.

Watching them, Cash said with a chuckle, "I love those kids."

"I'd like to have a couple someday." As soon as the words left her mouth, Tracy felt a red-hot blush heat her cheeks. She had said it quietly but didn't dare meet Cash's blue eyes.

"Me too," Cash said before turning to the others. "Tracy hopes her editor will allow her to extend her magazine article to include Triple C-Central and West by mentioning all of you, including photos of you and your ranches."

"Really?" Chloe asked with interest.

"Free advertisement," Derek commented as the others agreed.

"Yes, that's what I thought too," Tracy replied. "My editor's name is Gerald Moles. He arrived a little while ago and I think being here is a sign he might approve the idea. But *Ranchers and Ranges* owner, Kirk Devereux will have the final say."

The Coopers were well aware of the magazine. Thus, the article was the topic of discussion on the walk from the helicopter to the barbecue. They found Cooper, Colton, and Austin grouped in front of Coop at a picnic table with Abilene on his knee and a dog at his feet.

"Happy birthday, Tracy!" Coop called.

"Thank you, Coop," Tracy said.

"Meet Crockett," Coop said in reference to the dog.

"Hi Crockett." Tracy leaned over and petted the cattle dog's head. "I have a German shepherd named Dude."

Coop said, "Crockett and I need to meet Dude."

Wishing that could really happen, Tracy said, "Dude would love this ranch."

As Coop spoke to the rest of his family, Cash said to Tracy, "If your editor allows you to continue working on the article, you're welcome to stay with me."

"Thank you, Cash," Tracy replied, her heart racing at the idea. "But I'm due to pick up Dude at the doggy daycare in the morning. They stay booked up and won't have room for him on such short notice."

"Stay here tonight and we'll go get Dude in the morning," Cash said casually. "We can bring him to the ranch for a visit."

Tracy said shyly, "I miss him, and I think you'd like each other."

Practically stomping her way toward them, Donna came to a stop and said, "You'd best get over to Gerald before he leaves, Tracy. He's not happy."

CHAPTER TWENTY

"*W*hat's not to be happy about?" Winston Smith demanded.

With a scruffy beard, needing a haircut, and overweight he stood with his hands clenched in Tammy Dalton's small living room. The diminutive lady with gray hair and sharp, bluish-green eyes glared at him from the sofa, where she sat with her swollen foot propped on a pillow.

"Everything!" Tammy snapped. "I can't drive a stick shift with my injured foot and even if I could, I can't walk to my truck, Winston. You won't take me to the hospital in Colorado Springs and I can't call 9-1-1 because you claim to have misplaced my cell phone."

"I make scrambled eggs every morning for you from the chickens I provided. I cook for you every evening," Winston shot back. "I told you there's nothing to be done for a sprained ankle. It wasn't my fault you tripped over that rug."

"My foot could be broken and not just sprained. I need to have it x-rayed," Tammy argued. "I didn't know that rug was there until I slipped and fell in the middle of the night," she reminded him. "Why was it all crumpled up between my bedroom and the bathroom anyway?"

"I bought a nice rug for you, but of course you don't appreciate anything I do, Tammy."

"Winston, you being a friend started out all right, but being my caregiver is not working well," Tammy said. "I think I'd be better off on my own. You should leave."

"You just said you can't get around on your own," Winston reminded her cajolingly. "If you could lend me some money, I could pay my cell phone bill and we could get the service turned back on."

"What happened to the money I've paid you for looking after me up until now? Never mind. Drive me to the bank and I'll get the money."

"Oh now, don't be silly. Save yourself the trouble of trying to make it to your truck," Winston said. He was sick to death of putting up with her demands. "Everybody from Wild Horse to Kit Carson knows you and your dead husband buried cash for years all over this property. Just tell me where at least one stash of the money is buried. I'll go pay my cell phone bill and be right back."

"Buried money?" Tammy asked. "What are you talking about, Winston?"

"You're a Dalton. Outlaws often buried their money to hide it from lawmen back in the day. I figure you buried yours in the yard to hide it from the IRS," Winston said. "You live like you're poor. But I still remember when your son and his wife took that expensive vacation out to Arizona which ended in a helicopter crash."

Tammy winced. "We aren't outlaws and we didn't bury money in the yard."

"But when she worked at the bank, my daughter, Donna, said it was rumored—"

"Donna? I thought you said your daughter's name was Brenda."

Winston silently cursed himself at the slip and didn't reply. "It's rumored your husband made all kinds of money before his oil well dried up."

Tammy stared at him. "So that's why you're here."

~

"Is Gerald still here, Jacob?" Tracy asked as she, Cash, and Donna met up with him.

"He's over at the kegs refilling his cup," Jacob said as they stood near the stage.

Through a throng of people dancing to a fast song and others in line near the grill waiting for steaks or burgers, Cash glanced toward the kegs. He spotted a guy sticking out like a sore thumb due to his business casual attire. Had to be Gerald. What was the editor's problem? Why drive all the way out to the ranch only to leave before touching base with the owner?

"What's he unhappy about?" Tracy asked, taking the words out of Cash's mouth.

"Jealous," Jacob whispered to Tracy and inclined his head toward Cash.

"Ask Gerald yourself," Donna muttered and then smiled at someone behind them.

"She's back!"

Cash watched the man who'd just spoken wrap his left arm around Tracy's waist and tug her close. An unfamiliar emotion slammed Cash in the gut. He couldn't remember ever feeling such a jolt. What the hell? Probably six foot tall with a yellow pompadour slicked straight back, the man completely ignored Cash as he grinned down at Tracy.

"Gerald, I'd like you to meet Cash Cooper, owner of Triple C Ranch-East," Tracy said and eased out of Gerald's grasp. "Cash, this is Gerald Moles."

"Nice to meet you, Gerald," Cash said and offered his hand.

Gerald pulled his eyes off Tracy and blatantly stared at his empty left arm. Grinning, Donna jiggled her way into Gerald's loose embrace. With a frown, Gerald handed Donna his beer and glanced at Cash. This guy was as arrogant as they came.

"Cash Cooper, man of the hour." Gerald finally acknowledged Cash with a sarcastic ring to his voice. He shook hands with Cash and said, "Quite the entrance." Releasing Cash's hand, Gerald retrieved his beer from Donna, and raised it in Tracy's direction. "Happy birthday to my best journalist."

"Flattery will get you nowhere," Tracy said firmly.

Cash could tell Tracy was serious and Gerald was well on his way to being drunk. "We're known for our barbecues," Cash said to Gerald as the smell of grilled beef wafted all around them. "Have you eaten?"

"No," Gerald said moving away from Donna and with only a cursory glance at Cash. He chugged his beer, handed Cash his empty cup, and said to Tracy, "They're playing our song."

The flash of surprise in Tracy's turquoise eyes told Cash that she had no song with Gerald just before he pulled her away from Cash into the crowd of nearby dancers. It was a slow song and Cash did not watch.

"Let's dance, Cash," Donna said and grabbed his arm.

"No, thanks," Cash said, pulling his arm from her.

"Boss," Jeff called, coming his way.

Cash left the dance area and walked toward Jeff. "What's up?"

"Some guy named Gerald something, driving a Tesla, made quite the entrance," Jeff said as they stopped to speak.

"Gerald Moles," Cash informed him, noting Jeff's ironic choice of words. He waved to some friends in the distance and spoke to a couple who passed by him and Jeff. "Let's keep moving," he said, wanting to hear what Jeff had to say. They headed toward the café where Cash saw Kellie, Cristen, and Teresa. Sam was behind the grill with Bob. Bob was Chase's ranch foreman and his wife, Teresa, was Kellie's sister. Cash greeted everyone and ensconced among these trusted friends, he asked Jeff, "What kind of entrance?"

"Beau and Ed said Moles arrived late and refused to park his car in the field."

"So where did Moles park?"

"The driveway," Jeff replied.

"I take it the driveway was full by the time he got here?" Cash asked.

"Yes. But he backed his car in between a big SUV and the split-rail fence. Stupid," Jeff said and shook his head. "He'd been much better off in the field where there's endless room."

"Did he say why?" Sam asked.

Turning to his dad, Jeff replied, "Said he didn't drive his new white Tesla all the way out here just to get it dirty and his shoes dusty in a damn pasture. Then he called Tracy to complain."

"Seriously?" Bob asked with a genuinely perplexed frown. "Did he not know there might be dirt and dust on a ranch?"

"He must not get out of the corporate office much," Sam said.

"Or visit the ranchers and ranges featured in the magazine he works for," Jeff added. "Anyway, the guys said Tracy hurried out to the front gate."

"How did she react?" Cash asked.

"Ed said she looked embarrassed, and Beau said she mouthed an apology," Jeff reported.

Cash glanced at the dance area and noted the strained expression on Tracy's beautiful face. When Tracy's eyes collided with his, he saw in them all he needed to see. Saying he'd be right back, he walked straight to Tracy.

"I'm cutting in," Cash informed Gerald Moles. Not giving the man a chance to protest, Cash took hold of Tracy's left hand as she held it out to him. Cash tugged her into his embrace and danced her away from Moles.

"Thank you, Cash," Tracy whispered. "I wish I'd never invited Gerald."

"As I recall, it was my idea," Cash said and then chuckled. "He looks pissed."

"Maybe Donna can sidetrack him," Tracy said as Donna took her place with Gerald.

"I doubt it. No contest between you and Donna."

Tracy blushed at his compliment. They finished the slow dance and danced a fast one as Cooper Brevard, holding his little cousin, Courtney Cooper's hand, joined them near the stage to dance. After walking the children back to their parents, Cash escorted Tracy to the barbecue grill.

"How do you like your steak?" Sam was asking Gerald. "I grill 'em rare to well done."

Instead of answering Sam, Gerald said to Cash, "I understand your brother and sister are open to being interviewed by Tracy and photographed by Jacob."

Cash clenched his jaw and casually hooked a thumb into the front pocket of his jeans. As Gerald had ignored Sam, instead of answering him, Cash asked, "Gerald Moles, have you met Sam Reynolds, my ranch foreman?"

"Hello, Gerald," Sam said.

"Hello," Gerald replied with only a cursory look at Sam and directed his attention back to Cash. "I told Tracy that she and I will head to the Springs tonight and discuss the angles."

"There are no angles, Gerald," Tracy said. "As I see it, we put Cash on the cover, much like how he's standing now, maybe with a Triple C Ranch-East corral behind him." When she smiled at Cash, he instinctively knew she was thinking of the oil painting of him when he was eighteen. "I have the story almost finished," Tracy told Gerald. "When and if they agree and it's convenient for them, I can interview Chase and Jade Cooper and then Derek and Chloe Brevard. Jacob can take photos and I can add their quotes to Cash's article."

Gerald chuckled, but it wasn't a friendly one. "As I see it, we'll discuss it in my office."

"As I see it," Cash began with a glare at Gerald for his abruptness to Tracy, "time to eat a steak." With a smile at Tracy, he swept a hand toward the grill. "Tell Sam how you like yours."

Tracy turned to Sam with a smile. "Medium please, Sam." To Cash, she said, "I'm ready to find a seat and eat."

"Let's do it, birthday girl," Cash said and held out his arm. Tracy slipped her arm through his. "You know how I like mine, Sam."

"Medium and medium rare coming up," Sam said. "And you, sir?" he asked Gerald.

"Well done," Gerald mumbled.

"I thought so," Cash said in a way that made Gerald scowl as he endeavored to determine if Cash meant the steak or having turned the tables on him.

A giggle escaped Tracy, and she whispered, "*Well done,* Cash."

CHAPTER TWENTY-ONE

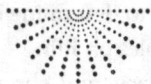

"Come join us, Jacob," Tracy called a few minutes later from the picnic table.

She'd felt the tension in Cash's muscular body as they'd danced and when her arm had been looped through his. He'd sat at a picnic bench and tugged her down beside him, somewhat strategically, at the end of the table. Gerald had joined them but had to sit across from her instead of beside her. Donna followed and predictably plopped down beside Gerald which put her across from Cash. When Jacob arrived with his plate, he slid onto the bench next to Cash. Reaching across Gerald for a saltshaker, Donna jiggled her amply exposed breasts which Gerald ignored. Jacob couldn't say enough nice things about his week on the ranch. He and Cash talked as Gerald smirked.

"Mighty tasty brownie, Tracy," Coop said as he walked up to the picnic table, munching one with pecans on top. "Kellie says you were a big help today."

"Thanks, Coop. It was my pleasure," Tracy said. After helping make croissants, she'd baked half a dozen tins of brownies.

"She makes a mean chicken salad croissant too," Cash said and grinned at her.

"Coop, please take my seat," Jacob said and giving up his

place next to Cash, moved to the other side of the table beside Donna.

"Thanks, Jacob," Cash said and patted the bench beside him.

"Coop, I believe you met Donna Smith earlier in the week," Tracy said as Coop sat next to Cash. "This is Gerald Moles from *Ranchers and Ranges*. Gerald, this gentleman is Crawford Cooper, patriarch of the Triple C Ranches."

"Heard about you, Mr. Moles," Coop said coolly to Gerald who lifted a hand in greeting. Then ignoring Gerald, Coop asked, "What time are your fireworks tonight, Cash?"

"Whenever we're ready," Cash said, cutting a side eye and frown at Gerald who hadn't appropriately acknowledged or even replied to Coop. Tracy figured Cash might explode at any time due to Gerald's continued rudeness, especially when it came to his beloved grandfather. Looking back at Coop, Cash said, "The guys who set off our fireworks are just waiting for me to tell them when. You ready, Coop?"

"I'm ready." Coop grinned and clapped his hands for emphasis.

"The *big* fireworks will be on top of Pikes Peak shortly before ten tonight," Gerald said. Cash ignored that jab to the ranch fireworks as he pulled out his cell and texted. Looking across the table at Tracy, Gerald urged, "We should be going so we don't miss that show, Tracy. Are you all packed up?"

"I want to capture Cash's fireworks," Jacob said. "Then I'll head back to the Springs since I need to drive the ladies who won the contest into town."

"As Tracy's assistant, I took it upon myself to check in with the contest winners," Donna said importantly and leaned into Gerald, pushing her breast against his arm. "I made sure the ladies got packed so they'd be ready to go whenever we are."

"Jeff told us Cash suggested the ladies pack up this afternoon because it would be dark and harder to do so after the fireworks," Jacob said. "So, I drove the van around to the cabins and we loaded the luggage."

"I was speaking to Tracy," Gerald said to Jacob and Donna.

"You go ahead, Gerald," Tracy said evenly. "I have the Mustang."

"Are you spending another night in our cabin, Tracy?" Donna asked pointedly.

"No," Tracy said, fairly certain that when Cash invited her to stay, he didn't mean alone in her cabin. Maybe not in Cash's bed, but somewhere in his house. "I agree with Jacob, I prefer to see Cash's fireworks so I can include them in the article."

Tracy had never seen this side of Gerald: the arrogant rudeness nor the barely concealed anger. He'd always been easy to work with in the office. Then again, this was Gerald's first time being around her in Cash Cooper's intimidating presence.

"The Mustang has to be returned to the rental car location, Tracy," Gerald said.

"Tonight?" Tracy asked in surprise. "I was planning to pick up my dog and return the car tomorrow morning."

"Tonight, by nine o'clock," Gerald informed her.

"Jacob, you can drive a stick, can't you?" Cash asked.

"I sure can, Cash," Jacob said. "Donna, you can *assist* by driving the ladies back to town in the van."

"What about Tracy?" Donna's voice had a jealous ring to it.

Cash looked across the table, not at Donna, but at Gerald and said with finality, "I'll drive Tracy home when she's ready."

Tracy wasn't sure if the explosion came from the fireworks, Cash, or Gerald. Since the early evening sky lit up, she guessed it was Cash's fireworks as Jacob snapped photos. In order to face the fireworks, Cash got up and strategically changed positions on the bench seat of the picnic table, placing his back to Gerald. She and Coop followed Cash's lead. Cash placed his arm on the table and flattened his hand against her long hair.

With the bursting of the fireworks, Cash's hand moved up her back to her shoulder, and he tugged her closer to ask, "Are you gonna lose your job because of me?"

Next to his ear, Tracy said just loudly enough for him to hear, "If I do, I have a couple of side hustles I can pursue."

Cash leaned back, grinned at her, and asked, "Like what?"

"Besides chasing chickens and baking brownies?"

"Yeah, besides that."

"I love massages and I've learned how to give a delightful one." Without skipping a beat, she followed up with, "And I have a children's book series I'd like to finish and see published."

"Is that right?"

"It is."

With a grin as hot as a firecracker, Cash said, "Will you give me a *delightful* massage?" Before Tracy could answer, a big boom sounded, and the little girl named Abilene stumbled into Cash. "Hi, sweetheart," Cash said, immediately scooping her up and settling her on his lap.

"Uncle Cash," Abilene said and smiled at him.

"Abilene," her twin brother, Austin, called. "You let go of my hand."

Cash saw Derek striding toward them and waved at him. "We got 'em, Derek."

Derek waved back and headed in the opposite direction to Chloe and Cooper, a few picnic tables away. Coop tugged grandson, Austin, onto his lap and they looked to the sky. Tracy smiled, thinking how blessed this family was to live in such proximity, enabling them to physically share the love they had for each other. Yet, with their ranches a few miles apart, they also had privacy and led their separate lives. Tracy sighed with deep longing and felt a tug on her hair. When she glanced back at Cash, Abilene held a lock of Tracy's hair in her little hand.

"Hi, Abilene," Tracy said with a smile. When Abilene smiled at her, Tracy instinctively held out her hands. With a brief glance up at her Uncle Cash, who nodded, Abilene wiggled into Tracy's arms. Tracy hugged the little girl to her heart and reminded her, "My name is Tracy."

"Tracy," Abilene echoed and picked up a lock of her hair again.

"You have beautiful hair, Abilene," Tracy said.

Abilene touched her dark-blond hair. She nodded at Tracy and a smile lit up her darling face. Abilene leaned against Tracy's chest and Cash's hand flattened to Tracy's back, this time underneath her hair. The fireworks display soon ended in a fantastic finale of red, white, and blue bursting across the night sky. Even amid these sensational sights and sounds, Tracy could not remember ever experiencing such serenity in her soul.

"You have beautiful hair too," Cash whispered to Tracy before standing up. Abilene reached for him, and Cash tucked her into his left arm. He held out his right hand to Tracy and tugged her off the bench. "Coop, you and Austin coming with us?"

"Yup," Coop replied, standing Austin to the ground and taking his hand. "I'm riding home with Chase and family."

At the mention of a ride, Tracy remembered Gerald. She looked over her shoulder for the first time since the fireworks began. He was gone. Cash shrugged. When they turned the children over to the Brevards, Tracy felt a pang as Abilene and Austin waved goodbye to her. Next they bid farewell to Chase, Jade, and their kids. Coop hugged Tracy before leaving with them.

"We can go get Dude in the morning, but you're staying with me tonight, right?" Cash asked her and with a crooked grin, added, "Or as long as you want."

Tracy's heart pounded and she told the irresistible rancher, "If you have room."

Cash chuckled. "I think I do. I'm heading out front to help Beau and Ed," he told her. "If your bag is in the

Mustang, I can get it for you while I'm there and give the car keys to Jacob."

"The keys are in my purse in the café," Tracy said. They met up with Kellie, Cristen, and Teresa hard at work and Tracy gave Cash the keys. As there was much to do after such a big party, Tracy offered to stay and help the ladies. Before leaving, Cash pulled her into his arms. Flirting with him, she said, "Full disclosure, I'll miss you while you're out front."

"Full disclosure, you can stay in the bedroom of your choice. Okay?"

CHAPTER TWENTY-TWO

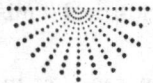

"*O*kay," the gorgeous redhead whispered with a shy smile.

Cash pulled Tracy to him for a kiss. Her turquoise eyes closed and her full lips, so sweet and supple, invitingly parted. Sliding a hand under her glossy, thick hair to the nape of her neck, he hugged her and then reluctantly let her go. Before she could change her mind about spending the night, he jogged away from her. He gave Sam, who was helping Kellie, Teresa, and Cristen, a wave. He sprinted past Jeff and Larry who were expertly rounding up guests like the wranglers they were and herding folks toward cars parked in front of the house. He met up with Jacob in the driveway and popped open the trunk of the Mustang. Retrieving Tracy's packed bag, he gave the car keys to Jacob and stashed Tracy's bag in the foyer of his house.

"Thanks for everything, Cash!" Jacob called as he headed the Mustang toward the ranch gate and highway. "You and Tracy take care of each other. Hope to see you soon!"

"Sure thing, Jabob," Cash said and waved.

Donna was driving the van directly behind the Mustang and, like Jacob, was on the opposite side of the vehicle from Cash. In Donna's case the passengers blocked most of her view. Good. Earlier, she'd frowned and ignored Cash as all the contest winners, getting into the van, had thanked him saying they'd be back. As for Donna, he hoped he'd seen the last of her. On the flip side, he was glad Diane and Joyce had been able to spend time with Chloe and Derek and their kids during the barbecue. Those two ladies had hugged him and assured him they'd see all the Coopers again. Now, the contest winners were all waving out of the van windows, once again shouting out *thank yous and see you sooner than laters*.

"Please come back again." Cash smiled as he waved goodbye. Other departing guests called their thanks and farewells as he continued to the front gate, his thoughts on Tracy. What bedroom would she choose?

"You're just in time, boss," Beau said, leaning against the split rail fence next to Ed.

Under driveway lamps and moonlight, Cash saw Gerald Moles. Surely getting dust all over his shoes, he was pacing back and forth on the driver's side of a Tesla in the open space where the SUV had been parked. Spinning on his heel, Gerald glared at Cash and pointed to the driver's door of the white Model 3 electric vehicle. It was the cheapest model Tesla made.

"What are you going to do about that?" Gerald demanded.

"About what?" Cash asked, coming to a stop a few feet from Gerald and his Tesla.

"That gouge!" Gerald's voice and the finger he was pointing both shook.

Beau walked around the car holding a bright flashlight which they always had on hand to escort people to their cars. He shone the light against the car door where Gerald was pointing. Cash couldn't see anything and said so. Gerald flipped on his cell phone flashlight and held it a couple of inches from the door.

Ed joined them and said, "We specifically told this gentleman he could not park here because the driver of the

SUV would have difficulty opening his door wide enough to enter his vehicle."

"I can see that without the SUV even being here," Cash said.

"We can't detect any damage to this gentleman's car, boss," Beau said and winked.

"Right here," Gerald blared, stabbing his finger against the bottom of the door. "See? Or are you all completely blind?"

Turning on his own cell phone flashlight, Cash leaned over and squinted. He realized the complaint involved a smudge on the white paint. Beau had winked because it was a speck of mud and not a scratch, much less a gouge.

"Who was driving the SUV?" Cash asked as he stood up straight.

Ed snickered. "Owen Custis. His son, Sully, was with him."

"Okay," Cash replied. "I talked to our good friends, Owen and Sully, earlier."

"I'm calling the Colorado Springs police," Gerald spat.

"The El Paso County Sheriff's Department has authority out here in the country," Cash said helpfully.

"I think 9-1-1 will know who to contact," Gerald said smugly, preparing to call.

"When the deputy arrives, tell him you blocked the SUV door of retired El Paso County Sheriff Owen Custis," Cash said evenly. Owen Custis, highly respected and admired by law enforcement and local ranchers alike, consulted with and assisted Derek in his horse business in training Percherons for mounted officers.

"Cash, maybe you could call your brother-in-law, Derek, to get his take on this situation," Beau suggested.

"Yeah." Ed looked at Gerald and said, "Since Brevard worked with Custis as a deputy sheriff for a number of years, he'll know what to do."

Ed and Beau both chuckled. Cash held his cell phone flashlight to the door again and, using his thumb, flicked away the dirt. He shined the light from the spotless door to Gerald's face as the man's mouth fell open. Cash stood, turned off the light, and shoved his phone into his back pocket.

"We're done here," Cash said, hands on his hips and facing Gerald.

Squaring off with Cash in an aggressive manner, Gerald said, "I can kick your magazine article to the curb and have Tracy fired with a stroke of my computer key."

"I doubt it," Cash said. It was one thing to threaten him, but not Tracy. "Your boss personally called me to set this up. He and my father were college roommates."

Gerald visibly flinched. "Kirk Devereux?"

"Kirk Devereux is the owner of the magazine which makes him your boss. Correct?" Cash asked with feigned patience. Gerald didn't answer. "Do your research, pal," Cash said. "This is not Triple C's first rodeo in *Ranchers and Ranges*. It's a follow-up in honor of my deceased parents."

"Let's go, boss," Ed said to Cash with an emphasis on the word boss.

Gerald had looked worried since the mention of Devereux. "Tracy isn't who you think she is," he said, switching the subject away from his employer.

Cash clenched his jaw and narrowed his eyes. "Who do I think she is?"

With scorn in his voice, Gerald said, "An innocent little girl from the sticks."

Having been the man who'd taken her virginity twenty-four hours earlier, Cash defended her innocence. "I know that's exactly who Tracy is."

"No way." Gerald laughed mockingly as if Cash didn't have a clue. "Tracy Dalton has spread her—umm—self to half the men in the Springs."

Besides his intimate, firsthand knowledge that Gerald was lying, Cash would not allow him to slander Tracy. He reared back his fist, but Beau caught his arm in mid-strike preventing him from landing the punch. Ed also grabbed Cash and they walked him back a few steps.

"He wants you to hit him, Cash," Beau said.

"Then he'll tell his boss you started a fight," Ed said, holding on to Cash.

"Get the hell off my ranch, Moles," Cash growled, shrugging off Beau and Ed. "Or I'll kick your sorry ass off it and have *you* fired!"

"What's going on?" Tracy called out, hurrying toward them.

"Somebody dented my car and Cooper is threatening to kick my ass if I don't shut up about it and leave," Gerald said.

"Son-of-a-bitch!" Cash barked.

CHAPTER TWENTY-THREE

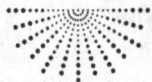

"**C**ash!" Tracy stepped between him and Gerald. Facing Cash, she placed her hands on his hard chest. The rugged rancher in his cowboy hat, red button-down shirt, and blue jeans pooled around his boots, splayed his large hands to the belt fastened by his Triple C buckle. She whirled on the man wearing slacks and loafers. "Gerald, both Beau and Ed told you to park in the field. If your car was dented, it's your own fault."

"It's not dented," Cash growled, protectively standing right behind her.

"She wasn't talking to you," Gerald sneered at Cash. "She's talking to me."

Tracy frowned at Gerald. "Not only have you been rude since the moment you arrived, but now you're lying about your car. What's wrong with you, Gerald?"

"It's this showboater and his ranch." Gerald inclined his head toward Cash and asked dismissively, "You know he inherited all of this. Right?"

"I know Cash, his wranglers, and other staff work long hours every single day to be excellent stewards of this ranch." Conviction rang in Tracy's voice. "They make that hard work look easy as they teach and entertain their guests. At the same time they're sharing their knowledge and respect of the animals, the land, and the natural resources with us city folk."

Gerald ignored what she'd said and reached for her. "Let's get back to the city where we belong, Tracy."

"I'm not going anywhere with you, Gerald," Tracy said incredulously. Retreating a step from Gerald, she placed her back against Cash's muscular chest. "Nor am I going to continue working with you."

"What do you mean?"

"I mean if Mr. Devereux won't give me a different editor, I'll quit."

"You can't quit in the middle of an assignment," Gerald warned her, beads of sweat showing on his temples and making his yellow pompadour wilt.

"I sure can, and I'll tell Devereux you're the reason why," Tracy said.

More casually, Gerald said, "Up until this assignment, we've made a great team. I enjoy working with you, Tracy."

"Boss, didn't this guy just claim Tracy had spread herself to half the men in the Springs?" Beau asked as Ed nodded and glared at Gerald.

"What?" Tracy gasped and looked at Cash.

Cash raised his chin, glared past her at Gerald, and gritted through his teeth, "Yes, he did."

"It's three against one and these bastards are lying, Tra —" Gerald began.

"No!" Tracy's right hand smacking Gerald's face exploded simultaneously with the fireworks bursting into the sky atop Pikes Peak. "It's *four* against one, Gerald," she seethed with fury, fists clenched at her sides and shaking from head to toe. "Leave!"

Cash shot a shielding arm in front of Tracy and swept her behind him. Presenting a solid wall of security Beau and Ed, arms crossed over their chests, stepped up on either side of Cash.

"Moles, you've been told to go. Twice," Cash growled as

Tracy elbowed her way in between him and Beau. "I suggest you do so while you're still in one piece."

Gerald yanked his car door open and slid behind the wheel. Starting his electric vehicle, he made a silent and anticlimactic exit from the ranch onto the highway.

Beau chuckled and asked, "Did that prick just give us the finger?"

"Yeah, I think so." Ed laughed. "From a safe distance."

Cash grinned down at Tracy and asked, "Is my girl here a spitfire or what?"

"Hell, yes, she is!" Beau hollered.

"Hell, yeah!" Ed howled even louder.

Tracy smiled at the compliments and gave the men a playful curtsy. Her heart flip-flopped wildly not at the scene with Gerald, but the fact Cash had referred to her as *my girl*.

When all the guests were gone, Beau and Ed shut the gate across the driveway. Tracy didn't recall it being closed during the past week and guessed it was due to the trouble with Gerald. Cash took her hand, and they started toward the house. Sam, Jeff, and Larry met them halfway there. Beau and Ed, more than Cash, filled them in on the scene with Gerald. Sam, Jeff, and Larry each added a story or comment of their own about Gerald, none of which were favorable. Thus, Gerald Moles was unanimously declared banned from Triple C Ranch-East.

Bob and Teresa had already taken the back road to Triple C-Central by the time Sam said good night and walked home to Kellie. Beau wrapped an arm around Cristen, and they veered off to his truck. Jeff drove himself, Ed, and Larry to the bunkhouse.

Cash opened the front door to his house and, like the gentleman he was, let Tracy enter the foyer first. He locked the door and checked an alarm system which showed everything was secure for the night. Near the front door, he showed her how to take off her boots using a bootjack which he kept next to a coat rack. With their boots and hats off, he looked around and rubbed his forehead.

"I left your bag here in the foyer." Cash cocked his head, and she detected a hint of vulnerability in his voice as he asked, "Did you give it back to Jacob?"

"No."

"Where is it?"

Tracy bit her lower lip and said, "In the bedroom of my choice."

A sexy grin lifted the corners of Cash's mouth before it came down on hers. His hands slid under her arms and her feet left the floor. Arms around his neck, he cupped her fanny.

The tongue-searching, body-molding kiss was a prelude to passion.

When Tracy's feet touched the floor again, she headed straight for the staircase. Cash caught up with her and grasped the seat of her dress. She giggled, wiggled free, and raced up the stairs. He laughed and chased after her. In his bedroom, she'd left her purse next to a dim lamp on the dresser and her bag on the floor at the end of his bed.

"Wanna watch what's left of the Pikes Peak fireworks?" Cash teased.

Tracy shook her head. "You're the only fireworks I want, Cash."

Cash placed his hands to her face, and as they kissed, he backed her up against the side of the bed. He took hold of her short dress near the hem and eased it up her thighs. Tracy shivered. As he tugged the dress up her ribs, Tracy's desire for him soared. She raised her arms so Cash could pull the dress over her head. He did so and she gave her hair a shake around her shoulders as he tossed her dress to the end of his bed. Before the fully clothed magnificent male, Tracy stood clad only in her barely there navy-blue satin bra and matching G-string panties.

"Show me what you want, Tracy," Cash said, his hands splaying on his tapered waist.

Tracy began unbuttoning his shirt. He let her. She pulled the front of the shirt out of his jeans to finish unfastening it.

As he shrugged out of his shirt, she struggled to undo his belt buckle. He unbuckled it for her. Then stopped. With her heart thundering, she unbuttoned the top button of his jeans. He let her. With a grin up at him and a tug she popped open the remaining buttons of his fly. His brow cocked and his blue eyes narrowed. He waited. She pushed his jeans down his hips and thighs to his feet. He stepped out of the jeans and stood before her in snug boxers.

"I want the big, bad stallion," she whispered.

Tracy boldly cupped her hands to the long, hard bulge stretching the front of his boxers. Cash unfastened her bra, peeled it off her, and dropped it. He reached around her, grasped the comforter and sheet and tossed them toward the end of his bed.

"Does the little spitfire filly understand if she gets in this bed, she won't be able to walk when I'm done with her?"

Tracy feared she might faint on the spot. "She understands."

Cash hooked his thumbs into the sides of her panties, pulled them down and off her. With her panties around his index finger, Cash twirled his hand spinning her panties off across the room. Tracy moaned and tried to shove him into the bed. It was like pushing against a mountain. He waited. She pulled his boxers down, and when his manhood was fully exposed, she shyly wrapped her hands around him. Cash groaned. He stepped out of the boxers and only then did he let her shove him into bed. This experienced man was as irresistible as he was seductive.

"Come a little closer." Cash snared her wrist and yanked.

"You're a lot of potent masculinity for a tenderfoot novice to handle, Cash Cooper," Tracy admitted, landing in bed beside him.

Cash's chuckle was deep and mesmerizing as he guided her to stretch out on top of him. Giving her goosebumps, one of his hands slipped under her hair at the nape of her neck and his other hand flattened to her back. He brought her lips to his for a kiss as his knees came up between hers, spreading her legs to the outsides of his. She opened her mouth to his tongue as he positioned his manhood to her most secret place. Cash slowly eased all the way into her.

"Saddle up, cowgirl," he whispered.

Straddling Cash's hips, Tracy sat up, placed her hands on his broad shoulders, and smiled down at him. "Let's ride, cowboy."

CHAPTER TWENTY-FOUR

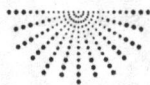

"There's my apartment." Tracy pointed it out after they'd turned left onto West Fillmore Street.

Cash grabbed her finger and lifted her hand to his lips. What her hands had done to him the previous night in bed would make him hard right now if he didn't refocus. Tracy smiled at him, and he released her hand as he drove his truck along the outside of the apartment complex sequestered behind a tall, black wrought-iron fence. Yup. He'd been here once before, but nothing and no one he cared to remember.

"Do you want to stop by your apartment before we pick up Dude?" he asked her.

"No, let's get him first," she said. "Dog Party USA is just past Coronado High School and around the corner on Mesa Road."

"Dog Party USA is the name of the boarding place?" Cash asked and chuckled.

"It is." Tracy's eyes sparkled as she placed her hand on his arm and laughed.

This woman's slightest touch stirred his libido like a snake charmer rousing a cobra from a basket. Her turquoise gaze captured him. Her every smile made him want another. Her sexy giggle made him grin. He hoped if they stopped by her apartment, she wouldn't stay. He'd replied to a text from Kirk Devereux that morning mostly for Tracy's benefit. He owed her that. But he had to admit if the magazine owner allowed her to continue her story it would benefit him, too, because he liked having her on his ranch. When her story was done, what then? He guessed they'd cross that bridge when they came to it.

"There it is," Cash said, seeing a sign that read *Dog Party USA.*

"Yes! Yay!"

Cash turned into the parking lot of a large, stucco building. The front of it was welcoming with a tall portico and benches facing each other on opposite sides of double glass doors. At the back of the structure a fenced-in grassy field, with some smaller dogs in it now, was obviously where the *dog parties* took place. He backed into a parking spot facing the building and turned off the engine. This was a first for him. Never had he taken any woman on errands, much less to a doggy daycare.

"Want me to go in with you or wait here?" he asked.

"Wait here, Cash. Dude will be excited. I'll tell him about you before you two meet."

Cash watched the cowboy boots walk the spectacular girl away from him and toward the kennel. Her cinnamon hair bounced across her slender back. He could feel the thick texture of those waves between his fingers. A skintight white tank top hinted of her beaded nipples, making his mouth water. Her rounded fanny swayed in snug blue jean short-shorts and his hands itched to caress her soft skin. She vanished into the building and only minutes ticked by, but it felt like hours. His entire body ached for Tracy. His craving to have her in his arms pulled him out of his truck. Walking around to the front, he leaned against it, crossing his feet at the ankles.

"Hi Cash," came a female voice from somewhere behind him.

Cash glanced to his left. Hell. He folded his arms over his chest. "Hi Rusty."

"What are you doing here?" the strawberry blonde asked, holding a pink leash with a tiny dog at the other end of it. The yapping and snarling started instantly. Prancing forward, the dog nipped near the heel of Cash's boot. When Rusty pulled on the leash, the dog nipped at her too. "You don't have a dog."

"I brought a friend whose dog is here," Cash replied.

"Oh," Rusty said. Looking down at her dog, showing its little teeth between yaps and snarls, Rusty said, "Be quiet, Foo-Foo, you remember Cash." Cash remembered this was just one of the reasons he'd been in and out fast at Rusty's apartment. "A female friend?"

"Yeah."

"So that's the way it is then."

It wasn't a question and Cash didn't respond. Straight ahead, Tracy emerged from the building. On a black leash, a black and tan German shepherd walked obediently at her side. Cash lowered his head and looked at Tracy over the top of his sunglasses. He smiled and she waved. As Tracy and Dude neared, he leaned away from the truck, which put his back to Rusty. Hoping she'd take that as a cue to leave, she didn't and her dog continued to yap.

"I'd back your dog up if I were you," Cash said to Rusty.

"Is that your friend?"

"Yup."

Rusty was attractive enough, but she didn't have Tracy's winning personality, nor was she drop-dead beautiful like Tracy. The grimace on Rusty's face said she knew there was no comparison. Instead of leaving or backing up, she yanked the leash on her dog which increased the yipping.

"Dude, this is Cash," Tracy said, stopping a few feet away. Her eyes flicked to Rusty, and she politely said, "Hello."

"Cash hates dogs," Rusty told her, around the noise and nipping.

Cash knew Tracy knew better. Not only had he told Tracy he was thinking of getting a dog, but she'd also seen him with Crockett. Because of Rusty's misinformation, instead of introducing her to Tracy, he walked further away from her. Reaching Tracy and Dude, Cash held out the back of his hand. Dude sniffed and seemed to approve. As Rusty's dog continued its tirade, Dude silently sat down on his haunches beside Tracy.

"Shake?" Tracy prompted Dude.

Dude looked at Cash and lifted his right paw. Cash shook it. "Nice to meet you, Dude." Not wanting the German shepherd immediately being forced into the truck, Cash squatted down in front of him at eye level. "Want to go for a—"

The yapping and snarling escalated to the point it cut Cash off. Cash had had enough of Rusty's intrusion. When he stood and turned to Rusty, Dude stood as well and barked at the other dog. Just once. It was a loud and deep woof, and one was all it took. Rusty's dog squeaked, pranced around behind her, and quieted. Dude's big brown eyes looked up into Cash's eyes as if communicating he wanted to hear what Cash had to say to him.

"Good dog," Tracy praised Dude's obviously well-trained behavior.

"Want to go for a ride?" Cash asked the German shepherd. Dude gave a happy jump. Cash petted Dude's head and Dude placed his front paws on Cash's thighs.

"Down, Dude," Tracy said. Without hesitation, Dude sat down between her and Cash.

"Good luck holding onto Cash after he's taken you to bed. He's a confirmed bachelor," Rusty said, glaring at Tracy. "Cash will kiss you goodbye and never look back." With that, she turned away, held up her middle finger over her shoulder, and stalked toward the stucco building.

"That's twice in less than twenty-four hours I've been flipped off," Cash said.

"We," Tracy said. "Because of me."

"No." Cash shook his head. He walked to the passenger's side of the truck and opened the front and back doors to the cab. "Because of me."

Holding Dude's leash with her left hand, Tracy placed her purse on the passenger's seat. Turning back to Cash, she said, "We both have our detractors, don't we?"

"And our wingmen, like Beau, Ed, and Jacob," he pointed out, relieved that she wasn't upset with him. When he lowered his head to kiss her, she wrapped an arm around his neck and stood on tiptoes to kiss him. Sliding his left arm around Tracy's slim waist, Cash felt Dude nudge his furry head underneath his right hand. He scratched Dude's head. Here in the parking lot, under somewhat aggravating circumstances, Tracy made everything okay. His heart whispered to him. When Cash raised his head, his voice was husky as he said, "I love—dogs."

Tracy gazed up at him with a glistening in her eyes and whispered, "Me, too, Cash."

"Yeah." Cash had almost said he loved her. Because he did. "Okay, hop in." Tracy trustingly handed him Dude's leash. As she climbed into the truck, he gave her cute derrière a familiar pat. "That goes for you, too, Dude. Hop in." The dog jumped into the back seat and Cash said to him, "I've got a ranch and I hope you're gonna like it." He carefully shut the doors, walked around the truck, and slid in behind the wheel. Dude sat in the middle of the back seat and stuck his head between them.

Damn, if this didn't feel right too.

"Next stop, my apartment," Tracy said as they headed that way.

"Just a pit stop?" Cash asked.

"We'll see," she flirted with a sideways grin.

"Your bag is back at my ranch ya know."

"Because you hid it."

"I put it in the closet for you."

She grinned and he soon turned into the drive leading up to her fenced-in apartment complex. When he came to a stop, she gave him the code to open the wrought-iron gate.

"Keep to your left and we can enter my place through the garage," she said.

"Okay." Cash followed her directions. She took the door opener out of her purse and clicked it. He pulled up to the garage as it opened and asked, "Where's your car?"

"I don't have one. You can park your truck in the garage if you want."

Cash did so and hands still on the wheel, he swung his head toward her. "How the hell do you get around, Tracy?"

"I Uber it," she said and hopped out of the truck. She and Dude met Cash at the back door of her apartment, and she unlocked it. "Come on in."

Dude ran ahead and Cash followed them. Tracy led him past a washer and dryer, turned right and at the end of a short hall, swung her hand toward a sofa in the living room. Cash sauntered forward and stopped near the front door as she continued around a countertop on her left. She entered the kitchen and looking over the top of the counter at Cash, she filled Dude's water bowl. At the other end of her kitchen was a breakfast nook table for two. Dude lapped up his water as Cash placed his hands on his hips.

"What do you mean you Uber it?"

"I work from home," Tracy said. "When I go on assignment, the magazine sends me in a car with Jacob." Shrugging, she added, "This last time, with all the contest winners involved, Donna convinced Gerald to let her go with us to assist. She went in the van with Jacob, but Gerald had scheduled a meeting with me, and I missed the van. So, he rented that car for me."

"Gerald sent Donna to keep an eye on you," Cash grumbled. "Moles made you miss the meeting so he could impress you with that Mustang."

"He asked if I wanted a Tesla and I declined."

"Good call. We don't have plug-ins for electric cars. How do you get your groceries?"

"I have ready-to-prepare meals delivered once a week," she explained. "And the grocery store is just across Fillmore

Street, so I walk over there. If it's snowing or raining, I Uber it."

"How did you drop off Dude last Monday?" Cash asked and at the mention of his name Dude walked to him.

"Uber."

Cash held up his right hand, to indicate he'd heard enough about Uber, and shook his head. "Let's see the rest of your apartment."

"Okay. It came furnished," she told him. Meeting back up with him in the living room where a flat-screen TV was situated in front of the sofa, she said, "This is where I watch movies." She pointed to two built-in bookshelves with a small desk and a cane-backed chair between them. "This is where I write and edit my articles for the magazine." Crooking her finger, she guided him down the hallway and past a bathroom into the bedroom. The bed was queen-sized, and on the left was a lamp on a nightstand. Standing at the end of her bed, she said, "This is the only bedroom and that ends the tour."

"Nice." Cash smiled.

"Thanks. My grandmother gave me two thousand dollars for a graduation gift and offered me her truck too. But I explained I would not take her only means of transportation."

"You need a car." Cash sat down on her bed and crooked his finger. "Am I the first guy to be on this bed since you moved in?"

"You know you are," she told him, walking closer.

"Good." He grabbed her hand, lay back, and pulled her onto the bed next to him.

"Let's kiss," she flirted.

"Yeah, let's have a cinnamon kiss." Cash rolled on top of her, and the German shepherd barked. "I'm not gonna hurt her, Dude."

Dude walked across the bedroom and put his chin on the mattress. He blinked and stared at them. Cash cocked a brow and told Dude to lie down. Dude trotted across the room and curled up in a dog bed near the window. When Cash lowered his mouth to hers, Tracy wound her arms around his neck and kissed him with abandon. Cash settled himself between her legs and she threaded her fingers through his hair. He pulled up her tank top and unfastened her bra. He kissed his way to her breasts and when his lips closed over a nipple she moaned.

"Yes. More, Cash."

Cash tugged her shorts and panties down and she kicked them off. He unfastened his belt and fly and shoved his jeans to his thighs. Since she'd told him about being on the pill, he'd made no further mention of a condom. Tracy met his every in-and-out thrust. Faster and faster, he escalated until she shivered, her orgasm squeezing him internally. Her heart pounded against his chest, and she clung to him as he thrust hard and deep. Spilling himself inside her, Cash groaned from the ecstasy fulfilling his every need like never before. He kissed Tracy before rolling off her.

"That was a quickie to christen your bed, spitfire," he said.

"You sparkle me, big'n bad."

"Sparkle you?"

"Yes, that's how incredible it feels. Like I've been sparkled from the inside out," she whispered. "I love—it."

He smoothed a silky cinnamon lock of hair off her cheek. "Me, too, Tracy."

CHAPTER TWENTY-FIVE

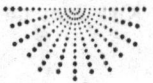

Tracy knew this bed and bedroom would never feel the same without Cash in it.

"I hear my cell phone somewhere," she said, crawling out of bed.

Cash rolled out after her and buttoned his fly. Tracy stepped into her panties and shorts and grabbed her tank top. By the time she found her phone, it had stopped ringing. She listened to the message as Cash swaggered into the living room. He opened her front door with Dude at his side. One of the best things about this apartment was the small, concrete front porch patio which provided a fabulous view of Pikes Peak. Blue skies, white clouds, and a summer breeze made the setting perfect. Cash nodded in appreciation and stepped onto the porch. With her phone to her ear, Tracy followed him and Dude. As the message ended, the expression on her face caused Cash to tilt his head in question.

"What's up?"

"This is up," Tracy said and tapped her phone to replay the message. "Listen."

"Tracy, Kirk Devereux. I've heard great things about you from Cash Cooper. I asked him about expanding your story to include the other two ranches and he said you also hoped to do that. His family is on board, so let's go for it. I've touched base with Jacob,

*and he is excited to return to the Triple Cs. Gerald and Donna,
however, voiced creative differences and have been reassigned.
Therefore, if you have any questions, please contact me directly.
Come fall or winter, I see your Triple C Ranch story on the cover
and taking up most of the magazine. Congrats."*

Tracy clicked off the message and asked, "Did you do
this?"

"I replied to a text Kirk sent me asking how the week
went."

"*Kirk*?"

"He and my dad were college roommates," Cash replied.
"I said you and Jacob were a pleasure to have on the ranch.
He asked if the rest of my family would grant interviews
and be available for photos. I told him yes."

"Cash, I don't know what to say," Tracy admitted.
"Except thank you so much. I figured *come Monday*, I would
be fired."

"I know I teased you about that, but I had a hunch you
wouldn't be."

"He must have gotten into it with Gerald."

"I don't know." Cash reached his hands above his head
and stretched. "Kirk didn't mention him or Donna and
neither did I."

Tracy nodded. "To go from thinking I was about to be
fired to being told my article will appear on the cover of
Ranchers and Ranges is the best news ever."

"A reason to celebrate," Cash said.

Dude barked as though agreeing and Tracy said, "Dude
wants to go on a walk."

"Let's take him. Then how about I take you out to dinner
before heading back to Triple C-East?"

Even though her bag was at his ranch, the way Cash
had phrased that question, Tracy didn't know if she was
still included in heading back to Triple C-East. "Sounds
wonderful. How about I give you a massage as my thank
you?"

"You don't owe me a thank you. But hell, yes." Cash said

and grinned. "I'll take you up one of your side hustles. At my ranch?"

"Yes," Tracy whispered, her spirit soaring.

Putting Dude on his leash, they walked through the complex and out the front gate. Tracy told Cash they'd show him a beautiful view along their usual walk. When he offered to hold Dude's leash, Tracy gave it to him. He took her hand, and she smiled up at him as they moseyed along. This joy must be how people, who had found the person for whom they'd been waiting, felt. She hadn't known she'd been waiting for someone until Cash entered her life.

Slicing a shortcut through the empty campus of Coronado High School, they turned west again. Trekking along Mesa Road took them to the point, about a mile from the apartment, where she and Dude always lingered before heading back.

"From any angle, just like Pikes Peak, it never gets old," Cash said at an overlook boasting an incredible view of Garden of the Gods Park. As Dude sat down, Cash looked north to south.

"Did you know the Europeans referred to Garden of the Gods as Red Rock Corral?" Tracy asked. "With all the dark red and pink sandstone, that name makes sense."

"Yes," Cash agreed. "I did know that. I also know that back in 1859, two men who helped survey the site, which was caused by the shifting of the Rocky Mountains and Pikes Peak, decided it would be a great spot for a beer garden." He chuckled. "Because of the formations like Balanced Rock, Three Graces, and Steamboat Rock, one of the men apparently declared it was a place fit for the gods to assemble."

Tracie nodded and laughed. "I remember coming across that story while working for the magazine. In the April 5, 1893, issue of Colorado's oldest newspaper, *Golden Transcript*, a writer, named Helen Hunt Jackson, an activist on behalf of improving the lives of Native Americans, was said to be riding past a cabin of a prospector in the area and stopped to admire his garden. The two people tending the beautiful garden told her their names were Jupiter and Juno. Helen Hunt Jackson said, 'Then this must be the Garden of the Gods.'"

Cash turned to her and said, "Being smart is part of what makes you so sexy."

"Thank you, Cash," Tracy said, feeling a blush stain her cheeks.

"Since you aren't being fired, what happens to your other side hustle?"

Tracy shrugged. "My series of children's books stays on the back burner for now. But I won't give up on my dream to publish them, giving hope to abandoned, neglected, or abused kids." When Cash turned to her with his brow creased in concern, she explained, "I was fortunate to have my grandparents. But many children who lose their parents, whether it's due to an accident like a helicopter crash, substance abuse, illness, divorce, incarceration, or countless other reasons out of a child's control, aren't so lucky."

"Let me guess, your books feature a German shepherd," Cash said.

"Yes, named Dude."

"You write stories about boys and girls who have every reason to fail but give them positive messages as to why they can succeed."

"Yes, exactly." Tracy was taken aback and repeated to him, "Being smart is part of what makes you so sexy, Cash."

Cash pulled her into his arms and whispered, "Tracy, to me you're more beautiful than Garden of the Gods."

She swallowed hard. "As it so happens, my favorite attraction in Garden of the Gods is Kissing Camels," she said, in reference to the iconic red rock formation that appeared to be two camel heads kissing high in the sky. "Some say it's the longest kiss in history."

Cash grinned and said, "Let's kiss."

"Let's." Tracy stood on tiptoes and Dude patiently waited beside them as they kissed in the shadow of Garden of the Gods. Then with a wave at the camels, she said, "I'm starved."

"How does Southside Suzy's sound?"

"The steak and burger restaurant downtown?"

"Yes."

"I've never been there. Is it good?"

"It better be. Their beef comes from Chase's cattle ranch."

CHAPTER TWENTY-SIX

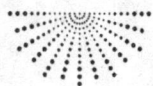

"*A*ll packed?" Cash asked, standing behind Tracy in the doorway of her bedroom. He'd been thankful on their walk not to have run into Rusty again. But that had been only a fleeting concern. He was focused on Tracy and enjoying every minute in her presence.

With a look here and there, Tracy said, "Yes, my totes are full."

Cash had placed what he'd describe as a couple of beach bags in the back seat of his truck. Tracy had said the small bag she'd taken to his ranch was the only real suitcase she had. After Tracy had fed Dude, Cash had packed his dog food and bed, into the back seat as well.

"Glad they're full because I might never bring you back here," Cash said.

Tracy giggled that sensual, flirty laugh that always made him smile. Turning to him she said, "I guess Dude and I would just have to Uber it back into town."

Cash cocked a brow and repeated, "You need a car." He called Dude and walked down the short hall to the living room. "Dude, you ready to go for a ride?" Cash asked, picking up his leash. The German shepherd barked and trotted to him. Cash fastened the leash to the collar and Dude stood obediently at his side.

"Are you sure Dude will be welcome at Southside Suzy's?" Tracy asked, her purse over her shoulder. "We could swing by later and pick him up."

"He'll be fine if we eat outside on the patio," Cash assured her, clipping Dude's leash onto his collar. "It's the perfect weather for that."

"Okay."

Tracy picked up her purse and they headed out the back door to the attached garage. Dude jumped into the truck like he belonged there. As Tracy crawled into the front seat, Cash gave her sexy bottom his familiar pat. Backing his truck out of the garage, she closed the door. Taking I-25, ten minutes later he pulled into a parking spot in front of Southside Suzy's. Everybody, from downtown business owners and employees, to staff from the nearby hospitals, to professors and students from the local colleges, to the workforce at the El Paso County Courthouse, ate here. With Dude's leash in one hand and Tracy's hand in the other, Cash walked toward the fenced-in patio of the restaurant.

"Cash-man!" Richard, a loyal friend and leader of the Sons of Steel Motorcycle Club, called after parking his Harley. Wearing the colors of one of the five most dangerous clubs known, the tall, black-haired man with a black beard gave them a wave and walked toward them.

Richard was the longtime boyfriend of Suzy. Suzy's father, Vincent South, had owned this place for decades. Shortly after buying it, he'd totaled his Harley on the highway in front of Triple C Ranch-Central. Along with Coop, Cash's dad had rushed to his rescue. Vincent, also known as Vince or Butcher, supposedly because he wore a white apron like a butcher, was a great friend or a mean bastard, depending on who you talked to. In any case, Vince had not wanted law enforcement involved after he'd crashed. Cash's parents and grandparents had patched him up, fed him a steak dinner, and hauled him and his motorcycle back to the Springs. Vince had bought all his beef from

Triple C ever since and their steadfast bond was unbreakable.

"Big Dog!" Cash called to Richard using his motorcycle club name. Dude barked just once as Richard and his two bodyguards, Blade and Tommy-Gun, approached.

Normally Richard shook Cash's hand and gave him a tug against his chest. But with respect to Dude, he held out his hand to the dog first and said, "Being a big dog, you and I have something in common." Dude sniffed him and Richard petted his head.

"This is Dude," Cash said. "Shake?" Trusting Cash, Dude shook hands with all three bikers and then wagged his tail. Turning to the beautiful girl at his side, Cash was proud to introduce her and said, "I'd like you gentlemen to meet Tracy Dalton, Dude's owner."

"Hello," Tracy said, her dainty hand disappearing in the large hands of the formidable bikers as they gently shook with her. "It's nice to meet you all."

"Our pleasure," Richard said on behalf of himself and his men. "You guys here for dinner and drinks?"

"Yes, if Dude is allowed on the patio with us," Cash said.

"Absolutely," Richard said and snapped his fingers. "Lobo!" he called to the burliest biker of the club who was standing near the front entrance of the establishment.

Cash knew Lobo, who had named one of the horses on the ranch, was the unofficial bouncer. Typically, all it took was one howl from Lobo and whatever commotion might happen, didn't. Lobo came forward and greeted them with a grin that displayed his full set of upper and lower silver teeth. Cash introduced Tracy as his friend.

"Dude, this is Lobo," Richard said.

"Lobo is Spanish for wolf," Lobo told the German shepherd. "We're cousins, Dude."

"Shake?" Cash prompted Dude.

Dude, sensing he was in the company of friends, wagged his tail and shook with Lobo. Then, turning toward the four-foot-high fence that ran across the front of the patio, Lobo unlocked a gate to allow Dude access. Saying he'd check in on them later, Richard and his men left them to sit at the table of their choice. Cash chose a corner table next to the fence where Dude could sit away from other restaurant patrons.

"Who *don't* you know in this town?" Tracy teased him, but Cash caught the look of appreciation in the widening of her eyes.

Cash chuckled and a moment later, Suzy herself brought him a mug of his favorite beer and water with lemon for Tracy. With short, spiked hair and a splash of freckles across her nose, Suzy looked friendly. And she was to friends. Cash stood and they hugged. He introduced her to Tracy and when Dude raised his right paw without being prompted, Suzy shook.

"As you may have heard, I like big dogs, Dude," Suzy said, patting his head.

"Suzy, it's a pleasure to meet you and Dude obviously likes you too," Tracy said as Dude lay down under the table. "Dude and I have been separated for a week and we missed each other. Thank you for allowing him on the patio."

"Happy to have you here," Suzy replied.

"Tracy works for *Ranchers and Ranges* and is writing a story on Triple C-East," Cash explained. "We're heading back to the ranch after dinner so she can interview Coop, Chase and Jade, and Chloe and Derek later this week."

"Please say hello to the family for me," Suzy told Cash. As a slim teenage waitress with black hair approached with menus, Suzy said, "This pretty girl is Richard's daughter, Stella." Cash knew Suzy had no children of her own. But she placed an arm around Stella and said with obvious love and pride, "So that makes Stella mine too."

"Thanks, Suzy," Stella said with affection.

"Stella, this is Cash and his friend, Tracy," Suzy said, completing the introduction.

"Hi, Stella," Cash said as Stella nodded. "I've known your dad, Suzy, and Vince forever. Good to meet you."

"It's nice to meet you, Stella," Tracy said and smiled.

Smiling back, Stella said, "Nice to meet you both."

"Stella will take good care of you," Suzy said as Stella handed them the menus. Turning to Tracy she added, "I'll be sure to buy a copy of the magazine when your story comes out."

"I'd be happy to bring you an autographed copy," Tracy offered.

"Cash Cooper, this lady is as sweet as she is beautiful," Suzy declared. Then with a look back at Tracy she said half-jokingly and half-seriously, "If this guy doesn't treat you right, you let us know, Tracy."

"I will," Tracy replied, going along with her and then smiling at Cash.

"Good to see you, Cash." Suzy patted his shoulder. "Thanks for stopping by."

Stella left with Suzy to allow Cash and Tracy to peruse their menus. Dude rested his chin on his front paws. When Stella returned she asked if Tracy would like something to drink in addition to water and took their dinner orders. Since Stella was under twenty-one, Vince showed up with another beer for Cash and one just like it for Tracy. The men hugged and when introduced to Tracy, Vince kissed the back of her hand. Vince was introduced to Dude and said he had something special for him. Vince sat down and spoke to them until Stella served their salads. He left with Cash's promise to come back soon with Tracy. Cash raised his mug and suggested they toast.

"What are we toasting to?" Tracy asked.

"Your magazine article bringing us together?" Cash suggested.

"Yes, absolutely. And to my first beer in honor of Garden of the Gods being a beer garden fit for the gods."

They laughed, clinked their mugs, and drank. Tracy made a cute face over the taste of her first beer but didn't choke on the dark brew. Cash sat with his back to a solid wood fence, thinking how happy he was to be here with her.

As they enjoyed their salads, Tracy was on his left, facing the street with Dude resting between them on the concrete patio floor. Stella came back for their empty salad plates and Cash scratched Dude's head. Looking up, he saw an expression between shock and dread cross Tracy's face.

"What now, spitfire?"

CHAPTER TWENTY-SEVEN

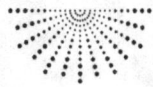

"*G*erald just pulled up in his Tesla and Donna's with him," Tracy said.

"Who *don't* you know in this town?" Cash teased, using her words.

"Ha. Ha," Tracy said softly hoping they didn't see her and Cash. "Maybe they'll sit indoors." But as Cash had said, it was great weather for dinner outside, so no such luck. The side door of the restaurant opened, and a waitress escorted Gerald and Donna onto the patio. At this angle, Cash was facing them straight on and they were on Tracy's left. "Do they see us?"

"Yes," Cash said, reaching a hand down to Dude. "Here they come."

A welt on his cheek, clothes rumpled, and yellow pompadour greasy, Gerald looked disheveled. Reaching their table with Donna, also unkempt at his side, Gerald blurted out, "You two got us reassigned."

"If that's the case," Tracy began, noting Cash had a grip on Dude's collar, "you got yourselves reassigned."

"It *is* the case," Gerald said with elevated irritability as Dude growled softly. "Devereux not only reassigned us, we're on probation. He called it a plan of correction for ninety days. He's sending us to a small satellite office in the middle of nowhere North Dakota," he sneered, his eyes oddly dilated. Tracy wondered if Gerald might be drunk, high, or both.

"The satellite office is a demotion after working in Colorado Springs," Donna sniffed and swiped away a spot of what looked like white powder on a nostril. "If Gerald doesn't take me along as his office assistant, I'll be on leave with no pay for the next three months." Jiggling her bosom almost out of her obscenely low-cut blouse, Donna placed her hand on Gerald's arm and patted it. "It's so cold in North Dakota, poor Gerald's electric car probably won't start."

Tracy remembered how Donna had initially appeared to come to her defense after she'd arrived late on Cash's ranch. Obviously, Donna's so-called assistance depended on who she thought could be the most useful to her at any given time.

"I hear North Dakota is beautiful," Tracy said sincerely. "I wish you both the best." She didn't know what else to say and hoped they'd move along.

"You're lucky I didn't tell Devereux you gave me this injury." Gerald stabbed a finger in his cheek as Dude sat up and barked. "Or you'd be out too."

"Tell him," Cash challenged. "I can't wait for Kirk to ask you what precipitated it."

"Teacher's pet, or magazine owner's, in this case," Donna snapped as Dude growled.

Gerald glared at Cash and then Tracy as he mumbled at her, "Uppity little bitch."

"Enough!" Cash stood up, with a firm grip on Dude's leash in his left hand.

"Or what?" Gerald asked, but cautiously retreated a couple of steps. "I don't see any cowboys to back you up today, Cooper."

"I don't need backup to deal with you. But I've got as

much back up here as I do on my ranch. So, take your alcohol and drugs, or whatever you're on and leave us the hell alone."

Lobo appeared at the gate. "Cash-man, everything cool?"

Gerald and Donna turned to Lobo, whose scowl, silver teeth, and tattooed muscles were on full display. Lobo's meaty hands curled into fists on a wide belt where he wore a sheathed knife on one side and a holstered gun on the other. A waitress walked up to the table and offered to seat Gerald and Donna.

"Watch your back, Cooper," Gerald said.

"You don't wanna tangle with me, Moles," Cash warned.

Gerald flinched and without another word, he and Donna slinked after the waitress.

"Everything's cool, Lobo." Cash tipped two fingers off the brim of his cowboy hat and sat down. Dude followed Cash's lead and Lobo returned to the entrance of the restaurant.

"Where did they sit, Cash?" Tracy asked.

"Toward the back of the patio."

"Should we go?" Tracy asked. "We can have Stella box up our food when she brings it."

"No," Cash said and placed a hand over hers, which she was wringing in her lap.

"Gerald and Donna have caused you more than enough trouble, Cash," Tracy said as he snared her right hand. "I think we should go."

"Wanna know what I think?" Cash asked.

"Yes," Tracy replied. Swiveling to a half-turn in her chair, she craned her neck as far as she could in doing her best to get a glimpse of Gerald and Donna.

Cash chuckled and tugged on her hand. "Hey, you."

"Hay is for horses," she whispered and swiveled back to him. Letting go of his hand, she grabbed her purse and pulled out her compact. Holding the mirror as if she were powdering her nose but actually trying to spot Gerald and Donna, she quietly confided, "I can't see them."

"You'd make a terrible spy," Cash said and laughed.

Tracy huffed. "I want to see how mad they look."

"Forget them and look at your steak instead. Here it comes."

Stella set their steaks and what she said was the house side specialty, sweet potato fries with a marshmallow-like dipping sauce, on the table. A metal bowl with sliced bites of rare steak went to Dude. Tracy's heart melted and she asked Stella to thank Vince. Though keenly aware Gerald and Donna were somewhere behind her, Tracy was as starved as she'd claimed and began eating. The steaks were delicious and the sweet potato fries were a treat. Although Dude had already eaten, he had no trouble finishing everything Vince had put in the bowl. They enjoyed their meal without further disruption. When Stella returned, she cleared the plates and asked about dessert.

"I can't eat another bite," Tracy said.

"Me neither," Cash said. "But I'll take the check whenever you're ready."

Stella shook her head and told them, "Suzy said there is no check for this table."

"Damn," Cash said in surprise, glancing past Stella toward the side door of the restaurant. "Stella, please tell Suzy that was not necessary, but thank her for us."

"Yes, sir, I will," Stella said respectfully. Cash peeled off a hundred-dollar bill from his money clip and handed it to the teenager. A stunned smile lit up her face. "Gosh, for me?" she asked, and Cash nodded. "Thank you, sir."

"This is from Dude," Tracy said, adding to Stella's tip by handing her ten more.

Stella smiled at Tracy and then at the dog. "Thank you, Dude. Come back soon."

Cash winked at Tracy and took her hand. As they said goodbye to Stella, Tracy inadvertently glanced at the back of the patio. Gerald and Donna averted their eyes. Walking to the gate, Lobo met them and unlocked it. Letting them out and locking the gate behind them, Lobo clapped Cash on the back and tipped his head at Tracy. With Cash holding Dude's leash, once they were on the sidewalk, Richard called to them from the front door asking if everything was to their liking. Stella came up beside her dad and he swung his arm around her.

"Everything was great!" Cash called and gave them a thumbs-up. "Thank you!"

Richard returned the thumbs-up. Stella showed her dad their tips and the big dog of the Sons of Steel placed a hand over his heart. Tracy waved and Stella waved back.

Once they were in the truck, Cash headed northeast. At the last gas station on the way to the ranch, he pulled in to fill up. The sound Dude made in the back seat told Tracy it was time for a potty break. While Cash attended to the truck, she and Dude jogged across the parking lot to a grassy lot. Dude did his business, and they turned back toward the gas station.

Tracy's heart almost stopped. Gerald and Donna had followed them. With her, and more likely Dude, out of his way, Gerald had confronted Cash. Gerald began hollering while Cash finished gassing up the truck. Donna came up behind Cash and shoved him. With Cash's right hand holding the gas pump, Gerald landed punches to his jaw and stomach. The behaviors of Gerald and Donna were so brazenly bizarre their actions had to be fueled by drugs. How long had these two been hiding their addictions? How long had they been masking the hostility that had surfaced on Triple C Ranch-East?

Upon being shoved and hit, Cash had barely moved but Dude took off on a dead run. Tracy could only keep up with the German shepherd for a few paces. There was no slowing him down and she had to let go of his leash. Dude picked up speed as Gerald drew back a fist again.

But Cash had dropped the gas pump and nailed Gerald square in the face, sending the unconscious man flying backward. Dude planted both front paws on Gerald's chest, landing him on the ground and bouncing his head off the pavement. Teeth bared and snarling, Dude barked as Donna stumbled over Gerald and fell across him. By the time Tracy reached Cash and Dude, Cash had replaced the gas pump into its slot, held his gun in one hand, and Dude's leash in the other. Seeing a nearly empty vodka bottle near Donna's hand, Tracy wasn't surprised.

An employee from the gas station ran toward Cash, shouting to him, "Sir! I called 9-1-1!" Arriving out of breath, he assured him, "Everything these two morons did was recorded."

"Thank you," Cash said to the gas station attendant as they stared at an unconscious Gerald and inebriated Donna on the ground. Dude barked, not sure about the attendant. Cash petted Dude's head. "It's okay, Dude. Thanks." The German shepherd quieted and sat.

Tracy's heart hurt seeing Cash's flesh under the stubble of beard was red, but at least the skin wasn't broken. Checking to make sure Dude was unhurt, she breathed a sigh of relief. Since they were out of the city's jurisdiction, an El Paso County Deputy zoomed into the gas station. As Gerald came to, another deputy pulled in right after the first one. With Donna sprawled in a debilitated stupor across Gerald's lower body, he scissored his legs, cursing her as he kicked her off him.

The first deputy called Cash by name and the second one kept Gerald and Donna in place. Cash told them what happened. With the attendant's help, they and the first officer on the scene watched the video which verified Cash's story exactly. When they exited the gas station, Gerald was sitting up, head hanging between his knees. The deputy who knew Cash spoke to the other officer who immediately cuffed Gerald. An ambulance appeared and loaded up a vomiting Donna. The deputy told Cash he'd be in touch. Cash thanked him and then Gerald was hauled off to the El Paso County Jail and Donna to a Colorado Springs detox facility.

Back in the truck, Cash headed onto the highway toward

the ranch. Along the way, Tracy apologized to Cash for the incident, which he said was certainly not her fault. Then she called Kirk Devereux, advised him he was on speaker, and told him the latest.

"They just went from demoted to dismissed," Kirk Devereux said.

Devereux also apologized for the magazine employees' behaviors and said a check would be in the mail to compensate Cash for his third of the contest expense. Cash assured him that wasn't necessary, but Devereux insisted. Promising to stay in touch with each other, the call ended.

"You *are* big'n bad!" Tracy told Cash as the countryside rolled by. "You knocked Gerald out cold even before Dude bounced his head off the pavement. You're seriously intimidating, Cash."

"Thanks for the assist, Dude," Cash said over his shoulder to Dude who was sitting behind them. Then to Tracy he said, "You never have to be afraid of me. You know that, right?"

"Yes, absolutely," Tracy replied without hesitation. "Nor do I plan to give you a welt across your cheek." She paused and then asked, "Would you feel better if I went back home tonight instead of to Triple C-East?"

"No." Cash swung his head toward her. "I want you to stay with me." He paused and added, "Unless you don't want to. In that case, we'll turn around and—"

"No, I want to stick with the plans we made for the coming week," she said and placed her hand on his thigh. "By the way, you never told me what you were thinking at dinner."

"Good timing," he said and closed his hand over her dainty one. "Last week you were part of the all-female contest winners' dude ranch experience. During the week to come, in addition to interviewing the others"—he nodded to Triple C-West as they passed it— "I was thinking you'll be able to observe our more usual dude ranch week on Triple C-East."

"I hadn't thought of that," Tracy realized. "Thank you for making it possible."

Cash asked, "What would you say about flying in the chopper with me next week?"

CHAPTER TWENTY-EIGHT

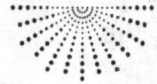

"Cash," Tracy whispered as they passed Triple C-Central. She shook her head. "I can't."

Cash figured that might be her answer as they sped east along the highway toward his ranch. Dark now, the light from the full moon and the truck's dashboard illuminated the concern on Tracy's beautiful face. Cash soon turned left into his driveway and steered around to the rear of his house. With the guests gone, he parked near the back door.

"Because of what happened to your parents."

"Yes," Tracy admitted. "I've never flown."

"In a helicopter?" he asked, and she shook her head no. "What about an airplane?" Again, she shook her head no.

"Are you mad at me?" she asked.

"No, of course not," he said. "Not tonight, because it's been a helluva day, but let's make time to talk about flying in my helicopter, *spitfire*."

"You'll never change my mind," she said as Dude rustled around in the back seat.

"Never say never, James Bond," Cash teased her, referring to the hit film from the eighties. He wondered if Tracy knew the back story. In her line of work, she might.

"James Bond? Earlier, you said I'd make a terrible spy!" she joked in return. "Did you know that before playing

James Bond for the final time, Sean Connery declared he'd never play the role again? The movie title, *Never Say Never Again* was in reference to his statement."

Loving not only how smart Tracy was but how fast they bounced back from their differences, Cash nodded, laughed, and hopped out of the truck. He let Dude out on his side and the German shepherd trotted off to the adjacent field. They unpacked the truck, stowing Tracy's bags and Dude's food and bowls in the kitchen. Tracy went back outside and called for Dude. Cash went with her, and they waited. She called again and still nothing. Cash let out a loud whistle, like the one he'd used to call Captain the day he'd met Tracy, and Dude came barreling out of the shadows.

"And that's how it's done here on the ranch," Cash said. Tracy put her lips together and no whistle was forthcoming. Dude skidded to a stop in front of them as she tried again. "So, we've got conquering the fear of flying and learning to whistle on the agenda."

"Not tonight, because it's been a helluva day—" Tracy smiled up at him— "but giving you a delightful massage is on my agenda, too, big'n bad."

Cash pulled her into his arms and asked, "Promise?"

"YOU PROMISED NO MORE DRINKING AND DRUGS, DONNA!" Winston blared into his cell phone, which Tammy Dalton thought was disconnected. "What good are you to me stuck in detox again? Up your nose, down your throat, or in your arm. Drugs and alcohol, the story of your life. I'm done with you." He listened and replied, "I hate you too!"

Winston ended the conversation with his daughter, blocked her number, and turned off his phone. Walking toward the Dalton house, he heard Tammy banging on a window.

"Winston!" she called.

"What's wrong now?" Winston asked, entering the house and locking the new double lock on the front door.

"It's bad enough the old windows in this house no longer open," Tammy replied, hobbling from the window to a chair. "Why did you cover them with tinfoil?"

"To keep the sun from waking you up early in the morning. So, you can take a nap in the afternoon," Winston said. "But I don't suppose you appreciate my effort on your behalf."

Tammy limped to a living room window, pulled back the lightweight curtain, and asked, "Why is the tinfoil on the outside instead of the inside, where I could take it down?"

"I didn't want to wake you up by working inside, so I went to the trouble of putting it on the outside." He hadn't mentioned needing money to pay his cell phone bill again and tried a different tactic. "You want to be well rested so we can leave on our road trip to Punkin Center soon, don't you?"

"Yes," Tammy said cautiously.

"Me too. Which I will gladly pay for once my social security check is deposited."

"Why are there new locks on my doors?" she asked with suspicion in her voice.

"Yes. We're in the middle of nowhere. Even the post office quit delivering mail, so now I pick it up for you since you can't," Winston said with a glance at her ankle. She could not be allowed to escape the house. Either the swollen ankle had to get worse or the other one needed to be injured. Today. "I put the locks on the doors for security reasons."

"I want to go to Colorado Springs to see Tracy like I told her we would," Tammy insisted and weaved sideways as she stood at the window.

"Of course, you do. And I'm going to drive you there in your truck."

"Good," Tammy said. "I want to stay with Tracy when we get there."

"Of course, we will."

"I'll pack," Tammy said, shuffling toward the privacy of the bedroom she refused to share with him. "Let's leave today."

"Why not?" Winston agreed and walked toward her. He'd kill two birds with one stone. When he purposely stumbled, it was over her bad ankle, and he took her down with him. "My arm! My arm!" Winston bellowed, rolling into a fetal position on the floor. Grabbing his right arm with his left, he accused, "You broke my arm!"

"You're the one who tripped!" Tammy cried, clutching her ankle.

"How do you expect me to drive a stick shift with a broken right arm?"

~

"WOULD YOU WANT A CAR WITH A STICK SHIFT?" CASH ASKED on Sunday afternoon.

"No, but I admire how you handled that rental Mustang."

On that note, Cash escorted her to his four-car garage and showed Tracy his own Mustang. Her mouth had dropped open in surprise and she'd covered her face in embarrassment, recalling how she'd asked him if he could drive such a car. Taking her for a drive, they pulled into a car dealership *just to look around*, he said. Since the dealership was closed, she didn't have to worry about him doing something rash. When he asked what her favorite car was of all the ones they'd seen, she was careful not to let on that she had fallen for the Cavalry Blue Rav4 with heated leather seats. Though a shade lighter, the color reminded her of Cash's blue eyes. Back home, they played in the hot tub before crawling into Cash's bed.

Bright and early Monday morning, she and Dude accompanied Cash to welcome the new dude ranchers for the week. It thrilled Tracy to be the lucky woman at Cash's side and she enjoyed the guests getting such a kick out of the

German shepherd's name being Dude. On Tuesday when Jacob arrived on Triple C-East, they saddled up, and along with Cash, met Chase on the back road to Triple C Ranch-Central. Cash left them in his brother's capable hands.

"Driving cattle is something I never expected to do," Tracy told Chase an hour later.

"That's what Jade said the first time she and I moved some Black Angus from one pasture to another," Chase replied with a smile. He'd brought along ranch foreman, Bob, and a couple of his main cowboys; Martyman, who was married to their Aunt Rachel, and Mean Pete who was married to Katy, Jade's assistant.

"Thank you for a great interview, Chase," Tracy said. Dude had stayed with Cash. The German shepherd was proving good at making friends with Cash's horses. But mixing Dude into a herd of cows on the move seemed like an unnecessary risk.

"I'm glad I brought my new video camera," Jacob said. "I know we can't use it in the magazine article, per se, but I may take some action shots from the film. Yes, thanks for your hospitality, Chase."

"My pleasure," Chase replied. The sun hovered high above Pikes Peak as Jacob snapped a final photo of Chase on his black stallion, Valor, with the cattle milling around a large corral in the background. Raising his right hand in a wave, Chase said, "Here come Cash and Dude."

Tracy, saddled up on Cinnamon, and Jacob on Chief, saw Cash with Dude trotting at his side. Cash obviously knew that by now, the cows would be safely inside the corral. Cash and Dude were accompanied by Jeff and Beau and ten dude ranch guests.

The previous day, all sixteen of this week's dude ranchers had practiced mounting and dismounting their horses and taken the typical short ride before lunch. Tracy had been there with Cash, and he had teased her about being an old hand at that now. Chase had texted Cash that he was going to round up a small herd of cows and relocate them into a corral for branding on Tuesday. He'd invited Tracy, Jacob, and Cash's dude ranchers to join him.

Now, the guests who weren't too saddle sore and wanted to ride to a real, live cattle ranch were in tow. Tracy's heart flip-flopped as the handsome owner of the dude ranch neared. Tall in the saddle and muscular in command, Cash was a force to be reckoned with and she loved every minute she spent in his presence. Dude had never had so much fun.

"How'd she do?" Cash asked his brother, inclining his head toward Tracy as he broke away from his guests, letting Jeff and Beau lead them toward the corral.

"She was a pro," Chase said regarding Tracy. "So was Jacob. I might have to steal 'em from the magazine and add 'em to my crew."

Reaching them, Cash said, "Jacob might be up for grabs, but I'm gonna keep Tracy on my ranch."

Chase chuckled. "Fair enough."

"I appreciate the compliment, Chase," Jacob said. Turning to Tracy, he asked, "Can you tell us what Kirk Devereux said when he called a few minutes ago?"

"Mr. Devereux said Gerald contacted him stating he didn't have enough money to bail himself out of jail. Gerald asked if someone from the magazine could bail him out."

"What did Kirk say?" Cash asked.

"He said, and I quote," Tracy began, "'Hell no, and you're fired, Moles.'"

"Kirk's a great guy," Chase said. "I'll bet there's more to the Moles' back story."

Tracy nodded and said, "Yes, Mr. Devereux said something about this being the third time Gerald's lack of good judgment had landed him in jail since he went to work for *Ranchers and Ranges* less than a year ago."

"Wow, three strikes. No wonder he's out," Jacob said and shook his head. "What a loser. Anything new on Donna?"

"Yes." Tracy told them, "The hospital permitted Donna to call the office to advise them she couldn't report to work due to being in detox. Evidently, she begged whoever she spoke with to send someone from the magazine to pick her up. They didn't do that but sent a cab. When it arrived, Donna was restricted from leaving. Turns out one of the doctors had placed her on a seventy-two-hour psychiatric hold for making homicidal threats against her father."

"Damn," Cash said and shook his head. "I can't imagine that."

"Me neither," Chase said, looking at his brother.

"I was hoping they'd be on their way to North Dakota soon," Jacob said.

"Me too," Tracy admitted quietly. "That's the downside to their being fired."

"Do either of you have a gun for personal protection?" Chase asked her and Jacob.

"I do," Jacob said. "Do you, Tracy?"

She shook her head. "No. But getting one is on my to-do list."

Cash said, "We'll add it to flying and whistling."

"I've heard those things are on the agenda," Tracy said. The way Cash had emphasized *spitfire* when he'd suggested making time to talk about flying was causing her to reassess. She'd thought back to the day they'd met. Driving that Mustang had been well out of her comfort zone. Since when did she not step out of her comfort zone? She smiled at Cash. "Cash thinks I need to take a ride in the Triple C helicopter."

"Definitely," Chase agreed.

They all dismounted at that point and Tracy hugged Dude. Chase led them to a huge barn where there were picnic tables used for meals by his cowboys. Some of his crew, she was told were out on the range rounding up more Black Angus for branding. Others were hauling cows to markets. Chase passed out water to anyone who wanted a bottle and gave Dude fresh water as well. Cash wed to the guests gathered around the corral admiring the cows.

"We'd better head back to Triple C-East or we'll miss the chow bell rounding us up," Cash said to his cowboys and dude ranchers. Jeff and Beau wrangled the guests back in the saddle and headed east. Jacob was staying in the bunkhouse again and left with them. Dude was ready to go too. But he remained close to Cash, looking up at him with nothing short of love and devotion in his big brown eyes. Cash petted his head and asked Tracy, "Is your interview over?"

"Yes, with Chase. Jade is making time for me tomorrow and then I'll head down the road to Triple C-West," Tracy said. "So, I'll go now before I completely lose my dog to you."

Cash chuckled, Dude glued to his side. "Thanks, Chase."

"Yes, thank you again, Chase," Tracy said. "I enjoyed herding the cows."

"You're welcome," Chase said. "Before I forget, Jade wants us all to do dinner on Saturday. Would that work for you guys?"

"Sounds good to me," Cash said. "Tracy?"

Tracy smiled knowing that meant she had at least one more day past Friday to spend with Cash. "Works for me."

CHAPTER TWENTY-NINE

"*Y*ou know ranch work starts before sunup," Cash said with a chuckle on Wednesday as he sat on the side of the big bed.

"I didn't hear the breakfast chow bell yet." Tracy covered her head with the pillow. She made a blind grab for him, caught his wrist, and tugged. The sheet lay so low across her naked back it barely covered her rounded derrière. "Come here, Cash."

"You stay in bed as long as you want, and I'll come back for you when the chow bell rings for lunch."

"I'll miss you." Peeking at him from under the pillow, Tracy said, "I'm only lingering in bed because once again I can barely walk."

"I'll miss you too." Cash grinned. The previous night they'd made love, fallen asleep, awakened in each other's arms, and made love again without a word. It occurred to Cash he always thought the words *made love* and not the words *had sex* when it came to Tracy. "After lunch, I'll drive you to Triple C-Central for your interview with Jade."

"Okay," she smiled, those mesmerizing turquoise eyes closing.

Cash tugged the sheet down and feasted his eyes. With cinnamon curls spread over her shoulders, her back tapering to her slim waist, and her fanny in full view, it took a will of iron not to roll back into bed with her. With a kiss to a soft butt cheek, he stood and strode naked to the shower. When she joined him, making love to her steamed the mirrors more than the hot water. After their wet and wild romp in the shower while he dressed, she pulled on one of his Triple C tee shirts. She crawled back into bed but this time it was with her laptop. She blew him a kiss and he walked out of the bedroom with the image of Tracy in the middle of his bed. Right where she belonged. At least in his opinion.

"Come on, Dude," Cash called over his shoulder and smiled when he realized the dog was already padding up behind him. "We'll see you later, spitfire."

"See you and *your* dog later, big'n bad."

Cash chuckled and then grinned all the way through the house. There were two large bags of dog food in the kitchen, and he grabbed the unopened one. He hoisted the bag over his shoulder and put his cowboy hat on his head. He and Dude made it to the café just as the breakfast chow bell clanged. It was another beautiful day with no humidity. He loved life. How long had it been since such a thought had consciously crossed his mind? Since Tracy entered his life. Since Tracy was on his ranch. Since Tracy was in his bed. Yeah, since Tracy.

"Morning," Cash said to Kellie and Sam.

Yesterday, Cash and Tracy had fed Dude in his kitchen before the three of them headed out. But today, he figured since Dude was with him, he could eat outside too. The previous day, the German shepherd had made friends with every last one of the guests. This dog was made for dude ranch life. Finding two tin bowls in the outdoor kitchen, Cash filled one with water and one with dog food. He placed them near the back table in the corner where he and Sam usually sat.

"Morning," Kellie said as Cash joined Sam in the serving line for breakfast burritos. She placed a crispy strip of bacon on Cash's plate. "That's for Dude."

"She likes the dog better than us," Sam joked as Kellie laughed.

Cash chuckled on the way from the serving line to their table. He set his plate down and crumbled the bacon into Dude's bowl. Dude looked at him as if to say thanks and gobbled up the treat and food. Dude ranchers began arriving, ready to eat and ride. Acknowledging Cash and Sam, those who took seats closest to them also said hello to Dude. Others across the café asked about Dude and some called to him. Thus, Dude made the rounds and shook hands. Like a boss.

"YOU'RE A GREAT BOSS," TRACY SAID TO KIRK DEVEREUX AS they spoke on the phone. She'd crawled out of Cash's bed and was sitting in a two-person leather chair near the hearth in his bedroom. "Thank you for your unfailing support regarding Gerald and Donna."

"I gave them more chances to redeem themselves than I should have," Devereux said. "They had me fooled as to what they were capable of, and I regret that."

"I think they had all of us fooled for a while," Tracy agreed.

"I can assure you Gerald was not responsible for your Triple C Ranch assignment. So don't feel you owe him anything if he should contact you. As a longtime friend of the Cooper family, I knew you'd be a good fit to do the Triple C story. Once again, I apologize for any trouble Gerald and Donna caused you and Cash."

"No apology necessary at all, Mr. Devereux," Tracy said sincerely. "But I understand the need to offer one. I've apologized to Cash for the trouble they caused as well."

In Devereux's opinion, Gerald and Donna were a liability to the magazine's good name. Their belongings had been packed up and remained in the hands of security at the front desk of the *Ranchers and Ranges* office building.

"While I hope we've seen the last of Gerald and Donna, I want to thank you for sticking with us, Tracy," Devereux said. "You're not only an excellent journalist, but you're also brave. Let me know when you and Jacob finish up on Triple C. I already have new assignments lined up for the two of you."

"Really?" Tracy asked. Normally, she'd be thrilled. But suddenly all she could think of was that those assignments wouldn't be on Cash's ranch. "Where?"

"Since you're covering Triple Cs, here in the middle of Colorado, your next assignments will take you to all four corners of the state." The excitement in Devereux's voice would have been echoed in Tracy's too—before she'd met Cash. "You might not even be in Colorado Springs during the holidays. In the meantime, I'll be searching for a new editor to fill Gerald's spot at the magazine. Take care, Tracy. Talk to you soon."

They hung up with the word *brave* resounding in Tracy's head. If she were brave, she'd hop in that helicopter when and if Cash asked her. Cash Cooper was the brave one. She'd never forget his calm in the face of the calamity at the gas station. He'd warned Gerald Moles not to tangle with him. And Donna Smith? Cash had let her know in a firm but not unkind way he was not interested in her from day one. Like Kirk Devereux, Tracy hoped they'd seen the last of Gerald and Donna.

All four corners of the state. Tracy's shoulders sagged.

Working on the interview with Chase, she gazed around at Cash's king-size bed, the walls of Western art, the big archway to the bathroom area with the horse trough, and the rustic French doors open to the balcony and hot tub. The room, the house, the ranch—all of it a class act with the right amount of wild cowboy just like the man who owned it.

Cash will kiss you goodbye and never look back. Tracy's eyes stung.

Maybe she shouldn't look a gift horse in the mouth. Professional assignments to all four corners of Colorado might distract her from the personal devastation that surely lay on the horizon. Right now, here on the ranch with Cash, was Christmas in July. By the time the actual holidays rolled around, she could very well mean nothing more to Cash than another notch in his bedpost. She glanced at his bedpost before she could stop herself. No notches. Still, she closed her eyes and wondered how quickly he'd forget about her after she was gone. Should she mention the upcoming travel assignments to him? And feel her heart shatter when he shrugged? A word from Cash and she'd turn down the assignment. She could ask Kirk Devereux to let her take over Gerald's job as editor. Not only would that allow her to stay in the Springs, but she'd have more time to dedicate to writing and illustrating her children's books. Picking up her cell, she punched in a number. Voicemail.

"Grandma, I hope you're feeling well," Tracy said. "Call me before you leave Punkin Center and let me know you're on your way to Colorado Springs. Maybe I'll have the chance to introduce you to Cash Cooper." She finished in a whisper, "I've fallen in love with him."

"YOU'RE IN LOVE WITH HER, LITTLE BROTHER," CHASE said, out of Tracy's earshot.

"Yeah, I know," Cash replied.

Chase and Jade had arranged their schedules to include lunch with tours of the house and stables. They'd been kind enough to invite Jacob to join them as well as Katy, Jade's friend and receptionist.

Over lunch Jade told them she had arranged, with a set of parents and a set of guardians of two clients who were progressing well, to have photos taken of the children riding horses. To protect their identity, the photos would be taken from the back and with the children wearing riding helmets. Tracy and Jacob were both appreciative of the trouble Jade had gone to on their behalf and of the magazine. Katy had spoken up saying that was Jade's nature. Chase and Cash wholeheartedly agreed. Jade had explained equine therapy was designed to reduce anxiety and depression. The connection with a horse could not only help a struggling child develop empathy and affection, but it could also increase a child's confidence and self-esteem. Jade wanted people to know about equine therapy and to trust the horses trained to help traumatized children.

After lunch, Tracy and Jacob left on a tour with Jade and Colton. Jade started with her in-home therapy office and then they moved on to Katy's office. With an adjoining door to Jade's office, in Katy's office, Chase had installed a private door to the outside for clients. Then Tracy and Jacob headed out to the stables with Jade and Colton where the trained thoroughbreds and ponies were housed along with other Triple C-Central horses.

"Jade and Tracy seemed to hit it off right from the beginning," Chase said.

"Yes. Everybody loves Jade. You're a lucky man, Chase."

"I know it."

Standing behind the wet bar in the den, Chase placed crystal tumblers on the counter as Cash stood opposite him, with Dude at his feet. Chase poured two shots of his finest bourbon.

Little Courtney had gone down for her nap after lunch. Per the baby monitor, she was sound asleep in the nursery. Good thing, because according to Chase, the little girl knew at least a hundred words and was good at putting two or three together in short sentences.

"At least Courtney can't repeat any of this conversation," Cash joked.

"Yeah." Chase chuckled. "For now."

With a smile at Courtney via the baby monitor, Cash said, "I want one. Or two."

"Not that it matters, but Jade and I like Tracy. She's genuine. She fits."

"Coop, Sam, and Kellie have all said the same thing about her."

"Reason to celebrate," Chase said. They raised their tumblers and clinked. "The turn of events in this relationship with Tracy is a first for you, Cash."

"Yeah, I don't know how it happened so fast," Cash admitted. Though he'd never thought of himself as a confirmed bachelor, neither had he ever thought of himself as being in love. "I'm still getting used to the idea."

"It just happens." Chase chuckled and shrugged. "When you meet the right woman, somehow you know in your gut she's the one."

Cash tilted his head and asked, "That's how it happened with you and Jade?"

"Oh, hell yes." Chase nodded. "When I opened my front door and found her standing on the porch, I could have sworn there was an aura floating around her." He smiled and added seriously, "I had no idea what we'd face or if things would work out, but I remembered what Dad always told us."

"If it's worth fighting for, be a warrior, not a deserter," Cash said.

"Yes. Sounds like to me you've been fighting for her from what you've told me about the two people at her magazine who are sitting in jail and detox," Chase said. "What about Tracy?"

"Tracy stood with Beau and Ed and me against Moles when he started trouble and she wound up smacking him across the face."

Chase chuckled and nodded. "So, she's fighting for you too."

"What's your best advice?"

"Don't let her be the one who got away."

CHAPTER THIRTY

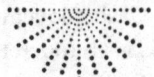

"*W*hat's on your agenda today?" Tracy asked, lying in Cash's embrace early Thursday morning.

"Ropin' and rawhide," he said around a stretch and a yawn.

"What do you mean?" she asked as Cash's arms closed around her again.

"Marty fix-it-man Martinez, or Martyman for short, and Mean Pete, who you met the other day, are herding some of Chase's cattle over here this morning. The dude ranchers were so interested in the cattle, we're gonna demonstrate for them how a cow gets branded."

Tracy was falling more in love with this man, his ranch, and his family every day. "I'd love to include that in my story."

"Done," Cash said. "While Chase's crew is keeping the guests busy, my guys will pack up the covered wagons. After lunch, we're riding out to the fishing pond for an overnighter."

A pang pierced Tracy at the thought of being separated from Cash. She slipped her leg between his and snuggled closer. "Gee, I hope you don't get lonely on your overnighter."

He grinned at her. "I won't if you sneak into my tent like last week."

"Done."

Cash rolled on top of her, and she eagerly spread her legs for him. "Wanna sparkle before the sun comes up?"

"Yes, I'd stay in this bed with you all day."

"Don't tempt me, spitfire."

Tracy lost herself to Cash's lovemaking. She savored his every nibble to her neck, each touch that tingled all the way to her toes. He kissed his way across her breasts and down her tummy. As his tongue circled her belly button, his hands cupped her fanny, lifting her to his lips. When he'd first introduced her to this most intimate of kisses, and every time thereafter, she nearly lost her mind from the ecstasy. This morning she clutched the sheets and moaned his name as rapture seized her body, heart, and soul. Cash rolled to his back, and she lovingly kissed his hard inches before saddling up for the ride she wanted only with Cash.

And oh, how they rode.

"YEEHAW!" CASH WHOOPED AND TOSSED THE LARIAT.

In the saddle on Captain, Cash lassoed another good-sized calf on the first try. He bailed off his horse and Martyman handed him the branding iron. Mean Pete held the animal as Cash pressed iron to cowhide. When released, the calf jumped up and trotted off, in the long run, none the worse for wear. Cash swung himself back into the saddle and lassoed the next calf.

"Yeehaw!" Tracy hooted, standing outside the corral while waving a dainty fist over the Elsa hat on her pretty head. Dude and Crockett flanked her like guard dogs.

"Go, Cash!" Jacob yelled and filmed.

Cash flashed a grin at Tracy. Brains and body, the woman oozed smart and sexy. Never had he enjoyed roping as much as he did today with this one-of-a-kind redhead cheering him on. For a couple more days she was all his. Then what? As much as he'd like to, he couldn't just toss a rope around her and tie her to him.

"Taught him everything he knows," Coop called, only half joking as he stood on the other side of Tracy and Crockett.

The Australian sheepdog and German shepherd barked as the guests surrounding the corral clapped and shouted their appreciation of the show. Cash, atop Captain, took off his hat and placed it to his chest in thanks. Martyman and Mean Pete bowed. With the show concluded, Cash rode to Tracy. As he neared, Tracy stepped up onto the bottom rail of the corral. He leaned down, swung an arm around her, and kissed her. The crowd hooted and hollered even more. Wow! That had never happened before—because never before had there been a woman whom he'd kissed in front of guests. He held Tracy all the more tightly and she placed a hand to her hat to keep it from falling down her back. Since the first night they'd made love, they'd been inseparable. The more they made love, the more Cash could not get enough of her.

Kellie rang the chow bell for lunch and with a chuckle against Tracy's lips, Cash let her go. He rode Captain out of the corral, dismounted, and with a pat to the horse's mane, turned him over to Larry. The branding done, the cows in the corral would be taken to graze and driven back home by Coop, Martyman, and Mean Pete after lunch. Even though Sam, Jeff, and the wranglers had finished packing for the overnight camping trip they always let the guests line up for meals first. But within minutes, all were feasting on Kellie and Cristen's delicious beef barbecue sandwiches, coleslaw, potato salad, and baked beans. Cash, Tracy, Coop, and Sam were joined at the table in the back corner by Martyman and Mean Pete.

Mean Pete, who lived on Chase's ranch with Katy and was a stepfather to her sixteen-year-old son, Finn, said, "It's nice to see you again, Tracy. My beautiful wife, Katy, said she enjoyed meeting you."

"Thank you," Tracy said. "Katy is a sweetheart. She spoke highly of you telling me what a great dad you've been to Finn."

"Finn's father was in the Army and died when his parachute failed to open," Mean Pete said with respect in his voice. "I love our boy, Finn, like he was my own flesh and blood."

"I've been where Finn was," Tracy said. "I write and illustrate children's books for kids who have faced similar struggles but find hope and a happy ending like Finn."

Cash smiled to himself noting how Tracy had captured the attention and admiration of every man at their table. "Tracy lost her mom and dad in a helicopter crash when she was little. Her grandparents raised her." Cash heard and saw the appreciation around the table for this accomplished young woman deepen. He wondered what a happy ending looked like to Tracy.

"Thank you." Tracy smiled and then to Mean Pete she softly said, "Katy told me how you met on Triple C-Central." Her turquoise eyes widened as she'd heard some facts about Mean Pete and Katy's introduction which had been under terrifying circumstances. But they'd survived and thrived. "Knowing you were coming to Triple C-East today, the first thing Katy said to me was that Mean Pete would be one of the nicest people I'd ever know. And she was right."

"Aw, shucks," Mean Pete said shyly. "Thank you, Tracy." Then looking at Cash, he said, "I like this girl, Cash."

"Me too," Cash said and winked at her. "Mean Pete, I remember you saying that same thing about Katy the day she happened to use your phrase of batshit crazy."

"Yes, sir." Mean Pete grinned. "I knew Katy was my girl right then and there."

Martyman said, "Tracy, I hear you're headed to Triple C-West tomorrow." Marty and Cash's Aunt Rachel lived near Mean Pete and Katy. "To interview Chloe and Derek?"

"Yes," Tracy replied. "Chloe is taking me on a tour of the original house and the new bed-and-breakfast she and Derek built. Then Derek said he will introduce me to the Percherons he trains for law enforcement."

"Let's saddle up, everybody," Jeff called from the far side of the café. "Wagons are ready to roll."

"Ready to rock and roll, spitfire?" Cash asked Tracy.

"Count on it, big'n bad."

CHAPTER THIRTY-ONE

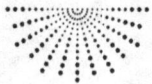

"I've had the best days of my entire life here on your ranch," Tracy said that evening as she and Cash toasted marshmallows over the campfire outside their tent.

Moonlight reflected off Turkey Creek Pond. Frogs croaked near the water, katydids chirped in bushes, and occasionally a turkey gobbled in the distance. The dinner bell had clanged hours ago, calling folks to fill their plates and bellies with spareribs, burgers, or freshly caught fish. Many of the dude ranchers had tried their hand at fishing and the bigger fish were turned over to Cristen to fry. Other guests had gone horseback riding or hiked the nearby hills during the late afternoon and evening. Most had since settled in for the night. Here and there, you could see a couple sitting in front of their tent or hear a voice followed by a laugh. Tuckered out, Dude had curled up on the ground between Cash and Tracy and was softly snoring. In Tracy's opinion, this life was idyllic. If she could stay on this ranch instead of traveling to those other ranches in the four corners of the state, she would do so in a heartbeat. She vaguely wondered what kind of work she'd be qualified to do on a dude ranch.

"It's been great." Cash raised a marshmallow out of the

fire. Hot and gooey, he let it cool before popping it in his mouth. Tracy pulled her marshmallow out of the fire and blew on it.

Cash grinned at her. "You're here during a great time of the year. A little hot during the day," he acknowledged, but it's a whole different story during the winter."

"What do your guests do in winter?" Tracy asked and bit off half of the marshmallow.

"Besides the mandatory chicken chasing?" he teased.

Tracy laughed, but not too loudly. "Yes, besides that."

"Weather permitting, we horseback ride. In summer and winter, we shoot skeet, sometimes with a longtime friend of mine named Sullivan Custis, who goes by Sully."

"If I remember correctly, he's the son of the former El Paso County sheriff, right?"

"Right. Owen and Sully both own ranches here in the country." Cash smiled and nodded. "When we get a good snowfall, we take people on snowmobile adventures. Instead of hiking, we snowshoe and when the pond is frozen solid, people can ice skate."

"That sounds wonderful." Tracy ate the other half of her marshmallow, figuring she would be miles away come winter. She pictured countless pretty women holding tight to Cash as they zipped across his ranch on a snowmobile. Instantly, she rebuked herself. This was his ranch, and he had no obligation to her. "I can imagine how beautiful the ranch is covered in snow."

"It truly is," Cash said with humble honesty ringing in his deep voice. "I've contacted the architects who Derek hired to build Chloe's new bed-and-breakfast."

"Really?" Tracy tilted her head. "Why?"

"I haven't told anybody else this yet." Cash looked at her and confided, "But I'd like to build a lodge next to the cabins. I'd have it constructed in the adjacent lot we use for extra parking and pave a driveway out to the main road."

"How exciting." Tracy turned sideways in her chair and said, "You are a man of vision."

Cash shrugged. "I'd like the lodge to offer a grand hall with comfortable sofas and chairs for lounging around a roaring fireplace. I'd have a full bar and offer gourmet dining." Cash gestured as he spoke. "There would be tall windows for admiring the view year-round and for watching the snow fall on Pikes Peak. I see sleighs pulled by Percherons, taking guests on rides."

"Wow, Cash. That sounds amazing," Tracy said. "Truly impressive."

"The cabins have been refurbished and it's time to further upgrade the ranch with a lodge," he replied.

"How many rooms would your lodge have?"

"Ten, maybe a dozen, I'm thinking."

"That means more horses? And staff?"

"Yes. I'm going to talk to Sam and Jeff about it. And I'll run it past Chase and Derek to get their ideas too. Chloe gave me some great suggestions when I refurbished the cabins, since she and Derek had just built the new bed-and-breakfast." Cash paused and his blue eyes captured Tracy. "I know what I want. And you're the first person to hear about it."

"I'm honored." Tracy placed a hand over her heart and smiled. Then sliding marshmallows on both their sticks, she handed Cash his. "Let's toast to your new lodge," she said and touched her marshmallow to Cash's. "It will be fantastic."

"Heck yeah," Cash said. "Speaking of a full bar and toasting, let's also toast with a nightcap of something stronger than the water we've been drinking all day." Handing her his marshmallow stick, he ducked into the tent. Coming back with tin cups, he poured two shots of whiskey. "To you and the lodge, Tracy."

Tracy touched her cup to Cash's and said, "To you and the lodge, Cash." They swallowed their shots and toasted their marshmallows. "What's on your agenda for tomorrow?"

"Besides you?"

"Yes." A hot blush burned through Tracy's entire body.

"Sam's in the shop tomorrow so Ed will take some folks skeet shooting," Cash said. "Jeff and Beau are escorting others on a cattle drive on the other side of the highway." Who knew the Triple C Ranches extended to the other side of the highway? "Larry will be around for those who want one last ride on their favorite horse."

"What about you, Cash?"

"Since there is no barbecue or fireworks like we had last Friday for July 4, Chase and I will offer helicopter rides for $200 per passenger."

"I don't know how you keep it all going," Tracy said.

"Sam, Kellie, and Jeff do their parts, but I'll need to hire someone to run the lodge once it's built."

Tracy raised her hand and said only half-jokingly, "I'll take that job."

"You're hired."

"I accept."

It was the middle of the night when Cash woke.

"Tracy?" he said softly, seeing that her cot was empty.

He blinked to make sure as his eyes adjusted to the moonlit darkness. She was gone. Images of her falling into the lake, facing a lone coyote, or stumbling over a snake shot through him. His heart pounded as he swung his legs off the cot. When his feet touched the ground, he realized Dude was inside the tent. Before they'd gone to bed, Cash had secured a ground stake outside the tent and Tracy had clipped the dog leash to it so that Dude could come and go.

"Where's Tracy, Dude?"

The German shepherd sat up, but Cash noted Dude didn't seem alarmed. And though the dog walked to the opening of the tent, he didn't bark. Cash got off the cot and covered the few paces to join Dude. In the distance, emerging from a copse of trees, he saw her. She wore a sleeveless white nightgown. However, this one wasn't sheer like the one she'd been wearing the night her laptop had fallen and held her hostage. As she made her way toward them, her cinnamon hair tumbled around her shoulders and the white gown billowed around her cowboy boots. With the moon and stars overhead, she appeared like a cowgirl angel sent from heaven to rescue a lonely rancher. Was he lonely? He hadn't noticed it until she burst into his life. Cash suspected he'd feel all alone, even in a crowd of people, if Tracy were no longer with him.

He glanced down at Dude, put his finger to his lips, and taking hold of Dude's leash, moved him to the left of the tent opening. They waited mere seconds before Tracy silently dipped into the tent. She stood for a moment, no doubt letting her eyes adjust to the darkness as Cash had when he awakened. Hidden in the pitch-black corner, Cash carefully nabbed the back of her gown just as she took a step toward her cot. Hauled up short, she stood stock-still. To Dude's credit, he didn't make a sound. Tracy tugged on her gown, Cash held tight.

"Cash?" she whispered. "Cash, help. Something has a hold of me."

Stepping out of the darkness, Cash let go of Dude's leash in preparation for placing his hand over Tracy's mouth in case she screamed. "Me."

Tracy fainted. Cash caught her. Dude licked her hand. She giggled. He groaned. The dog curled up with a sigh.

"You scared me, Cash Cooper."

"You scared me, Tracy Dalton," Cash scolded. "Don't you know you can't go wandering around in the woods by yourself? Especially at night. What were you thinking?"

"I had to tinkle and the trees—"

"You had to what?"

"Tinkle." She sat on her cot and pulled off her boots. "Number one."

"Next time you have to take a piss when we're camping,

you tell me. And why were you in the trees when we have outhouses?"

"Because the outhouses were too far away. I was afraid I'd wake someone tramping through the campsite to get there and back."

Cash sat down on his cot, wondering when he'd ever been so personally concerned about a woman's welfare. Never. "Come here."

"No," she said with one of her sexy giggles. "Why should I?"

"So I can turn you over my knee and spank you."

"Ooh, okay," she flirted, stepped over Dude and lay across his lap.

Cash flipped up her gown and placed his hand on her naked fanny. If only they'd been in his bed at home. "I'll settle for your pinkie swear not to leave me in the dark like that again."

Tracy sat up, shifted herself in his lap, and hooked his pinkie with hers. "I swear."

CHAPTER THIRTY-TWO

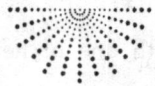

"Chloe, I can't thank you enough for taking time to show me your beautiful home," Tracy said.

"As Cash may have told you, Uncle Chester built this house back in the day," Chloe said. She had beautiful blue eyes and wore her long, black hair in a ponytail. They sipped sweet tea in a comfortable den while twins, Austin and Abilene, played with toys on a thick carpet.

Earlier, Austin had taken Tracy's hand and showed her the racetrack he'd received when turning three. The track wound here and there and he stayed busy racing his cars on it. Abilene had said she remembered Tracy from the night of the fireworks. Abilene had happily cooked up some pretend treats for Tracy in the tyke-sized kitchen she'd requested for her third birthday.

"The arched bridge over the indoor goldfish pond in the foyer is one of my favorite things about your house," Tracy said, watching the children play.

"Mine too. We filled it again once the kids were big enough not to drown in it. They picked out the goldfish and named them."

"The dumbwaiters in the foyer and kitchen must have come in handy when this was the bed-and-breakfast," Tracy said. "Cash told me when you and he were in elementary school you'd hop in a dumbwaiter and race each other to the second floor."

"Yes, big brother Chase was too cool to ride in the dumbwaiters. But Cash and I would race, and Chase would declare the winner." Chloe laughed and then sobered. Tracy was vaguely aware of a frightening event involving one of the dumbwaiters. But that was Chloe's story to tell some other time, so Tracy didn't ask about it now Chloe brightened again and said, "I'm blessed to have Cash and Chase for brothers."

"Definitely," Tracy agreed. "They're both great and so is Jade."

"Yes, we love Jade."

"More sweet tea?" Rachel asked, coming into the den with a pitcher.

"Best sweet tea I've ever had," Tracy said, holding out her glass. "Thank you."

"Aunt Rachel is famous for her sweet tea. I think it's the main reason we have such good turnouts at our three annual barbecues," Chloe complimented her beloved aunt as she also held out her glass. "Thanks."

"You're welcome, girls." Rachel finished pouring and joined them.

"Thank you both for the tour of the new bed-and-breakfast," Tracy said.

"Your timing was excellent because our guests always check out by eleven a.m. on Fridays," Rachel said. "By the time you and Jacob arrived, they were all gone."

Chloe's phone signaled a text and she said, "Derek and Cooper are on their way to pick you up in the golf cart, Tracy. They'll meet you on the front porch and take you to the stables."

"Great. Thank you again for letting me interview you."

"My pleasure. Did you remember to wear or bring a swimsuit?" Chloe asked.

"Yes, I have it on under my clothes."

"Good, late afternoon is the best time for the kids to swim because the sun isn't so strong," Chloe said, walking her to the front door. "Even slathering on sunscreen, it's easy to burn. We'll meet you at the pool when you get back from the stables."

"Sounds wonderful." Tracy smiled, thrilled to be included.

She walked across the porch as Jacob came into view from around the side of the house. He'd already snapped a few photos inside when they'd first arrived and had gone with them to the new bed-and-breakfast when Rachel had given them the tour. Derek and Cooper pulled up in one of the golf carts used to travel from the main house, past the bed-and-breakfast, to the stables for the Percherons.

"Howdy," Cooper called and waved. The five-year-old, with his father's dark-blond hair and big brown eyes, was a miniature of Derek Brevard.

"Hop in and buckle up," Derek said.

Tracy and Jacob hopped into the back seat and buckled up. They all waved to Chloe and Rachel and then it was off to the horse stables. Derek, who'd grown up on a Percheron horse ranch in Texas, was an excellent guide. He toured them around the state-of-the-art stables as he told them about the docile draft horses known for their intelligence and willingness to work. Tracy asked questions and took notes as Derek explained how he and former Sheriff Otis Custis trained the animals for law enforcement. Percherons, with their calm temperament, made them an excellent choice for crowd control and patrol work in the city. In the country, these horses could take officers places cars could never reach.

"Thank you, Derek and Cooper," Tracy said as the interview and tour wound to a close.

"Yes, thanks," Jacob said as they piled back into the golf cart. As Derek and Cooper chauffeured them to the house, Jacob told Tracy, "I'm headed to a poker game in the bunkhouse on Triple C-East tonight. I can give you a ride there unless Cash plans to pick you up here on Triple C-West, Tracy."

"Cash said he'd be back for me. Have fun. Just don't lose all your money," she teased.

"Jeff said they play for nickels and dimes." Jacob chuckled. "I'll be heading back to the Springs in the morning. Do you need a ride?"

"I'm invited to dinner tomorrow evening, so no, I guess not."

"I'll touch base with you and thank Cash before I leave in the morning," he said.

Arriving back at the house on Triple C-West, Jacob thanked Derek again and left for the bunkhouse on Triple C-East. Derek dropped Tracy off near the back yard and then he and Cooper parked the golf cart. Tracy found Chloe, Rachel, Martyman, and the twins in a lagoon-like pool surrounded and made private by a rock wall. Martyman and Chloe were playing with the kids in the shallow end of the pool as Rachel lounged in the deep end on a dolphin raft. They called to Tracy, and Chloe pointed her toward the bathhouse, where there were fresh beach towels. Tracy removed her clothes and modestly wrapped a towel around her waist before emerging from the bathhouse. Rachel had switched to a chaise lounge, leaving the dolphin raft next to a pink flamingo raft. Picking out a chaise lounge next to Rachel, Tracy placed her towel on it and waded down cement steps into the heated pool.

Pets, Spike the German shepherd was poolside watching like the family guard dog he was as Scarlett the sleek black cat groomed herself at one end of a chaise lounge. Derek and Cooper soon joined the crowd, wearing swim trunks. The twins squealed seeing their father and brother. Tracy swam to the deep end and nabbed the flamingo. Chloe kissed her husband, hugged her son, and slid onto the dolphin. Derek and Martyman played with the kids.

"I hope Cooper and the twins aren't too much for you," Chloe said with a soft laugh.

"Not at all," Tracy said. "I want children when the time is right."

"Sometimes it happens when you least expect it," Chloe said as she gazed at her family. "And it all works out."

"Yes," Tracy said but didn't pry. Once again, she found herself thinking how much she enjoyed life on the Triple C Ranches. But it was Cash who tied it all together.

At the sound of whirring, Tracy looked into the sky. Cash was here. In the helicopter. Tracy gulped and swallowed hard. If this was her ride to his ranch, so be it. As far as she knew, no one else was aware of her terror when it came to flying and she was not about to embarrass Cash by declining a ride in front of his family. Wasn't it about time she controlled and conquered this fear? Who would she trust more than Cash to help her do so? No one. Tracy decided she'd climb into that helicopter and fly...if it was the last thing she did.

That's how much she loved Cash Cooper.

~

CASH SAILED ACROSS THE SKY AS THE FLAMINGO FLOATED IN THE water.

"Coop, is that girl on the pink flamingo not the hottest redhead you've ever seen in your life?" Cash asked. Although Coop wasn't a licensed pilot, in the off-chance Cash, Chase, or Derek were to become incapacitated while flying with him, they'd taught him how to land the chopper. "I mean in your whole entire life."

"You've brought home a lot of redheads, boy." Coop chuckled. "But of all the girls, no matter the color of their hair, Tracy is the most beautiful and the sweetest. Without a doubt."

Cash landed the helicopter far enough away from the back yard pool so as not to kick up dust. He and Coop hopped out, each carrying three pizzas, napkins, and paper plates, just delivered to Triple C-West and made their way to the rock wall. Rachel met them at the gate and opened it for them.

"What a nice surprise," Chloe said, wading out of the pool.

"Heck yeah! Glad to see you and the pizza," Derek said and laughed. "I'm starved."

"I'm starved too," Cooper said and swam to the steps of the pool.

Cash and Coop set the pizzas on the two tables under big blue and white umbrellas. Austin and Abilene, both wearing water wings even though they, too, could swim, followed their big brother toward the steps. Derek scooped up Abilene and Martyman plucked Austin out of the water. The men carried the twins up the steps, setting them carefully on dry land.

"Hi," Tracy called to Cash. Cupping her hands, she paddled her flamingo across the deep end to where he stood on the side of the pool.

Looking over the top of his aviator sunglasses at the gorgeous redhead in the white bikini surrounded by hot pink on blue water, he grinned down at her. "Hi."

"I missed you today," she said, reaching the side of the pool.

"I missed you too," he replied. "Do you have a towel?"

Tracy pointed to a beach towel on a chaise lounge, and he grabbed it. He held it out to her as she climbed the ladder out of the deep end. Her hair was in a clip high on her head and water ran in streams down her silky body. Had they been alone, Cash would have trailed his fingers along those rivulets. Tracy, all sexy smile and charming curves, stepped toward him and he wrapped the towel around her. When he pulled her closer, she tilted up her chin, and he kissed her. Then she tucked one end of the towel between her breasts.

Cash took her hand and they strolled to the umbrella tables as Derek, Cooper, and Rachel came from the direction of their outdoor kitchen with drinks and paper cups. Austin and Abilene were scooting child-sized chairs up to a miniature table with a red, white, and blue umbrella which was positioned between the two larger tables. Chloe was busy placing cheese pizza on paper plates for the children as Cooper set three juice boxes on the small table.

"Pinot Noir for the ladies," Rachel said, holding up a bottle and cups. Addressing Tracy, she asked, "Unless you'd rather have a beer?"

"Pinot, please," Tracy said, taking a seat at the table closer to her. "Thank you, Rachel."

"The first time Jade was here at the pool, she told Rachel and me Pinot Noir was the healthiest of all red wines because of the grapes it's made from," Chloe told Tracy as she sat at the other table in a chair closest to the children.

"Here you go, gentlemen." Derek gave Cash, Coop, and Martyman bottles of the Cooper family's favorite beer.

Coop and Martyman took seats at the table with Chloe as Rachel poured wine for the ladies. Then Rachel and Derek sat at the table with Cash and Tracy. Like everything else with Tracy, having this impromptu and informal meal with family felt right. Easy and fun. Like Chase had said, Tracy was genuine. She fit. Cash couldn't have wiped the smile off his face if he'd wanted to and he didn't want to. Every time he looked at Tracy, his feelings deepened. He was going to get her over her fear of flying...at all costs.

That's how much he loved Tracy Dalton.

After dinner, Chloe scooted back from the table and said, "Don't anybody rush off, but I know three little kids who need baths and bedtime stories."

"We need to get going too," Rachel said and began gathering up paper plates.

Martyman had gone to the kitchen area to get a black garbage bag and said, "Yup. We're headed out gallivanting early tomorrow morning as we do most Saturdays."

Tracy stood and picked up the empty plates and pizza boxes on their table. "What do you do when you're gallivanting?" she asked, stuffing trash in the garbage bag as Marty held it.

"We find yard sales or visit antique stores," Rachel said. "Then go to lunch."

"Always fun." Martyman nodded and asked, "You want to ride home with us, Coop?"

As they all lived on Triple C-Central, Rachel teased, "We're going your way."

"Cash, will you and Tracy be okay flying from here to Triple C-East?" Coop asked.

Cash looked at Tracy. "What do you say?"

"I say it's a party in the sky."

Cash looked at her over the top of his sunglasses again and winked. "That's my girl."

"I saw the Hummer you and Chase share parked at your ranch on the Fourth. I can drive it back here if you want me to copilot," Derek offered.

Cash said only half-jokingly, "Nah, I'll teach Tracy how to land."

Chloe said good night to Tracy and thanked Cash for the pizza. Cooper, Austin, and Abilene passed out hugs and then Chloe herded the children into the house. Martyman, Rachel, and Coop were next to leave. Then Cash helped Derek finish tidying up as Tracy ducked into the bathhouse and emerged in her tank top and shorts. Derek walked them out of the pool area and through the gate.

"See you at the family dinner tomorrow with Chase and Jade," Derek said.

"See you tomorrow," Cash said and snared Tracy's hand.

"Thanks again for the interview, Derek," Tracy called with a wave. "Good night."

As crossed the field to the helicopter, Cash expected at any second Tracy would stop walking and back out. To sidetrack her from her fears, he said the landing gear was called skids. He told her to always approach a helicopter from the front and not the back because the tail rotor spins so fast it's difficult to see and therefore dangerous. When they made it to the helicopter, he opened her door. She hesitated and he saw her shiver in the warm sun setting behind Pikes Peak. Fully knowing Derek would give her a ride, Cash decided on a lighthearted approach.

"Would you rather Uber it to Triple C-East?" Cash asked.

CHAPTER THIRTY-THREE

"*J*'d follow you into hell, Cash," Tracy admitted, heart thumping and knees shaking.

"Said the angel who takes me to heaven." Acknowledging her compliment as the vote of confidence it was meant to be, Cash said, "If we ever experience hell, let's escape it together."

"Together," she whispered, locking her eyes onto his blue ones.

"You'll never forget your first time," Cash said with a cocky grin.

Tracy gave him the sassiest smile she could manage. "No, I won't."

Cash pulled her close for a quick kiss. "Hop in and buckle up." Tracy climbed into the helicopter and with some minor assistance from Cash, she fastened her seat belt. He closed her door and sprinted around the front of the helicopter. Sitting next to her, he handed her a headset and put on his. Then he began hitting buttons, explaining what some were and that others had to turn green. "How much do you weigh?"

"Did I look fat in my swimsuit?"

"Hardly." Cash chuckled. "The chopper needs to know."

"One ten."

"I gauged your weight to be half of mine the day I met you," he said and placed his hand on her thigh. "You looked like the sexy spitfire you are in that bikini."

"Thanks," Tracy said, so riddled with anxiety she could hardly sit still in her seat.

"Green lights, plenty of fuel." The blades overhead whirred. "We're ready to fly. Okay?"

Tracy took a breath knowing this was her last chance to bail. She glanced out the window at the ground. It was right there. If she did this with Cash, the ground would be—"How high can this helicopter fly?"

"Max is 22,500 feet. We don't fly that high around the ranches."

"How fast can it go?"

"Up to a hundred and forty miles per hour. Cruising speed is a hundred twenty."

Tracy nodded again. "Okay." It was now or never. "Let's party in the sky."

Cash smiled, and the helicopter's skids left the ground. Farther and farther straight up into the air. Tracy said a prayer while holding her breath. She gripped her hands in her lap and looked down. Written atop the roof of the Percherons' stables in huge black letters was Triple C Ranch-West. The lagoon-like swimming pool quickly became a blue puddle and the floating flamingo a pink dot. The helicopter turned high in the sky, leaving the safety of the house, bed-and-breakfast, and stables in their wake. Quickly losing sight of the ranch, Tracy looked forward to avoid seeing how high above the ground they were.

Cloudless blue sky. Endless green pastures. Majestic rolling hills. Cooper ranch land.

"Next up is Chase's cattle ranch entrance, cowboys' bunkhouse, and stables for their horses," Cash said through the headset.

Tracy was seeing it all from a vantage point she could never have imagined. As Cash narrated, he pointed out Martyman and Rachel's house close to Mean Pete and

Katy's. Next, she saw Triple C Ranch-Central written in the same black lettering on the roof of the stables she knew housed the family's horses and those ridden in the equine therapy. To the rear of the main house was the four-car garage and big red barn. Coop's log cabin was nearby, situated close to Bob and Teresa's house, just as she remembered from the ground.

Through the sky they flew, like Colorado's state bird. She had written about the lark bunting in a couple of articles for the magazine. The bird always arrives in Colorado in April, spends the summer, and flies south in September. These summer days with Cash were priceless and few. And they were *flying* by. Where would they be, come September? It occurred to Tracy her hands were no longer bone-knuckle white. Her breathing had gone from being held and gulped to normal. She glanced at Cash for the first time since the skids had left the ground.

"Wow, Cash," she breathed, shaking her head in the wonder of it all.

Cash looked at her and grinned. "Yeah, I know. "I'm glad you're up here with me."

"Me too." Tracy's eyes stung with tears of happiness. "Thank you, Cash." Each beat of her heart echoed her love for this man.

"Anytime," he said. "Look up ahead, on the horizon."

Tracy faced forward again and glimpsed the distant edge of Triple C-East where they had left Dude with Sam, Jeff, and the other wranglers. Dude had ridden with Cash to drop her off at Triple C-West. But he'd jumped right back into the truck with Cash and returned home with him. Tracy knew Dude loved each and every minute of being on Cash's ranch as much as she did. When they returned to their apartment in the Springs, the German shepherd would surely miss the wide-open spaces, horses, cattle, even the chickens, and certainly the companionable affection from the friends they'd made. How would they ever survive without Cash Cooper?

"I see Dude with Sam and Jeff outside the bunkhouse," Tracy said and pointed.

"Yup."

They waved and saw Sam and Jeff wave back. On the roof of Cash's stables, she also noted Triple C Ranch-East written in the now familiar bold black letters. They flew over it, the café, the five cabins, the four-car garage, and the main house with its hot tub on the balcony. Cash flew above the empty adjacent field, then with a wide loop turning them back around to the west he began the descent. Above the exact spot where he had landed on the Fourth of July, Cash expertly lowered the helicopter. When the skids touched the ground, Tracy's smile was so big she thought it might split her face. Cash flipped switches, the motor ceased, and the blades overhead whirred to a stop. He took off his headset and Tracy followed suit.

"Cash," Tracy whispered. She tried to hug him, but her seat belt held her in place.

"Tracy," Cash mimicked and chuckled as she unbuckled her seat belt.

"Let's make love right now, right here in the—"

"Cockpit?"

Tracy looked between and behind her seat and Cash's and finished, "In the three passenger back seats. Cowgirl style!"

He inclined his head in thought and said, "No, but that would be a first."

"Never say never," she flirted.

Cash grinned and unbuckled his seat belt. He exited the helicopter and came around to her side, helping her out. So happy, so confident, and so in love, she flung her arms around his neck. Cash kissed her, lifting her feet off the ground and swinging her in a half circle. Putting her feet back on the ground, he grabbed her hand, and they made their way across the quiet backyard, which was currently devoid of wranglers and guests.

"Wanna go get *my* dog, spitfire?" Cash teased, nearing his truck.

Tracy laughed. "Yes, I'm sure he misses you."

～

"Yet another way you take me to heaven," Cash said, his voice husky.

Near the hot tub, Cash lay face down on a couple of extra wide beach towels tossed over the thick cushion of a chaise lounge for two. Tiki torches flickered in the corners of the balcony and candles glowed on tables. Soothing new-age music and soft lamplight filtered out through the open French doors of the master bedroom. Moon and stars danced overhead as Tracy's hands waltzed across his back. Naked and straddling his thighs, she'd started out by pressing her fingers into his lower back and slowly working her way up both sides of his spine to his neck. Then, down his neck and out to his shoulders, along his arms and ribs, she spread her magic.

"Is this your first massage with warming oil?" Tracy asked.

"This is my first massage ever."

"What?" she asked, the heels of her palms bearing down as her hands traveled across his lower back. "No way."

"Yes way," he groaned, loving each word she spoke and every move she made.

"You'll never forget this first time with me," she purred.

"No, I won't forget." He sighed with pleasure. "I hope it's the first of many."

"I hope so too."

Cash wondered if it was too soon to tell Tracy he loved her. He hadn't even known for two full weeks. He'd never been in love. Were there rules? He didn't want to scare her.

"What is warming oil?" he asked.

"The one I brought with me is a cinnamon essential oil," she said, her fingers splayed now as she pushed and pulled them across his flesh like a tide rolling onto the shore and retreating into the ocean. "Cinnamon essential oil can alleviate stiff muscles and ease aches in joints. It nourishes the skin and enhances circulation. It's supposed to decrease stress. But I guess you'll be the judge of that."

"Well, princess of the cinnamon kiss, it's doing all of that," Cash agreed, her elbows manipulating his muscles and eliminating knots he didn't know he had. The massage was every bit as delightful as Tracy had promised. But it was the woman, and not the oil she was rubbing into his skin, causing hot blood to pound into his lower body. He teased her with, "Did you know it increases libido?"

She giggled that sexy laugh. "I have heard that, not that you need it."

"I'll prove it to you if you let me roll over."

"Mmm...that is tempting. But you're not on cloud nine yet."

With that, Tracy ran her cinnamon-oiled hands gently over his slightly rounded butt cheeks. Cash wasn't sure how much more he could take. The pleasure rolled from head to toe and a low groan starting in his chest escaped through his teeth. Tracy slid forward until she was sitting on his buttocks. She leaned down and her bare breasts molded to his back. Cash was certain this angel had dropped out of the stars and through the clouds because what she made him feel mentally and physically was absolute heaven on earth.

"Is this part of a regular massage?" Of course, he knew it wasn't.

"From me to you, it is."

"Is it restricted to my back, or does it include my front?"

"Roll over now and find out."

Cash found out the massage most definitely included his front; chest, stomach, and lower. He ached, but it was from agonizing pleasure until she transported him into a sensual, hard throbbing, blissful paradise. Cloud nine? Oh, hell yes.

CHAPTER THIRTY-FOUR

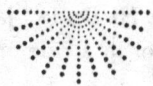

$\mathcal{R}$ainclouds hung low in the sky on Saturday morning as Tracy and Cash stood in his driveway.

"Dude, I have surprises for the two of you," Cash said to the German shepherd sitting between them before giving Tracy a cocky grin.

"What're the surprises?" Tracy asked as they waited for Jacob. He'd texted after enjoying one last ride on Chief and lunch with his wrangler buddies. He'd bid the guys farewell and was stopping by Cash's house to say goodbye before heading back into the Springs. "Tell us, Cash."

Cash chuckled and took a sip of the black coffee from the mug in his left hand. "You have to wait and see."

"Oh, come on," Tracy pleaded and took hold of his right hand with both of hers.

"Not telling you." He laughed and squeezed her hand. "But Dude's surprise is that he's invited to Triple C Ranch-Central this evening."

"Did you hear that, Dude?" Tracy asked and the dog barked.

"Colton wants a dog," Cash said and scratched Dude's head. Chase and Jade are considering a German shepherd because they like the way Dude and Spike interact with the kids. They know German shepherds are fearless and protective."

"Smart and loyal too," Tracy added.

"There he is," Cash said as the photographer turned off the main road and drove up the long drive. Jacob stopped his car close to the house and walked toward them. "Hi, Jacob."

"Hi, Cash. Hi, Tracy. Hi, Dude," Jacob said as he reached them. "I'm so glad I got in a ride on Chief before the rain falls."

"You two were a good match from the start," Cash said.

"Cash, I came by because I wanted to thank you in person for your hospitality. This has been the best ranch assignment I've ever had."

"You're welcome, Jacob," Cash said. "Come back again soon. The Labor Day barbecue is always a good time and you're invited."

"Thank you," Jacob said. "But Tracy and I might not be in town."

"What do you mean?" Cash asked Jacob, with a glance at Tracy.

Jacob looked at Tracy and asked, "Didn't Devereux tell you about our upcoming travel assignments?"

"Yes," Tracy replied. Because she'd pictured Cash shrugging and casually moving on when he found out she was leaving, she still hadn't mentioned the assignments. Too late now. She wished she'd confided in Cash on her own.

"What assignments?" Cash asked.

"Wait 'til you hear this." Jacob enthusiastically explained, "Between now and the first of the year, Devereux is sending us on ranch and range locations to all four corners of the state."

"Really? Where?" Cash asked, eerily similar to how Tracy had questioned her boss.

"Our initial stop is on the way to the northwest corner. It will be a range story in Lake County where Mount Elbert is the highest natural point of the Rocky Mountain range," Jacob said as the cloud directly overhead darkened.

"How long will you be gone?" Cash asked, looking from Jacob to Tracy.

"A while." Tracy didn't want to think about it.

"Right," Jacob said and nodded. "We'll have an expense account because Kirk said we may or may not make it back to the Springs after every assignment. Timing and interviews are still being worked out in some of the locations," Jacob told Cash. "Anyway, from Lake County, our first project of the four corners assignment takes us into Rio Blanco County in the northwest corner of the state where the White River runs smack dab through the middle of a rancher's land. I can't wait to try fly fishing in that river."

"Cool," Cash said. Tracy detected the chill in Cash's deep voice.

"Definitely," Jacob agreed. "From Rio Blanco County, we head down to the southwest corner for another range story. For that second story, in Montezuma County, Tracy will interview a geologist, a paleontologist, and an anthropologist. I'll photograph the interviews, surroundings, and prehistoric rock carvings called petroglyphs, which are located in Mesa Verde National Park."

"Sounds interesting," Cash said. As he raised his coffee mug to his mouth, Cash pulled his hand from Tracy's grasp and adjusted his mug.

"We just found out," Tracy said, not knowing what to do with her hands.

"Like this morning?" Cash's voice sent an icy shiver through Tracy.

"Well, umm...no," she replied softly.

"After Montezuma County, for our third assignment, we drive due east across the bottom of the state to Baca County for another ranch story," Jacob said. "Tracy will interview a rancher whose land touches state borders with Kansas, New Mexico, and Oklahoma."

"Wow," Cash said and looked at Tracy. "Is that right?"

"I don't know." Tracy felt the tension in Cash's body without even touching him.

"Yes, that's right, Cash," Jacob said, missing the friction. "After that, sometime around Christmas or New Year's we will have made a full circle of the state. Our fourth and final project is in the northeast corner on a horse ranch in Sedgwick County. Weather permitting, we're scheduled to ride and hike the Pony Express Trail through the sandstones and visit Fort Sedgwick. That fort was the deserted military post portrayed in the movie *Dances with Wolves*. Devereux wants Tracy to give the story an old West spin."

"Does he?" Cash asked her.

"I guess," Tracy replied.

"I guess Dude will become a semi-permanent resident of Dog Party USA," Cash said and with a spin of his left wrist tossed the remainder of his coffee onto the ground. At the sound of his name, Dude nuzzled up against Cash's leg and Cash petted his head.

"Cash, thanks again." Jacob extended his hand and Cash shook with him. "Tracy, I know you said you don't need a ride today, so I'll see you back in the office next week. We can work with Devereux on finalizing details of our assignments."

"Okay," Tracy said, feeling sick to her stomach. Jacob stepped forward and gave her a hug. She hugged him back and said, "Bye, Jacob. Drive safely."

"Will do. Bye, Dude." Jacob got into his car and waved goodbye to them out of the driver's window as he headed down the drive to the highway.

"When did Devereux tell you?" Cash asked her, not moving.

"Wednesday," Tracy said, looking up at him as a couple of droplets of rain hit her.

"Wednesday?" Cash repeated with a frown. "Talk about being left in the dark. Were you planning to tell me?"

"Cash, of course I was."

"Or were you going to ghost me again like you did after our first night together?"

"I didn't ghost you. I thought you'd ghosted me the next day."

"No." Cash shook his head. "Don't turn this around on me, Tracy. I'm not the one taking off to *all four corners of the state*."

"I'm conflicted about it, Cash," Tracy said. How could she explain that she feared he'd simply go along his merry way when she told him?

"Conflicted?" He chuckled, but it wasn't a happy one. "Did you tell Kirk you were conflicted?"

"No."

"No," Cash repeated and nodded.

"Remember I told you I wanted to write children's books and work from home?"

"I remember offering you the job of running the lodge... on *Thursday*." Cash turned to her and frowned.

"I could do that, Cash, and write my books."

"Kirk told you about the assignments on Wednesday. I offered you that job the very next day. That would have been the opportune time to tell me you were leaving town instead of accepting the lodge job."

"Your lodge won't even be started by the time I leave."

"So, you're planning on going." It wasn't a question.

"I have to make a living, Cash."

"I understand. But if I knew I was getting ready to leave El Paso County and didn't know when I'd be back, I would have told you."

"I didn't know if you'd care, Cash." Tracy's throat ached and her eyes stung.

Under a day's growth of beard, Cash's jaw clenched. "I don't know either, Tracy." At the harsh tone in Cash's voice, Dude whimpered.

"Where did you see me going tomorrow?" Tracy asked.

"I said you could stay as long as you wanted. I didn't see you going anywhere."

"Then you should have said something, Cash."

"You should have, too, dammit."

Cash threw his mug. It hit the blacktop side road close to where he'd plucked her off the ground while riding Captain. The mug smashed into pieces like Tracy's heart. Her stomach hurt, her hands trembled, and her knees shook.

"I don't know how to make this right, so Dude and I will leave."

"Good timing," Cash growled as rain fell in torrents. "Here comes your ride."

Tracy tore her eyes off Cash and looked toward the highway. Two vehicles slowed and turned under the Triple C Ranch-East sign. The car in front was a Cavalry Blue Rav4, followed by a dealership car. Cash jammed his hands into his front jeans pockets as Tracy gripped her hands at her waist. When the vehicles came to a stop in front of Cash and Tracy, Dude stood up and barked. The gentleman driving the Rav4 Crossover SUV exited the car and, smiling, ran forward through the downpour, dangling keys.

"Is this the pretty redhead you told me about who gets these keys?" the man asked Cash.

"She's the one," Cash replied and turned to Tracy. "Surprise."

"Here you go," the car dealer said to Tracy and placed the keys in her hands. "This brand spanking new Rav4 was special ordered for you and arrived this morning."

Flustered and stunned, Tracy looked at Cash and said, "No, no—I can't take it."

The car dealer looked at her, then at Cash and said, "It's bought and paid for so I hope one of you will take it."

"You need to get home, right?"

"I can Uber it, Cash."

"Maybe or maybe not with a wet dog," Cash said as the car dealer shrugged.

"I'll pay the Uber driver extra," Tracy said.

"Calvary Blue to your rescue, but suit yourself," Cash growled. Turning to the car dealer, he shook his hand and said, "Thank you." The salesman nodded and scurried in the rain toward the dealership car where a coworker waited to take him back into town. Looking at Dude, Cash said, "Gotta go, pal." Leaving the front door to the house open, Cash sauntered toward the side road. Dude trotted after him, but Cash slashed his hand toward Tracy and told the dog, "Stay." At Cash's command, Dude stopped in his tracks and sat in the pouring rain. Then to Tracy, as Cash walked around the corner, he called over his shoulder, "Take the SUV."

Tears streaming down her cheeks, Tracy stood in the rainstorm watching Cash vanish.

CHAPTER THIRTY-FIVE

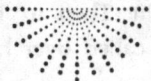

"*W*hat the hell are you doing here?" Winston hollered at his daughter and some guy, sniffing something off the backs of their hands while loitering at the edge of Tammy Dalton's property.

"Came to help you look for it," Donna said, walking forward.

"Look for what?" Winston played dumb. Pointing at the disheveled man following her, whose clothes had seen cleaner days, he asked, "Who the hell is he?"

"Gerald. My friend from the magazine who's been helping us," Donna replied.

Gripping the handle of a shovel, Winston said, "You were never supposed to bring him here, Donna."

With a sweep of her hand at the property, she said, "You're not getting anywhere finding it by yourself. Right?"

"None of your business." Winston watched his greed reflected in the unnatural gleam of Donna's eyes as she and the guy named Gerald observed the front and side yards where, at last count, a hundred and twenty-three freshly dug holes littered the ground. He'd been digging these holes for days, hence the tinfoil on the outsides of the windows. "I don't need your help."

"Where's Tammy Dalton?" Donna asked, stepping over and around the holes.

"Who?" Winston asked stupidly, stalling. He glanced at the truck where his new pawnshop gun was hidden in the console.

"Tammy Dalton, like in Tracy Dalton," Gerald sneered. "Like in the Dalton Gang?"

Closing in on him, with Gerald at her side, Donna said, "Daddy dear, we all know you're hoping Tammy and her dead husband took after his outlaw ancestors and buried their money."

Tammy's husband was dead, thanks to him snapping the old geezer's neck. Nervously, Winston headed straight for the truck and said, "I'm aerating the soil as a favor for Tammy."

Donna's laugh was shrill to the point of maniacal. "So, you already murdered Tammy Dalton because she wouldn't tell you where she hid all her money?"

"I found out she didn't have no money," Winston said, sidling up to the truck.

"Yeah, right," Donna spat. "That's not what you said the last time we talked."

"If the old gal is dead, out here in the middle of nobody and nowhere, we can dig until we find it," Gerald said, studying the holes. "It's in a waterproof box of some kind."

"Y'all need to get," Winston said. Keeping his eye on them, he yanked open the passenger's door and reached toward the console.

"We'll *get* when we get our money," Donna said, putting her right hand inside her purse.

"I said there ain't no money!" Winston turned and threw the shovel at them.

"Whatever," Gerald said. "Thanks for the shovel to bury you."

Winston grabbed the gun out of the console as Donna pulled a pistol out of her purse. She was faster. Winston took the surprise bullet to the middle of his chest. Donna's crazed laugh was the last thing he heard before he hit the ground dead.

~

"I'M SURPRISED TO SEE YOU HITTIN' TOWN ALONE, CASH-MAN," Richard said at Southside Suzy's.

"Me too," Cash muttered, standing at the bar as he threw back another shot of whiskey.

Richard made eye contact with Vince who was drying glasses behind the bar. Cash had a feeling Vince had texted or called Richard and Suzy to come check on him. With that in mind, he pulled out his cell phone and turned it off without checking for messages or calls.

"Where's that beautiful redhead you introduced to us?" Suzy asked, concern in her voice.

"I don't know," Cash said as Richard and Suzy settled in on either side of him.

"How about something to eat to go with that whiskey?" Vince asked.

"Thanks, but I'm okay, Vince," Cash said.

He heard Suzy order something for him anyway and was vaguely aware of Richard and Vince sticking close by. As Cash drank, his mind wandered. Earlier, he had stalked to his stables. He'd grabbed Captain's saddle from the tack room and carried it to the horse's stall. Sam was running the store, had seen him, and asked where he was riding in the rain. Cash had paused as thunder rolled and decided it wasn't fair to Captain to ride him unnecessarily in weather as foul as his mood. Cash stood at the entrance of the stables, glaring through the pain and rain at the cabin Tracy had occupied as Sam stood beside him.

"Who agreed to that all-female dude ranch week, Sam?" Cash had asked his longtime friend that question again like he had the day they'd met Tracy Dalton.

"You did, boss," Sam had replied and placed his hand on Cash's shoulder.

They'd talked some, stood in companionable silence some and eventually closed the store. Cash had backed his Mustang out of the garage and driven around the house. The front door was closed now and the Rav4 sat where the car dealer had parked it. Wondering if Tracy was still in the house, he'd checked. The house felt oddly silent and deserted. He had found the Rav4 car keys on the hall table, but Tracy and Dude were long gone.

"Dammit," Cash had cursed, got back in the Mustang and peeled away from his ranch.

No sooner did he hit the highway than Cash received a call. It was from the Ranchers Gun Club and Shooting Range where he, Chase, and Derek were all members. Along with the Rav4, he'd ordered a Smith & Wesson M&P Shield EZ pistol for Tracy. He headed toward the gun club. The weapon would protect her if need be. Like the SUV, the gun was paid for so he might as well pick it up along with bullets. He'd ask Jeff or somebody to deliver it to her. In the parking lot of the club, he'd locked the pistol in the glove box of the truck.

Phone in hand, he'd called Chase and told his brother Tracy was gone so not to expect them for dinner. Chase had urged him to come to dinner anyway. Cash had thanked him and declined. In the Springs, he could call or run into any number of women to console him. He had passed the exit to Tracy's apartment and headed to Southside Suzy's. He'd barely made it to the bar when Delilah and Desiree had circled him as fast and tightly as they raced around a barrel. He'd been so gruff, they'd left in a huff. Cash had chuckled at his unintentional rhyme and then frowned, wondering at his own actions of chasing them off. Suzy had also left to take care of customers and Lobo had come for Richard.

"T-bone cowboy steak and baked potato," came a sweet and familiar voice.

Cash tossed back another shot, which Vince said was his last, and looked to his left. "Hi, Stella." He had an inkling Suzy had asked Richard's daughter to serve him, figuring he wouldn't refuse the meal if she were the one who set it before him. "Thank you."

"You're welcome," Stella said and smiled. "Enjoy and I'll be back to check on you."

Vince winked at her, smiled at Cash, and then said, "I heard this steak came from a ranch called Triple C-Central, so it'll be the best you've had."

Cash nodded at the kindness shown him. Pulling up a barstool, he sat and said, "You're the best, too, Vince."

Cash wasn't hungry and despite being fairly drunk, he wouldn't have ordered food. But his friends had gone to the trouble on his behalf, so he sliced up a bite of steak. He didn't receive a bill but knew about what his meal cost. After managing a few more swallows of his steak and potato, he smacked his money on the bar along with a hefty tip for Stella. However, he wasn't nearly sober enough to suit Vince. Vince snapped his fingers and the next thing Cash knew, Tommy-Gun and Blade were escorting him down the hall to Vince and Suzy's private office.

"Where are your keys, Cash-man?" Richard asked as two of his most trusted men maneuvered him toward a leather sofa.

"I can Uber it to my ranch," Cash replied. The irony of an Uber ride made him laugh.

"Keys, Cash," Richard said. "Otherwise, I'll call Chase or Derek to come get you."

"No, don't bother 'em," Cash muttered and handed Richard the keys to his Mustang.

"Good deal," Richard said. "Take a load off and sleep."

Cash closed his eyes and when he opened them again, it was Sunday morning. He sat up on the sofa and plowed his hands through his hair. The restaurant/bar was closed and quiet. His keys lay on top of a note that said his steak and potato were in a white sack in the office fridge. Cash figured he would have made it home all in one piece, but he didn't approve of nor was he in the habit of drinking and driving. Therefore, he was thankful his friends had stopped him from taking the risk of killing himself or someone else. Wondering what time it was, he pulled his phone out of his pocket and turned it on.

He had texts from Chase and Sam wanting to make sure he was okay. He texted back that he was fine. He had a hang-over, but he didn't mention that. Served him right. He also realized he had a voicemail from Tracy. He placed his finger on the message, ready to swipe and delete it. Since when had a woman driven him to drink? Never. But was that her fault or his? His.

Cash tapped the cell phone screen and listened.

"Cash, you said once I was brave. I'm sorry I wasn't brave enough to tell you that I love you. I'm sorry I wasn't brave enough to tell you about the travel assignment I didn't want and have since turned down. I can't stop crying. Dude won't eat. We're at my apartment. I love you so much, Cash. Dude loves you too. If we can at least be friends, please come see us."

Cash grabbed his cowboy hat off a table, got his food out of the fridge, and wrote a quick 'thank you' on the note. Keys in hand, he left the office and strode down the hall. The front door was such that it let him out and locked behind him. He strode down the sidewalk to his Mustang.

CHAPTER THIRTY-SIX

Tracy lay curled up on her sofa as Dude stared out the living room window.

"Cash isn't coming, Dude," Tracy said and blew her nose. She'd taken a shower this morning and cried. She'd blow-dried her hair and cried. She'd tugged on a tummy shirt and bikini panties and cried. "It's been twelve hours since I left him that voicemail."

Dude glanced at her and looked back out of the window. The German shepherd whimpered, then barked. Tracy sat up on the sofa and sniffled. When two hard knocks sounded on the door, Tracy wiped her eyes and stood. Dude loped across the room, tail wagging. The dog's reaction told Tracy exactly who was on the other side of the door. Heart pounding, Tracy raced across the room, unlocked the door, and flung it open.

"I love you, too, Tracy."

Cash Cooper. The love of her life. Tracy saw a flash of a brown cowboy hat on dark-brown hair. Brows creased over cobalt eyes riveted on her. Shadow of a black beard. Snug black tee shirt and blue jeans. White sack in hand. Leaning forward, he swept her up and into his arms.

"Cash," she breathed.

With her arms circling his neck and her legs clamping

around his waist, Cash walked into the apartment and kicked the door shut with a booted foot. Dude placed his front paws on Cash's right thigh and whimpered. Holding Tracy with the white sack at the small of her back, Cash reached down with his other hand and scratched the dog's head. Cash's mouth closed over Tracy's and she kissed him, pouring every ounce of her love into the man whom she'd feared never to see again. When he gently broke the kiss, she smiled at him. With a steely glare, Cash tilted his head and gave her a scolding, half grin.

"Do you always open the door in your panties?"

"Dude told me it was you."

"Yeah, I heard him." He looked down at Dude. "I didn't forget about you, boy."

Dude barked. Cash smiled at Tracy and patted her fanny. Tracy put her feet on the floor but kept her arms around his neck. Cash held her close and kissed her again. Tracy never wanted to let Cash go. Dude leaned against his leg. Tracy loosened her embrace and looked up at Cash.

"Thank you for coming to see us."

"Some little girl left me a voicemail crying and saying she loves me." He cocked a brow.

"That was me," Tracy whispered and hugged him again. Then tears trickled down her cheeks and between sobs she said, "I love you so much, Cash. I know I've brought you nothing but trouble. I'm so sorry for every—"

"I'm sorry too." Cash tossed the white sack onto the counter separating the small living room from the kitchen and cupped his hands to her face. "I'm a thirty-year-old grown-ass businessman and I should have been able to negotiate with you better than I did."

"I'm a twenty-four-year-old grown-ass journalist and I should have been able to communicate my feelings into words with you better than I did."

"This whole being in love thing is a first for me and if you give me the chance, I'll get better at it," Cash said and thumbed the tears off her cheeks. "I promise."

"This is my first time being in love and I promise to get better at it too."

"Just promise I'm your first, last, and only."

"My first, last, and only. I promise, Cash."

"I promise you're my last and only, Tracy." Cash kissed her again, and Dude woofed his approval. Cash snared her hand and strode to the counter. "Dude, that same little girl told me between sobs you aren't eating." Cash picked up the white sack and gave it a shake. Dude barked and licked his chops. "So, I brought you a steak and potato."

"Did you hear that, Dude?" Tracy asked, walking around the counter. Cash handed her the sack, and after cutting the steak and potato into bites, she emptied it on top of the untouched hard dog food into Dude's dog bowl. "Thank you, Cash," she said as Dude devoured the food. "Are you hungry?"

"I am now that I've seen you," he said. "Dude's eating last night's dinner."

Self-consciously, Tracy ran her fingers through her unruly hair and said, "I-I wasn't expecting you, so I don't have makeup or decent clothes on."

"And yet you're absolutely beautiful, and I love you." His grin was hot and cocky. "I'm wearing the same clothes I had on yesterday."

She said, "And yet I love you."

"The jeans are fine, but my shirt and shorts need washed."

"I'll do a load of laundry for us." The thought of washing clothes had been a chore far too difficult to tackle yesterday. But today, washing Cash's tee shirt and boxers with her clothes would be nothing short of a thrill. "Okay?"

Cash nodded, placed his cowboy hat on the counter, and pulled her into his arms. His mouth closed over hers and she ran her tongue across his lips. Their kiss deepened and his hands slid down her back and cupped her fanny. She wound her arms around Cash's tapered waist and slipped her hands into his back pockets.

"You didn't take the SUV like I told you," he said between kisses.

"I'll make it up to you," she whispered, standing on tiptoes as she kissed him.

"How?"

"I'll treat you to a pizza for brunch ."

"Okay." He patted her butt cheeks with both hands. He stood back and pulled his tee shirt over his head. "I need to take a shower before I take you to bed."

"Oh, so you think you're taking me to bed?"

"I know so."

"So do I," she giggled. He pulled off his boots and she admired him, from his thick, brown hair down to his sock-covered feet. "You know you're seriously gorgeous, right?"

His smile said he knew it. "If you say so."

"I say so." She led him to the bathroom and took a towel out of the linen closet. Placing the towel on the counter next to the sink, Tracy put her hands to his fly.

Cash touched a finger under her chin, and as she unbuttoned his jeans, he said, "I want to wake up with you in my bed from now on, not dream about you alone."

Tracy wrapped her hand around his wrist and looking up at him, said, "I want that too." Cash let her tug his jeans down and off. His desire for her was obvious, and she cupped her hands to the hard bulge in his boxers before stripping them off him. "I want you, Cash."

"If you don't agree to take the SUV, I don't take a shower and we don't go to bed."

"You drive a hard bargain," she said with a suggestive grin.

"You'd know."

"Give me your socks and we'll see what happens." Tracy laughed and turned on the water. "Shall I order a large pizza with everything?"

"Yes, and wings," Cash said, tugging off his socks.

With his socks, boxers, and tee shirt, she left him to his shower. Making her way to the living room, Tracy could hardly feel the carpet under her feet. Never had she been so happy, so relieved, and so full of hope for the future. She ordered the food, put Cash's laundry in with hers, and returned to her bedroom. Dude was sound asleep in his dog bed with a full belly, and she could have sworn there was a smile on the German shepherd's face.

Tracy dabbed on mascara and lipstick and brushed her hair. From the end of her bed, where she'd tossed it, she picked up a short sundress with a sexy, scalloped neckline dipping in a vee. The soft white dress was decorated with passion fruit berries the same reddish-brown as her cowboy boots and the berry leaves were turquoise. She'd ordered the dress while at Cash's ranch because he'd mentioned her eyes being turquoise and she knew it would go with the boots he'd bought for her. Finding it on her doorstep the previous day, she'd thought Cash would never see it. She shimmied into the dress now, elated that he would.

Returning to the kitchen, she set plates and napkins on the counter as the doorbell rang. Hurrying into the living room, she opened the front door to a slender pizza delivery man wearing the pizza chain's red and green collared shirt and matching ball cap. Probably about her age, he greeted her with a grin that grew bigger and toothy. She reminded him she'd paid online but would give him the tip in cash. She took the pizza and wings, set them on the kitchen counter, picked up his tip, and retraced her steps across the room.

"My name is Tad," he said, lounging in the doorway. "I don't think I've delivered to you before, Miss—" He paused, waiting for her to say her name as he accepted the tip.

"First time I've ordered," Tracy said. "Thank you."

"I would have remembered you," Tad said, looking her up and down as he leaned against the doorframe.

Grasping the doorknob as a sign for him to leave, she said, "Thanks again, Tad."

"Yeah, sure." With a glance past her, Tad instantly jerked

himself away from the doorframe. "Welcome." Swiveling on his heel, Tad skedaddled off the patio.

Tracy closed the door and turned to see Cash standing in the middle of the living room. In his jeans, shirtless and barefoot, with a scowl on his face and biceps bulging in the muscular arms crossed above his six-pack stomach, Dude stood at his side.

"Tad will never deliver here again," Tracy said with a laugh and shake of her head.

Taking in the passion fruit on her dress, Cash's gaze lingered on her cleavage. His eyes met hers as he sauntered toward her with a wicked grin. "You look good enough to eat, spitfire."

CHAPTER THIRTY-SEVEN

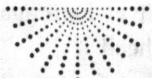

$\mathscr{I}$t was early afternoon when Cash heard the cell phone signal a text. He opened his eyes and saw Tracy's bedroom instead of his. After making love and eating the pizza and wings, they'd crawled into her bed. Neither had slept well the night before, and exhausted, they had napped.

Cash closed his eyes and yawned around a happy, satisfied grin. Tracy lay snuggled in his arms with her head on his pillow and her leg between his. She moaned softly and hugged him before rolling out of his embrace. He stretched and stacked his hands under his head as she picked her phone up from the bedside table.

"Cash, it's from my grandmother."

Opening his eyes again as Tracy sat up, with the sheet barely covering her breasts, he joked, "She's not at your front door, is she?"

"No," Tracy said, looking from the message on her phone to him.

"Isn't this around the time she said they'd head toward the Springs?"

"Yes, but her text says for me to please come home today."

"Call her."

Tracy scrolled to the number. She shook her head when the call went unanswered and said, "Grandma, it's Tracy. Please call me." She hung up and told Cash, "I've called her twice since she and Winston said they were going to Punkin Center. But it went to voicemail both times. Each time, a couple of minutes later, she texted back saying she was having a great time in Punkin Center with his daughter, Brenda."

Cash sat up and leaned against the headboard. "Punkin Center is where they were supposed to have been the past week or so. Right?"

"Right." Tracy nodded. "But if she wants me to come home, she's back in Wild Horse."

"Or she never made it to Punkin Center," Cash said. "Are there any neighbors or friends you could call to check on her?"

"No." Tracy rubbed her forehead. "Being so isolated is one of the reasons I tried to convince her to move here. She has no one."

"Except Winston."

"Yes." Tracy grimaced. "I've never been convinced his intentions were good."

"We've got nothing more important to do today than checking on your grandmother," Cash said as Dude rested his chin on the foot of the bed.

Tracy's cell phone signaled another text, and she said, "That will be Grandma texting instead of calling me." Tracy read it and this time, she quickly scooted out of bed.

"What did she say?" Cash asked, swinging his legs over the side of the bed.

"She said they never made it to Punkin Center because she sprained her ankle and couldn't walk. She didn't tell me because she didn't want to worry me. But she's out of food and Winston is gone." Tracy looked at Cash with a mixture of confusion and alarm in her eyes.

"Everything's going to be okay," Cash said.

Tracy nodded. When Cash handed her the pretty

sundress, saying he liked it, she put it back on. She grabbed his clean clothes out of the dryer and received a second text.

"Grandma says for me to rent a car and come alone."

"Call her again. She's obviously holding her cell phone." Stepping into his boxers and then his jeans, Cash pulled on his shirt and cocked a brow. "Ask why you have to come alone."

Tracy held up her index finger as another text came through. "She says she's not up to having company. She says she'll pay me back for the rental car."

"Forget that. Let's go."

"But what about me coming alone?"

"To face whatever is going on there by yourself? Hell no," Cash said, stepping into his boots. "Do these texts even sound like your grandmother?"

"No, they don't. I think someone else is telling her what to say or is using her phone."

"Text back that you're on your way. Alone."

Cash let Dude out and packed up his bowls and dog food. Tracy threw her freshly laundered Western clothes along with some other things into her bag. She locked the front door, and they headed outside to Cash's Mustang. Leaving through the front gate, to which Cash had remembered the code that morning, he headed straight for the interstate. They soon took a cutoff and headed to Triple C-East. Using his hands-free method of calling his brother-in-law, Cash contacted Derek. They listened to his advice.

Wringing her hands, Tracy said to the men, "Wild Horse is an unincorporated ghost town. There are no local police to do a wellness check, Derek."

Derek suggested they call the Cheyenne County Sheriff's Department to check things out. He said to be sure to mention his name as well as that of Owen Custis.

"How far away is the sheriff's department from your grandmother's house?" Cash asked.

"At least forty miles."

"We'll get there before the cops can."

Derek wanted to go with them. But he and Owen were in Denver delivering eight Percherons to the Denver Police Department. Transporting them on Sunday meant the horses would be well-rested for the police on Monday morning. In any event, Derek and Owen wouldn't be back at Triple C-West for several hours. Cash and Tracy thanked Derek and promised to keep him posted.

"Should we tell Chase what's going on?"

"He'd want to go, too, but he and Bob are in the north forty driving cattle and it would take him too long to get to Triple C-East." Indicting the glove box, Cash said, "There are two guns in there. Mine and yours. We're gonna fly and take them by surprise."

"WE'RE NOT GOING TO THE TROUBLE OF BURYING HIM," DONNA snickered, taking over where Winston had left off. She laughed as she and Gerald sat at the Dalton kitchen table. "Dear old daddy can burn when we set fire to the shed he painted with that flammable paint."

"I thought you said your father had already murdered the old woman," Gerald said.

"It was a guess. He was planning to burn the shed down with her in it after he found the money. He wanted her to sign the property over to him so he could live in the house. But obviously none of that happened."

"Just because I'm a closet junkie doesn't mean I'm a psycho killer like the two of you," Gerald said as he twirled Winston's gun around his finger.

"Don't..." Donna pointed her gun at him. "Don't ever call me a psycho again." When Gerald held up a hand, she set her gun between her cell phone and Tammy Dalton's. Gerald did the same and then they both snorted lines of coke off the table. As the feeling of power and energy hit her, Donna spewed, "Yeah, baby!"

"I'm not going back to jail!" Gerald howled. "I'm an editor!"

"You *were* an editor, Gerald. A lousy one," Donna snapped. "Your credentials were fake, and nobody at the magazine liked you. Why do you think Devereux planned to ship you off to North Dakota?"

"Because of you," Gerald said, his pupils enlarging into what detox had called cocaine eyes. If I hadn't gotten mixed up with you and this get-rich-quick scheme—"

"You wouldn't have blown through so much coke so fast?"

"I wouldn't have been fired," Gerald finished his sentence as he scraped another hit of cocaine into a line. "I wish you'd never found me working at that magazine."

"But you liked my get-rich-quick scheme enough to hire me, and now you're a jobless accessory to murder." Donna laughed in the way Gerald had said made his skin crawl. "Can't you see we have to kill Tammy and Tracy? Or don't you want your share of the Dalton money?"

"How does getting Tracy here equal getting the money?"

"That old bitch you locked in the shed will tell us where the money is buried when you put a gun to her Dalton Darling's head."

"Funny how you made sure I'm the only one the old woman has seen so far," he said. "Makes me wonder if you'll stab me in the back like your *dear old daddy* and Tracy."

"Winston had it coming to him, and so does Tracy."

"Too bad about Tracy, though. She would have been a sensational screw."

"You've got me, Gerald!" Donna spat. "I don't want to hear you speak her name again."

"Yeah, okay," Gerald said. He snorted his white line and shouted, "We're in godforsaken nowhere!" Wiping his nose with the back of his hand, he said, "By the time anyone comes this way, we'll be lost in the land of drugs aplenty living like royalty."

"Plenty of time to celebrate before we get to Mexico."

Donna got up from the table and as she walked into the living room, she stripped. Turning to Gerald, she flung her arms wide and jiggled her naked breasts. Seconds later he was on top of her in the middle of the floor. "We pull the trigger twice and light a match. Enemies are dead and evidence burns to the ground."

CHAPTER THIRTY-EIGHT

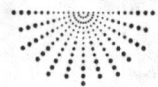

"*C*ash, there's the house," Tracy said in the helicopter while pointing toward the ground. In the distance, the two-bedroom home and small shed appeared forlorn and forgotten. "Is there room among the pine trees to land?"

"I see a spot where I can put the chopper down, but let's find out who else is here."

"What do you mean?"

"Look for a vehicle," Cash said.

"Is there something shiny on the windows of the house?"

"Yeah. Tinfoil?" he asked. "And holes in the ground everywhere."

"I see our old pickup truck," Tracy said.

"I see a white Tesla. Look, partially hidden in the *dust and dirt* of a grove of trees."

Tracy gasped and glanced at Cash. "Gerald Moles is here?"

"That son-of-a-bitch," Cash growled. With a perplexed frown, he looked at Tracy and asked, "What's his connection to your grandmother?"

"I don't—" Tracy stopped mid-sentence as the connection fell into place. "I do know."

Cash brought the helicopter down on a plateau behind a thick, taller copse of evergreens further from the house.

Shutting down the engine, they unbuckled their seat belts and exited the chopper. Cash came around to her side and handed her the Smith and Wesson he'd bought for her. Before leaving the ranch, Tracy had paid close attention as Cash demonstrated how to put the safety on and off the pistol. With the safety on, she slipped it into her purse.

"Tell me what you know," Cash said. Holding his semi-automatic Kimber Warrior .45 in his right hand, he grabbed Tracy's hand with his left one. They walked to the edge of the pine trees and stopped.

"The connection is Donna."

"To Gerald, yes. But how would she know your grandmother?"

"Her name is Donna Smith. Smith is such a common last name that it didn't dawn on me until just now that she is Winston Smith's daughter," Tracy said as Cash surveyed the area in all four directions.

"Then who is Brenda?"

"It's his fake name for Donna. I never met Donna back in the day because she's a lot older than I am and had left the area by the time I started riding the school bus Winston drove. But it all fits. Donna is the common denominator among my grandma, Winston, and Gerald. Since my grandmother sprained her ankle, do you think Winston asked them to come help him care for her?"

"Hell no. He doesn't care about your grandmother." Cash shook his head as they remained out of sight. "But what's the draw?"

"The draw?"

"What does Winston and or Donna want from your grandmother?"

"You mean like money?"

"Yes. I'm thinking all those holes in the yard that we saw from the air means somebody's looking for something. Does your grandmother have money, jewelry, treasure of some kind?"

"Like the Dalton Gang might have?" she asked, and Cash

shrugged as if anything was possible. "Not that I know of."
Staring at the house and then looking back at Cash, Tracy
said, "She and Grandpa didn't fully trust the bank and I
assumed they didn't have much money to put in a bank
anyway," Tracy said. "Then again, they did have an oil well
before it dried up."

"Could Winston have known about the oil well?"

"Yes, Winston's lived around here forever and must have
heard about it." Tracy watched Cash nod as if she had stumbled onto a clue. Tracy's grandmother's words of *look to these
walls* and *nest egg* echoed in her memory. "My grandparents
hid something inside the house."

"But Winston's been trying to find it outside," Cash said,
his eyes on the house. "How did your grandfather die?"

"He fell and broke his neck," she said. "Winston
happened to be passing by and saw him fall beside his
pickup. He gave Grandpa chest compressions."

"No. Winston was at the very least making sure your
grandfather was dead," Cash said. "Then Winston circles
back like a vulture and now your grandmother has fallen
and *at the very least* has sprained her ankle. I'm betting that's
not a coincidence."

Staying out of sight, Tracy looked up at Cash and said,
"When Gerald hired Donna at the magazine, I distinctly
remember he was the one who assigned her to Jacob
and me."

"She and Gerald are about the same age," Cash said.
"Could he be from Kit Carson too?"

"There was a Moles family in Kit Carson. I remember
because unlike Smith, Moles is not a common last name."

"Was there a son in the mix who could be Gerald?"

"I vaguely remember something now from years ago."
Tracy nodded slowly and continued, "Grandma said the
Moles' father went to prison for being a drug dealer, the
mother walked the streets as a prostitute, and a son took off
after high school." She looked at Cash and concluded,

"Gerald and Donna went to high school together, Cash. They've been working together from the start."

"It all figures," Cash agreed. "Right now, it's those three against the two of us but the sheriff and a deputy are on their way."

"What about my grandma?"

"They have her, Tracy." Cash pulled her into his arms and said, "But she won't tell them where the money is. They brought you here to make her talk."

"Dear God," Tracy gasped. "I can't believe this is happening."

"Me neither," Cash said, hugging her. "I think it's a safe bet that Winston killed your grandfather. Donna and Gerald are crazy. Jade would probably diagnose all of them as being psychopaths or sociopaths."

"As in psychopaths, it's biological, and in sociopaths, it stems from trauma?" Tracy asked.

"Exactly."

"Donna probably inherited it from Winston and who knows what happened to Gerald during his dysfunctional upbringing."

"They're on drugs and they're desperate. Dammit," Cash cursed under his breath. "If I'd known what we'd be up against, I'd have gotten the location from you and left you on my ranch."

"I wouldn't have given you the location." Tracy looked up at him and said, "Or let you come without me."

"I'm gonna call Sheriff Hunt and tell him what we know so far." Cash pulled his cell phone out of his pocket and made the call. After speaking to the Cheyenne County sheriff, he hung up and said, "Hunt and his deputy are ten minutes out."

"Cash, look," Tracy whispered as the front door to the house opened.

CHAPTER THIRTY-NINE

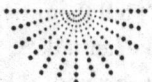

$\mathcal{G}$erald Moles opened fire in no particular direction and shouted, "Who's out there?"

Cash swept his arm across Tracy's midriff, pushing her farther into the trees and out of sight. "There's Donna," he said, seeing her dart from the back of the house toward the shed.

Moles spotted Donna, too, and hollered, "Where're you going, Donna?"

"Help me!" Donna screamed. "He's trying to kill me!"

Moles raced after Donna. Cash, holding his Kimber Warrior at his right side, stepped out of the evergreens to get a better look. Moles and Donna disappeared behind the shed. All was deathly quiet for several minutes.

"What's going on?" Tracy whispered on Cash's left side.

"Hell if I know," Cash said. "But at least they won't find the chopper over there."

A second later, a strangled female scream broke the silence.

"I think that was my grandma's voice," Tracy said, and before Cash could grab her, she bolted into the front yard of the house. "Grandma!"

"Tracy, stop!" Cash caught her and pulled her behind him. Flames shot up from the rear of the shed. "Stay here and hide," Cash said, and with his gun drawn, sprinted forward, jumping over the holes in the yard.

"Help," came a choked cry and coughing from inside the shed.

"I'm coming!" Tracy called from right behind Cash.

"Dammit, Tracy," Cash said over his shoulder. "I told you to hide."

Cash stopped short and grabbed Tracy's arm as Gerald Moles came into view. At the back of the shed, Donna stood holding a garden hose toward the flames. However, no water was forthcoming.

"Help me," Donna cried again, glancing at Cash and Tracy. "Your grandma's inside. Gerald's trying to kill her too."

"You backstabbing, lying bitch!" Gerald shouted.

Tracy took two steps forward before Cash yanked her safely behind him. Donna threw the hose down and ran toward them. Flames had already spread from the back of the shed to the sides. Another scream from inside the shed and Tracy broke free of Cash. Tracy raced toward the fire as Donna ran away from it. Moles swung his arm into the air as the women, running in opposite directions, were about to meet in the middle of the yard. Tracy was closer to Moles than Donna by at least six feet when he aimed his gun straight at Tracy.

BOOM!

The explosion from Cash's Kimber Warrior .45 blasted Moles off his feet and onto his back, sending the shot Moles had fired into the sky. Donna tried to throw herself into Cash's arms. Brushing past her, Cash ran toward Tracy and the burning building. Tracy was frantically hooking the hose up to the faucet on the side of the house. At the front of the shed, a shiny new padlock hung on the door.

"Mrs. Dalton, move away from the door," Cash called. "I'm going to shoot the lock off."

"Okay," came her fading voice, followed by coughing.

The shed was almost totally engulfed as Cash shot the

lock off and yanked open the door. Thinking on her feet, Tracy sprayed water on Cash and then at the flames licking the door. As Cash stepped into the fiery shed, Tracy rushed in close behind him with the hose, doing her best to keep the fiery inferno away from him. Cash picked Tracy's grandmother up off the floor and darted outside toward the house.

"Is she okay?" Tracy called over her shoulder as she continued to fight the fire.

"Yes," Cash said. "There's a dead body in the shed."

"Winston Smith," Tammy Dalton managed to say around another cough. Cash placed her in a lawn chair near the front door of the small house, and she told them, "Donna said the man who brought her here and locked me in the shed shot Winston in cold blood."

"Tracy, get away from that shed. It's been doused with some kind of accelerant," Cash said. Tracy tossed the hose into the shed where Winston lay dead and came running to Cash and her grandmother.

"Cash," Tracy cried and wrapped her arms around him. "Thank you, thank you, thank you, for saving my grandmother's life." Cash hugged her, let her go, and she embraced her grandmother. "Grandma, I'm so glad you're alive."

"Me, too," Tammy Dalton said and grabbed Cash's hand. Taking a deep breath of fresh air, she smiled at them. "If this here is Cash Cooper, he's a keeper."

"It is and he sure is," Tracy said.

"Thank you, Mr. Cooper. I'm Tammy."

"I'm Cash," he replied.

"Thank you, too, Tracy," Tammy said and took her hand as well.

"Have either of you spotted Donna?" Cash asked, but the women shook their heads.

Police sirens sounded and two cars from the Cheyenne County Sheriff's Department arrived in a dust-swirling stop at the edge of the yard full of holes. The officers exited their vehicles and approached with caution, hands on their guns.

"I'm Cash Cooper." Cash placed his gun on the ground and raised both his hands.

"Sheriff Hunt," the larger man said. Something caught his and the deputy's attention and they glanced int the direction where Cash knew the Tesla was hidden. Hunt spoke to the deputy, and gun drawn, the officer headed into the trees. Cash noted Hunt taking in Moles' dead body and the dying embers of the shed. "Looks like I should have brought the fire department and coroner with me."

"Yes, sir," Cash agreed, walking forward to greet him. "I shot that man on the ground a second before he fired the gun in his hand at Tracy Dalton. His name is Gerald Moles," Cash said as he and the sheriff met near the body.

"What's left of the Moles family is dead or in prison," Sheriff Hunt said.

"A second body inside the shed is Winston Smith."

"The school district fired Smith after one too many arrests for theft."

Cash and the sheriff shook hands, and Cash said, "Thanks for getting here so fast. My brother-in-law, Derek Brevard, speaks highly of you, Sheriff Hunt."

"Please call me James," the man in uniform said. "Derek is a great guy. Known him for a long time. I graduated from Coronado High School a couple years ahead of Derek. My department is in the process of buying some horses from Triple C Ranch-West."

"You won't be sorry. Derek and former El Paso County Sheriff Owen Custis turn out only the best-trained Percherons for mounted police all over the country. They're in Denver today delivering eight horses to the police department."

"I know there's a waiting list for his horses. Derek's got himself one helluva business for one helluva great cause."

"Yes, sir, he does," Cash agreed and turned toward Tracy.

"Sheriff James Hunt, this is Tracy Dalton," Cash said in introduction.

"Thank you for coming, Sheriff," Tracy said and introduced her grandmother to Hunt.

"Nice to meet you, Ms. Dalton," Sheriff Hunt said. "Folks, excuse me for a minute. I'm going to call for some backup, including the coroner and fire department." He moved a few steps away and made his call. Returning to them, he asked, "So tell me what went down here today."

"Sheriff," the deputy called before anyone could answer. With him was Donna. "Found this lady trying to leave in a dead Tesla."

"Is that right?"

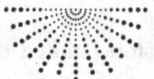

CHAPTER FORTY

"**Y**es. Sheriff Hunt, this is Donna Smith," the deputy said, glancing at Gerald's body. "Claims she was trying to escape being shot by a man named Gerald Moles."

"That dead body is Moles," Sheriff Hunt told the deputy walking past Moles.

"Ms. Smith says Moles shot her father, Winston Smith," the deputy reported.

"Yes." Donna nodded frantically. "Gerald shot my father in cold blood and hid his body in the shed right before he forced Mrs. Dalton into it."

"What are you doing here, Donna?" Tracy asked.

"Thank God you're okay, Tracy." Donna smiled at Cash. "You, too, Cash. Thank you for not letting Gerald kill me or Tracy," she said and reached a hand toward Tracy.

"Don't touch her," Cash ordered, clenching his jaw and narrowing his eyes at Donna.

"Take Smith's statement over there." Sheriff Hunt pointed to the deputy's vehicle as Donna lowered her hand away from Tracy. Turning back to Tracy and Cash, the sheriff asked, "What do you know about her?"

They told him about the attack on Cash at the gas station and Tracy ended with, "Donna was recently released from a detox unit in a psychiatric hospital in Colorado Springs. It may be important for you to know that she was held for seventy-two hours due to a homicidal threat she made against her father, Winston Smith."

Other details were added and Cash said, "Moles went to jail from the gas station. Donna must have gotten him out on bail. And I think somebody doused the shed with accelerant."

"So that's why Winston painted the shed," Tammy said. "He planned all along to burn it down with me in it."

Sheriff Hunt informed them, "Crime lab is on the way here and the fire chief can tell us what we need to know about the shed. I'll take your statements here, but I think I'm going to haul Donna Smith in for further questioning." Addressing Tammy, he said, "Ms. Dalton, an ambulance is also on its way to take you to the hospital in Colorado Springs."

"Perfect," Tammy said and took his hand. "Thank you, Sheriff Hunt. I'm sure I could benefit from x-rays and a boot or cast for my ankle."

A small army of first responders and other law enforcement were soon on hand. Sheriff Hunt was in command and took charge over the crime scene. Cash called Chase and Derek to let them know what had happened and to assure them all was well. He also called Coop who was taking care of Dude. The German shepherd and Australian cattle dog had become fast friends.

"Grandma, I can pack for you, and we will meet you at the hospital in the Springs," Tracy said. "What else do you need me to do before Cash and I leave Wild Horse?"

Tammy hadn't moved from her spot in the lawn chair because of her ankle, but she motioned to Cash and asked, "If you would help me inside, I want to show the two of you something."

"Of course," Cash said. He carefully plucked her out of the chair as Tracy went before them and opened the front door.

Inside, Cash placed Tammy on the sofa, and she said, "Now I know why Winston put that tinfoil on the windows. He didn't want me to see how he had torn up the ground digging for money that wasn't there."

"I wished I'd figured out sooner how evil Winston was," Tracy said.

"Tracy and I began putting two and two together once we saw Gerald Moles' car hidden in the trees," Cash said. "We all underestimated them."

"They lured you here, Tracy, to make me tell them where the money is," Tammy said, confirming Cash's suspicion. "I'm so sorry."

"What money?" Tracy asked.

"I'm getting to that." Grandma took her hand and pulled her down beside her on the sofa. She patted the cushion on the other side of her and Cash took a seat. "If not for you, Cash, Tracy and I would be dead," she said bluntly. "Thank you."

"You're welcome," Cash said to Tammy and looked past her to Tracy. "I love your granddaughter,

"I can see that. I can see she loves you too," Tammy said. "Don't you, Tracy?"

Tracy placed her left hand over her heart to reply, "With all my heart."

Cash reached across Tammy and took Tracy's hand. "If I thought she'd say yes, I'd put a ring on this finger." He stroked her ring finger.

"What would you say, Tracy?" Grandma asked.

"Yes." Tracy's heart raced, and she repeated, "Cash, I'd say yes a million times."

"Excellent," Tammy said as Cash winked and let go of Tracy's hand. "Now, here's what I need the two of you to know before the ambulance arrives." Tammy pointed straight across the living room. "Behind the cheap paneling covering that wall is where the money from the oil well is hidden."

Tracy nodded and glanced at Cash. Then they both

looked at the paneled wall. "What do you want us to do?" Tracy asked.

"When everyone outside is gone, tear that paneling down and put the money into pillowcases. It's all for you, Tracy. Grandpa and I insulated that wall of the house, a bit unconventionally, with the money we made from that well." A sigh escaped her, and she said, "We easily lived on our social security checks and bills were debited from our checking account. I can transfer that account to a Colorado Springs bank. We'll sell this place because I will never come back here."

"Grandma, that makes me so happy," Tracy said. "I've wanted you to come live with me in Colorado Springs since the day I left Wild Horse."

"I know, honey. But there was a method to my madness," Tammy said. "I'm not quite as eccentric as people may think. I felt I needed to stay here and guard the money until you were established somewhere safe and secure. There's nothing here for me now that you and Grandpa are gone." To Cash, she said, "A man who risked being shot to save my granddaughter's life and who proposed before he knew about the money sounds safe and secure to me."

"Thank you," Cash said.

"Speaking of saying yes to Cash a million times, there's at least two million dollars hidden in the wall." Tammy laughed and said, "She comes with a dowry, Mr. Cooper."

Cash chuckled. "That money's all hers, ma'am."

Tracy said, "Wait until you see Triple C Ranch-East, Grandma." With a smile at Cash, she added softly, "And the new Rav4 Cash bought for me."

Cash grinned. "I hope you'll both stay on the ranch with me, Mrs. Dalton."

"Tammy," she reminded him. "Thank you, I'd be delighted."

A knock on the front door sounded and Cash answered it. The paramedics entered with a stretcher. Tracy hugged her grandmother and then she was carefully placed on the gurney. She and Cash followed them outside to the ambulance.

"We'll see you in Colorado Springs," Tracy called to her grandma before a paramedic closed the ambulance doors. She turned to Cash and hugged him. "This has been the most terrifying day of my life. And the happiest."

Sheriff Hunt approached and said, "My deputy just left. He's taking Donna Smith into the office. Her story keeps changing and has more holes in it than this front yard. She's already asked for a lawyer. If she's not charged with anything, she'll be turned loose. Doesn't mean she won't eventually be charged. But even if she is charged with something right away, she could get out on bail. So, watch your backs."

"Yes, sir, we will," Cash said.

Tracy felt Cash's arm wrap around her shoulders. They thanked the sheriff and the fire chief, and eventually, one by one, the army disappeared from the property.

"Ready to tear down a wall?" Tracy asked Cash.

"Yes, but first I want you to know I'm serious about marrying you."

"I'm serious about marrying you, too, Cash."

"I know it's only been two weeks, but you're the one, spitfire."

"I knew you were the one the day we met, big'n bad."

"So did I." Cash smiled, kissed her, and wrapped her in his arms. Holding her he asked, "How about I come up with a ring and you come up with a wedding date?"

Tears trickled down Tracy's cheeks, and her voice shook with happiness. "Yes."

CHAPTER FORTY-ONE

"*I*n case of emergency, you'll have a gun at your fingertips. Just make a fist and jam your right hand through the thin paper directly across from the chain up here," Cash said on Triple C-East, with Tracy on his left and Dude on his right as they stood at the back door of the house. "There's a Glock on a shelf inside this wall."

"Got it," Tracy said, making a fist with her right hand. "Just punch through the paper."

"Right," Cash said. "Derek showed Chase and me this trick a few years ago. They both have guns concealed at their front and back doors too. The kids don't know about it, but even so, the placement is high enough off the floor they can't get to the gun," he explained, "Like Derek said, no bad guy who shows up at a house expects the homeowner to pull a gun out of the wall."

"No, I wouldn't think so," Tracy said.

Two weeks earlier, they had filled pillowcases with hundred-dollar bills in currency denomination bands of ten thousand. Tammy Dalton's sprained ankle had been properly treated and she'd been released from the hospital. Cash and Tracy had picked her up and settled her into his house. A home health nurse was seeing to her as well. Tammy had since transferred her checking account to the same bank

Cash and Tracy both used. But she would have no part of the money from the wall. Cash recommended his financial adviser and Tracy had invested two and a half million dollars into the stock market. Another fifty grand went into her checking account.

A week ago, Sheriff Hunt had called Cash to tell him that so far Donna Smith had only been charged with setting fire to the shed which indeed was painted with an accelerant. They suspected she shot Winston Smith and had found the unregistered gun used to kill him in the Wild Horse woods, but it was wiped clean of prints. They were building a murder case against her, but in the meantime, a lawyer had convinced a judge to let the arsonist out on bail. She was not to leave the state.

"C'mon, I want to show you where the gun is hidden at the front door," Cash said. "With the stables, store, café, and cabins out back, the front door is actually more isolated than the rear door of the house." With Tracy's dainty hand in his, Cash walked her through the house. Dude wagging his tail, knew the words *front door* and led the way. "Donna Smith is an angry, vengeful person. Like Sheriff Hunt said, we have to watch our backs."

"Yes," Tracy agreed.

"Here," Cash said in the foyer at the front door, lightly tapping the hollow spot where the gun was hidden in the wall. "I don't expect we'd have to reload, but I think there's a box of bullets in the drawer of that table. You know—the table where you left your car keys the day you refused to take your Rav4?"

Tracy smothered a grin at his teasing and said, "I love my Rav4."

"Yeah, yeah." Cash knew she did. "Just check the drawer for bullets, spitfire."

"Okay, okay." With a smile, Tracy pulled open the drawer and beside the bullets was a jeweler's box. "Cash." She glanced up at him. "Is that what I think it is?"

"Open it and find out," he said and noticed her hands

shake slightly. He loved her so much, he hoped he'd chosen well at the jewelry store. Tracy slowly opened the box, stared for a moment, and fainted against him. "Tracy," Cash said in surprise as he caught her.

With a huge smile and her sexy giggle, Tracy opened her eyes. "I love it!"

Cash chuckled and grabbed the box from her. As he knelt on one knee, Dude sat next to him. They both looked up at Tracy, and Cash asked, "Will you marry me, Tracy Dalton?"

"Yes," Tracy whispered. Dude barked, and Cash grinned. Cash removed the ring from the box. Tracy kneeled on both knees in front of him, and he slipped the ring onto her finger. Placing her hands to his face, she said, "I'd love to marry you, Cash Cooper."

Cash kissed her, stood, and pulled her into his arms. "The jeweler said this is a two-carat princess cut. Not only fit for the princess of the cinnamon kiss," he began as they both stared at the ring on her finger, "but with the shape being square, it reminds me of Colorado, where I found you and will always love and protect you."

Tracy's turquoise eyes shimmered with tears as she looked from her ring to him and said, "I will always love and protect you, too, north, south, east, and west."

"All four corners. Sounds good to me," Cash said and kissed her.

Familiar voices were heard as footsteps sounded on the porch. Cash opened the door to Coop and Tammy. It had been love at first sight. Coop liked to say Tammy was the only girl he cared to take to a barn dance and Tammy would reply Coop was the only man on her dance card. With them were Rachel and Martyman as the foursome had gone gallivanting and then to lunch. Cash hadn't seen his grandfather so happy in years. Thanks to Tracy, Cash knew such happiness.

"Look!" With excitement, Tracy held up her left hand and wiggled her fingers.

Cash told them, "You're all just in time to help us celebrate."

CHAPTER FORTY-TWO

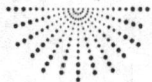

"*I* think we've selected the perfect photos to go with the different parts of our story," Tracy said.

"I think so too," Jacob agreed with a nod.

It was late Friday afternoon, and they were sitting on the sofa in Cash's living room. On the coffee table before them Jacob had placed his new laptop with an extra large screen. Dude lay snoozing near Tracy's feet. Since the trouble in Wild Horse whenever he and Tracy were separated, Cash had made a point to leave the German shepherd with her in his stead.

"I'm particularly fond of this photo of Cash in mid-air jumping from Captain Jack to the ground after lassoing one of the cows," Tracy said and pointed to it.

"One of the best." Jacob tapped his hand to his video camera. "It came from the video I shot while the wranglers were branding. That photo of Cash is being titled; *Roping'n Rawhide*." Turning to her, he asked, "Did Devereux tell you what he wants for the cover?"

"Yes." Tracy nodded and glanced at her engagement ring. "He wants Cash and me in the foreground saddled up on Captain and Cinnamon, with Dude sitting between the horses. In the background will be the Triple C Ranch-East house and the helicopter."

"With the words, *The Rancher Takes a Wife*."

"Right." Tracy smiled. She and Cash had gone into Colorado Springs to bring Kirk Devereux up-to-date on the shooting of Winston Smith by either Donna or Gerald, and Cash's defensive shooting of Gerald Moles. After that was thoroughly discussed, they had told him about their engagement. Kirk had congratulated them and insisted Tracy call him Kirk. He'd asked her to do so before, and now she did. "After we told Kirk we'd decided on a November wedding, Kirk said he wants the Triple C Ranches to be the December issue. You know you're invited, and I want you to take the photos."

"Yes. Of course, I'll be at the wedding and take photos," Jacob said. "So, we'll get the perfect one of you and Cash on horseback. You must admit, a Christmas issue with a wedding photo on the cover will be an attention grabber."

"Different anyway," Tracy said modestly.

"Devereux knows the magazine industry." Jacob held up his index finger and said, "He predicts that in the entire history of *Ranchers and Ranges*, it will be the number one selling issue, breaking all previous records. I agree with him."

"We'll ask Cash for his input when he gets here. He's done for the week and guests are gone so he should be home any time." When Tracy stood, Dude raised his head. "How about we toast to a job well done? I'll get three glasses and a bottle of wine from the wet bar."

"Need help?"

"No thanks, Jacob. Dude, you wait here with Jacob. I'll be right back."

Dude sat up and Jacob said, "Dude, let's get a video of you. Shake?"

Tracy left the wide-open, comfortable, country-style living room, crossed through the two-story foyer and passed the wide staircase. The ring bell announced there was movement at the front door right before a knock sounded. Tracy turned and doubled back a few steps to the foyer. From the living room, Dude barked as she opened the door.

"Donna!" Tracy gasped. The woman had the same crazed look now as she'd had when she screamed about Gerald trying to kill her in Wild Horse. Her back to the living room, Donna instantly slapped Tracy hard across the face.

"That's for Gerald," Donna said. "Yeah, he told me how you repeatedly hit and kicked after the barbecue while Cash's men held him down on the ground."

What? Dude barreled toward the foyer as Donna shoved Tracy sideways and stepped into the foyer. Dude jumped on Donna, planting his front paws on her back and knocking her face-first against the carved horse on the railing of the staircase.

"Dude, come!" Tracy ordered the snarling, barking German shepherd. "Now!" Dude obeyed and retreated to Tracy's side. She grasped his collar. "Why are you here, Donna?"

"It's payback, bitch," Donna spat, scrambling to her feet. "Because of you, I'm out on bail while the sheriff tries to pin Winston's murder on me. And yes, I killed that lying loser and yes, I'm glad he's dead. I woulda killed Tammy too. But not Gerald." The woman's pupils were dilated and her eyes frantic and darting. "Now, I have no father, no job, no boyfriend, no money, and no place to live." She screamed, "And it's all your fault, Dalton Darling!"

"Jacob, call 9-1-1 and Cash," Tracy said over her shoulder.

"Already done," Jacob said, calmly walking forward as he filmed everything.

Twisting around and shocked to see Jacob, Donna shouted, "I hate you as much as I hate her, Jacob! I might as well go to prison for three murders as one." Including Jacob with a glance and laughing maniacally, she sneered, "At least I'll have three hots and a cot in jail."

Donna yanked a knife out of her pocket which brought a new round of barking and snarling from Dude. Donna lunged at Tracy, but Dude leaped between them. With a sharp whimper, Dude fell to the floor. Baring her teeth, Donna raised her hand and charged Tracy with the bloody knife.

BANG!

Cash raced down the wide hall from the rear of the house as Donna stumbled backward falling flat on the floor. Staring at the Glock in Tracy's hand, Donna's mouth opened and worked soundlessly. With a bullet hole in her chest, the punched hole in the wall seemed to be the last thing Donna Smith saw as she took her final breath.

"Tracy!" Cash yelled as she crumpled to her knees beside Dude.

"Cash, help us," Tracy pleaded, tears streaming. She set the gun on the floor and placed her hand to the chest wound oozing Dude's blood. Cash knelt beside them, gathering Tracy into his strong and comforting embrace.

"Are you okay?"

"Yes," Tracy cried. "But she stabbed Dude."

Cash gently released Tracy and pulled off the neckerchief from around his throat. Speaking softly and encouragingly to Dude, he pressed the cloth to an inch-long gash to stop the bleeding. Dude's breathing was shallow, but Tracy's fierce defender was conscious.

"Dude, you might have a nicked vein, buddy," Cash said at the blood loss. "Lie still."

Jacob had run to the kitchen and hurried to them with a bowl of water and paper towels. With Dude's head in Tracy's lap, Cash carefully cleaned away the blood while keeping pressure on the wound. Jacob left them long enough to step outside and wave two El Paso County cruisers out on the highway toward the front porch.

The sirens brought Sam, Kellie, and Jeff running from parts nearby. Beau and Cristen weren't far behind, and they closed protective ranks around Cash, Tracy, and Dude. Kellie, being a nurse, examined the gash and said Dude would need stitches. Sam was already on his cell to the veterinarian the ranch used. Sam hung up, saying the vet was on her way.

"Did you hear that, Dude?" Tracy asked. "The doctor's coming. You'll be okay."

Two deputy sheriffs entered the house while an ambulance turned into the driveway. Within minutes, Derek who had seen the cruisers pass Triple C-West, arrived with Chase. Jacob handed over his video camera to the deputy sheriff in charge.

"Sir, here's what happened," Jacob said.

"I'll be damned," Chase said to Derek in the foyer. "See that." He indicated the paper broken over the hole in the wall and the gun lying on the floor.

"I knew that trick was bound to come in handy one of these days," Derek said.

"Take a look, Derek," the deputy said to his former partner in the sheriff's office and handed him the video camera.

Derek and Chase both watched the film, and Chase asked, "Have you seen this, Cash?"

"No, but I saw most of it firsthand," Cash replied, beside Tracy and Dude.

"Open and shut case," Derek said as the deputy nodded.

"You know what we learned from this?" Cash asked Tracy, who shook her head.

"Never bring a knife to a gunfight."

EPILOGUE

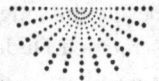

FIVE YEARS LATER

$\mathcal{C}$ash opened the oversized rustic door below the large wooden sign reading *Cooper Lodge*.

"Come on, Dude," Cash said to the treasured dog at his side. With stitches and antibiotics along with plenty of love and attention, Dude had quickly recovered.

Since opening the lodge three years ago, conveniently located just down the road from the house, they had been booked out months in advance. Additional employees had been hired and more horses purchased. The dude ranch business was booming as Uncle Clarence used to say. Cash liked to think his uncle would be proud of how Triple C Ranch-East had grown. He and Dude stepped out of the July sun and into the air-conditioned lobby. Decorated in what Cash referred to as cowboy comfortable, with leather sofas and matching chairs, along with coffee tables, end tables, and built-in bookshelves, the lodge lobby warmly welcomed guests.

Beau and Cristen had gotten married and taken over the café. Sam was in charge of the shop full time and Kellie was head chef in the lodge's dining room with a great staff of cooks and waitresses. To all of the family and friends, this lodge was a second home. It was also the headquarters of Cash's beautiful wife. He grinned as she emerged from her manager's office where she not only ran the show at the lodge but penned and drew her children's books. Catching his eye, Tracy's smile was nothing short of radiant. Dude bounded toward her.

"I saw you pull in beside the lodge," Tracy said. Staying at the office door, she scratched Dude's head as he nuzzled her hand before trotting past her. As to the box tucked under Cash's arm, she asked, "Whatcha got there, handsome?"

"Something just arrived with the name Tracy Cooper on it."

"Hi Cash," called the receptionist behind the desk. She had recently met Jacob, and as Coop had pointed out she and Jacob were sweet on each other. "I can't wait until Mr. and Mrs. Devereux and Jacob are here to celebrate the Fourth of July next week with us." With a glance around, she whispered. "And to interview and photograph our VIPs."

"Same here," Cash said. Then reaching Tracy, he added just for her, "Even the Colorado governor and his staff can't compare to the July Fourth week when I met a certain redhead who stole my heart."

"Awww shucks...I missed you today, cowboy." Tracy slipped a hand through his arm and pulled him into her office. Cash set the box on her desk and kissed his wife.

"Daddy," squealed their three-year-old daughter. From across the office, where she'd been playing with a dollhouse and petting Dude, she stood up on the plush carpet covering the polished, hardwood floor. With blue eyes the same shade as his and red curls bouncing around chubby cheeks, she came running with Dude at her side. "Hi, Daddy."

"Hi, Carly." Cash chuckled and scooped her up in his arms. She'd been named after her her great-uncle Clarence Carl Cooper and nicknamed after her mother. "How's my *wild*fire?"

"Good, Daddy. I missed you."

"Like mother, like daughter," Tracy said. Then pulling the tape off the cardboard, she opened the box and smiled. "My new book."

"Let's have a look."

Kirk Devereux had published the Triple C Ranch article in *Ranchers and Ranges* at Christmas time as planned. However, as to the wedding photo on the cover, Cash had made a slight change, from two horses to one. The issue, an all-time best seller, displayed Tracy in a white version of her Elsa hat, cowboy boots, and white flowing wedding gown sitting sidesaddle on Captain with Cash seated behind her in a black cowboy hat, tux, and boots. Dude sat beside Captain and framed covers hung on walls in the lobby as well as Tracy's lodge office and in Cash's home office. The family had bought a dozen boxes and distributed copies to staff, guests, and customers. They'd also set the magazines out at annual barbecues for neighbors and friends.

Reverend Miller had performed the marriage ceremony in the same country chapel where the Cooper children, both young and grown, had been baptized. Devereux had been sorry to lose Tracy as a journalist but had happily put her in touch with a publisher of children's books when she felt she was ready. Jade, as a child therapist, had written an endorsement that appeared on the back of her books. Tracy opened her latest book titled *Carly and Dude Go to the Rodeo.*

"What's it about?" Carly asked.

"Carly and Dude meet a little boy who's lost," Cash said, so proud of his wife and daughter. "They help him find his way back to his mom and dad at the rodeo."

"Did someone say rodeo?" Coop asked as he and Tammy came to the office door.

"I did." Cash turned with a grin. "Come and see Tracy's latest book."

Coop and Tammy entered arm in arm. Once she'd arrived on Triple C-East, Tammy had never left. Oh, she lived with Coop in his log cabin now on Triple C-Central, but that's as far as she'd gone. She and Coop, so in love, were adding years to each other's life.

This evening was a private and casual family dinner before the VIPs and big fireworks display to come the following week. Cash heard the voices of his brother's children, Colton who was nine now and the spitting image of Chase. Courtney, at seven, was as blond and lovely as Jade. The kids rounded the corner of the office with their folks trailing behind them.

"Hey everybody," Cash said and let Carly down to collect hugs.

"You told us hay is for horses, Uncle Cash," Colton joked as Courtney and Carly hugged.

"Hey, everybody," Derek called at the door.

"Not you, too, Uncle Derek," Courtney said with a giggle.

"Hay is for horses," Carly echoed Colton.

"That's right, Dad," Cooper said, and at ten was the oldest of the cousins.

"Austin. Abilene!" Carly squealed, hugging the eight-year-old twins.

"Is anybody hungry?" Tracy asked and received a bunch of I ams and yeses.

"Well then, anybody who doesn't want to eat hay tonight —" he scooped up Carly, grabbed Tracy's hand and sauntered to the door, "better follow us."

As usual, the dining room was full of dude ranch guests, bed-and-breakfast guests, as well as customers from near and far who'd heard about Cooper Lodge.

They met up with Rachel and Martyman in the dining room where tables had been scooted together, covered with snow-white tablecloths, and set for sixteen. Cash sat at one end of the long table and Chase sat at the other end. Coop and Tammy took seats near Cash and Tracy. Derek and Chloe sat toward the opposite end with the rest of the family filling in the middle.

This was Triple C Ranch land, and cattle ruled.

Thus, steaks, prime rib, and burgers were served, along with side choices of baked potatoes, mashed potatoes, fries, broccoli, squash, corn on the cob, and asparagus.

Cash gazed down the long table and when everyone had been served, he raised a glass of sweet tea, made according to Rachel's famous recipe and said, "This family has come a long way in the last decade. I love you all."

"Hear, hear," Chase agreed, raising his glass.

Others echoed the sentiment and Coop took Tammy's hand, saying, "I'm blessed beyond measure to be here with Tammy to see it."

Cash smiled at Tracy, who gave him a nod. "Come Thanksgiving, Tracy and I will celebrate our anniversary and add a baby boy to the family."

These were Triple C Ranch people: wranglers, cowboys, and cowgirls. Thus, as Cash kissed his wife, hoots, hollers, and clapping broke out with guests and staff joining in on the celebration.

"Wonderful," Tammy said with tears in her eyes.

"Congratulations," Chloe and Derek called from down the table.

"Yes, congratulations," Chase said as Jade blew them a kiss.

Rachel and Martyman echoed the congratulations with heartfelt smiles.

"What's his name going to be?" Coop asked with all the kids wanting to know too.

With a smile back at Cash, Tracy replied, "Dalton."

"Dalton Cash Cooper," Cash said and swallowed the lump in his throat as spirited applause and whoops of approval sounded around the table.

For dessert, cherry and apple pie were among the favorites. Ice cream and cake were popular too. The younger children soon grew restless and sleepy, so the older kids and adults pushed back from the table. Cash and Tracy escorted the family to the lobby where hugging and handshakes took place before they parted ways. Didn't matter they'd see each other in the coming days. They were together now and never took their time together for granted.

When Cash and Tracy arrived home, Cash filled the tub in the bathroom attached to Carly's bedroom and Tracy placed the little girl in the warm water. Carly splashed and played, making her parents laugh. After Tracy dressed Carly in pink unicorn pajamas, Cash carried her to a new, double-wide recliner near the fireplace in the master bedroom. Sitting with Carly on his lap, Tracy snuggled up on his left. Dude lay down on the right side of the chair and sighed.

"Hot tub under the stars later tonight, big'n bad?" Tracy flirted.

"If you read us your new book first, spitfire." As Cash cuddled Carly, Tracy read. Carly and Dude were sound asleep as she reached the last page. With a scratch to Dude's head, a kiss to Carly's curls, and a wink at Tracy, Cash closed the book and whispered, "The end."

A LOOK AT: CHARLEY COOPER

TRIPLE C RANCH BOOK FOUR

Enter the captivating world of contemporary western romance, where love and danger collide amid the rugged terrain of the Rocky Mountains.

After losing her mother during a harrowing attack that shattered her world, Charlotte "Charley" Cooper finds herself at a crossroads. Alone and vulnerable, her fragile existence is thrown into chaos when she is contacted by the owners of the prestigious Triple C Ranch in Colorado Springs.

Sullivan Custis owns a thriving business in addition to a thirty-thousand-acre ranch in the countryside. Living a busy but secure bachelor's life, he doesn't expect to cross paths with his gorgeous new neighbor—or become in danger of losing his heart.

But as Charley's flower shop becomes the epicenter of a series of gruesome murders, the once idyllic landscape of Old Colorado City turns treacherous. Determined to protect Charley, Sullivan urges her to seek refuge on his ranch. Yet, as tensions mount and Charley vanishes, Sullivan finds himself in a race against time to rescue the woman who has captured his heart.

Immerse yourself in this riveting tale of love and suspense, where passions burn brighter than the mountain peaks and loyalties stand taller than the pines. Grab a copy now and surrender to the jaw-dropping allure of this extraordinary western romance story.

AVAILABLE NOW

ABOUT THE AUTHOR

Lynn Eldridge is a former president of the West Virginia Chapter of Romance Writers of America and earned an honorable mention in their Golden Heart Contest. Lynn is the author of several historical and contemporary romance novels, including *Desire in Deadwood*, *Remember the Passion*, *Tame the Wild*, and Skyrocket *to Surrender*. Her latest novel, *Hearts and Mountains*, is a 2023 Spur Award Finalist.

In addition to her writing career, Lynn is a licensed clinical therapist and dedicates one day a week in an outpatient behavioral health facility in Charleston, West Virginia.